THE ORPHAN
MOTHER

ALSO BY ROBERT HICKS

A Separate Country
The Widow of the South

THE ORPHAN MOTHER

A novel

BY ROBERT HICKS

GRAND CENTRAL
PUBLISHING

NEW YORK   BOSTON

Copyright © 2016 by Labor in Vain, LLC.

Cover design by Anne Twomey
Cover illustration by Bridget Davies
Cover copyright © 2016 by Hachette Book Group, Inc.

Grand Central Publishing
Hachette Book Group
1290 Avenue of the Americas
New York, NY 10104
grandcentralpublishing.com
twitter.com/grandcentralpub

First Edition: September 2016

Grand Central Publishing is a division of Hachette Book Group, Inc.
The Grand Central Publishing name and logo is a trademark of Hachette Book Group, Inc.

The publisher is not responsible for websites (or their content) that are not owned by the publisher.

The Hachette Speakers Bureau provides a wide range of authors for speaking events. To find out more, go to www.hachettespeakersbureau.com or call (866) 376-6591.

PCN: 2016942112

ISBNs: 978-0-446-58176-9 (hardcover), 978-0-446-57613-0 (ebook), 978-1-455-54173-7 (large print), 978-1-478-97094-1 (signed edition)

Printed in the United States of America

RRD-C

10 9 8 7 6 5 4 3 2 1

In Memory of Tom Murdic
I can still hear you

THE ORPHAN
MOTHER

PROLOGUE

MARIAH

December 12, 1912

To the shabby house on Columbia Avenue they came, the four of them, all in black, narrow ties fastened with jeweled stickpins about their necks. One wore engraved cuff links, real gold, she suspected, just like a white man's. Their shoes were burnished and clean, and they all wore socks. As they stood on her doorstep she looked them up and down, thinking, *I made you. It is because of me that you can wear a tie.*

"Mrs. Mariah Reddick?"

The man asking was small, with quick nervous gestures and a pencil-thin mustache. He looked bewildered and kept glancing around and past her into the depths of the house, as if he were expecting some other Mariah to step forth. He spoke with borrowed confidence.

"Yes."

"I'm Reverend Erastus Cravath," he said. "From the university. Now *your* university."

"I figured that's who you be. But I didn't figure you'd come yourself."

"Miss Mariah—"

"Mrs. Reddick."

"Mrs. Reddick, then. We've come because we've just received a letter from—well—we've received a certain letter, and we wanted to come ourselves to ascertain the veracity of the claims and to meet you, according to the terms of the bequest."

"If you think I'm fooling in that letter, you just need to talk to my lawyer," Mariah told him, leaning now against the doorframe.

"We don't think that at all," one of the others interrupted, craning forward earnestly. "Not at all. But the terms of the letter made it quite clear that there was an additional request, that a representative of the university should meet you in person. So here we are."

At that, Mariah nodded. "You gentlemen have come a long ways. You want to come in?"

"We would indeed," the second one said. "Pardon the intrusion, Miss Mariah—Mrs. Reddick."

Mariah stepped back from the door, but the man, Parmalee Edwards, kept talking. "Just to be clear and legal and so forth, you *are* the Mariah Reddick whose attorneys wrote us last week?"

"I am Mariah Reddick, I just said it. Don't know another one," she said. "Come on in. Wish you'd sent me a note or something, I don't got much to feed you with. I baked this morning, so I still have some cold biscuits around."

One by one they followed her in, stickpins glittering. The house felt very full when they were all inside, sitting uncomfortably in the small parlor: two on an old sofa of a certain age, the other two in armless mule-eared chairs. They left the armchair by the fire for her. Edwards followed her back into the kitchen to help with the biscuits and the tea. ("We cannot have her serving us," he had whispered to the others.) "Really, ma'am," he said, "we are just fine. No need to trouble yourself."

"No trouble at all," Mariah told him, laying out plates and biscuits and heating water for the tea. She had set out tea for others for nearly eighty years, she could do it again for herself and her important guests.

When they were all settled, teacups in hand, biscuits to the ready, a fire now blazing in the hearth, Erastus Cravath got down to business.

"Mrs. Reddick, we are amazed at your generosity."

"No trouble at all," she said.

"The school's never seen a gift of this sort...never. This is going to change everything for us. We shall have a new library, the Reddick Library, how does that sound to you?"

She laughed. "I ain't never sat in a classroom or a library, not even in a Negro school like your'n. No sir, you don't need to put my name on nothing."

"We could have a new dormitory, even a new chapel—the Reddick Chapel?"

Her face tightened, and suddenly the kindly old lady had disappeared. Now she became fierce and formidable, and they were perhaps beginning to understand how this frail former slave might have amassed such a fortune.

"I don't want no chapel and no dormitory. I want things just the way the lawyer spelled out. Spent a long time figuring this through, and that's how I want it to go."

"But this kind of generosity—surely there's some way of recognizing your charity and good works?"

"You know your Bible, Reverend Cravath," she said. "Matthew 6:3. Jesus says when it comes to giving, *But when you give alms, do not let your left hand know what your right hand is doing.* I don't want a mention of me or a building named after me. God help you if you ever name a chapel after me."

They all spoke at once, voices tumbling over each other. "But Mrs. Reddick, think of the example you're setting—"

"—a shining example for both whites and for Negroes, if they knew what you've done—"

"You have a higher responsibility," Cravath interrupted, "to set an example to others of how men and women of color have risen from the depths of despair and broken the chains of slavery to rise to the pinnacle of prosperity!"

"Look around, Reverend. It look to you like I'm living in any pinnacle of prosperity? When I was allowed to choose, I chose to live my life the way I chose to live it. I'll die the same. That I got money don't say nothing about my life."

"And that's how you wish to be remembered?" the reverend asked. "Your obituary—that is, if the white folks decide you are even worthy of an obituary—will tell of another broken-down former slave, a penniless Negress who served her white family faithfully, and really nothing more."

"That may be," she admitted.

"What an opportunity you are letting slip away."

Mariah stood up and walked to the window to the left of the parlor stove, and then back to her seat. She took the last biscuit and cupped it in her hand like it was something precious and not to be eaten, like she was saving it for someone.

"I had a son once. He was all about opportunity. Hardworking young man who hoped and dreamed of a better future. This thing I'm doing is the opportunity he should have had, it's *his* opportunity. Not mine. If I can just help other young Negroes like him, that's my opportunity, Reverend."

"May I ask why you're not bequeathing your fortune to your son?"

"He died. Long time ago now." She looked directly at him, gray-eyed and clear, and did not look away.

"I'm sorry for your loss."

"So am I."

"We just want to tell you how very grateful we are, how much we want to recognize your enormous generosity—"

"Then do what I ask. Nothing more."

"As you wish." His face pinched sour and tight. He was not a man used to being turned down by other Negroes, Mariah thought.

"Reverend, I'm a simple midwife. I bring healthy babies into this world—that's what I do. I don't know nothing about educating and teaching and speeches. My neighbors just need to know me as the midwife. Nothing more. Imagine the world if the bottom rail was the top rail, hear me? I'm good being on the bottom rail."

This was the world, the life, she had chosen. Perhaps once she could have had fine clothes and diamonds and a trip to Paris or London, but she had remained true to a world that had chosen her. And she had found joy in it, bringing new life into this world. No matter how flawed it all was, no matter how filled with anger, prejudice, and death, there was nothing as sweet to her as the fontanel of a newborn. The possibilities that existed in a baby! The places and the dreams and the hopes that such a child would have! No library or chapel could equal it.

A penniless Negress. Nothing more. This is how you will be remembered. His words rang true. She would choose to seem just another poor broken-down Negress. She saw nothing wrong in that, nothing to be ashamed about. In this small way, she would live and die as she wished. That was a sort of freedom.

"You want more tea?" she asked them. "I can still find the roots myself. This here tea you can't find in a big city."

They nodded and thanked her.

It pleased her that she was using the tea service she'd gotten long ago, in another world, with a delicate pattern of leaves chasing each other across its surface. She had nothing new: her possessions now were few, and growing fewer. For many years she had saved every penny she could to put into the endowment, to give to this university of strangers who did not know her and would never know her name.

5

This was not about names. This was, always and forever, about that one child—that hope, that possibility—who had hoped someday the world could get better, for Negroes especially, but maybe even for whites, too.

She stood up. "I'll go get the tea," she told them. "And I'll bring out more biscuits. It's a long trip back to the city."

CHAPTER 1

MARIAH

July 2, 1867

That morning, just as the world stirred in a light breeze, there had been a difficult birth. The new mother gasped in pain, but at bedside Mariah listened beyond that, she listened to the air around her, trying to breathe so slow and light that she could hear only the blood in her head. She heard the rest of the world clearly, the sounds of cutlery on plates in the nearby fancy house and the rattle of feet far off out on the street. When a baby was on its way, right when it was about to enter her world, Mariah became vigilant, her senses more powerful. She was the guard at the gates, the lioness with her nose in the wind and her teeth bared. *It's a hard, hard world, child. You will need help.* And then she heard the servants whispering in the kitchen by the woodstove. She heard, out in the street: *Won't be no nigger speeches here, you mark my words. They'll lose the gumption, you'll see. They'll run away. They don't know what's coming.* One of the maids—Emma May, whom the family had brought from Nashville—whispered to one of the kitchen boys, *Go run and get Dr. Cliffe.*

She would have the whole thing finished by the time Dr. Cliffe staggered down the street. She took stock one more time: the sounds spun around her, none of them threatening. The way was clear and safe, the signs were right. *Come on, child, come into the world.*

She didn't believe in spirits, but whatever it was that charged the air between Mariah, mother, and baby—what the old souls had called *haints*—spoke. Now Mariah felt the threat, which she wanted to deny but couldn't. *This one isn't like the rest. There's something wrong. The life has flowed from her, the blood has gone.*

In all things but this, Mariah had left talk of haints and powers behind. That was old business, her mama's wisdom and tradition. Her mama had never known freedom.

Believe this, though: better get that baby out right now or it dead.

The top of the baby's head had appeared. She slid her long fingers on either side of the child's head, guiding and not pulling.

"Missus, here it comes. You got to help me now."

Evangeline, the magistrate Elijah Dixon's much younger wife, all of twenty-seven years old, had her eyes closed and would only shake her head. Mariah slapped her hard on her thigh, twice, and Evangeline struggled and clenched and wailed. The voices got louder but Mariah couldn't make out the words. The top of the baby's head had gone a deep, deep purple.

"Missus!"

Evangeline pushed. Mariah inserted her fingers between the baby's neck and the cord she knew must be drawing closed around its throat. The baby slipped a little farther out. Mariah could see the cord wrapped and knotted like a snake, and when she stretched it away from the child she thought she saw the purple fade. She coaxed the baby on, just a little farther, until the whole head had emerged.

"It coming, missus!"

She heard a voice behind her. Dr. Cliffe. *How did he get here so fast?* "The cord!" he shouted. "Step aside!"

Mariah knew what needed to be done and would not move

away. Where was her knife? Too late for that now. She got her teeth on the cord just at the side of the child's neck. She felt the baby's cheek on hers, smooth and soft. Afterward she would think of this as the true moment of the child's birth, when she bent down and felt him on her skin, barely alive but whole and true and human, his soft and crumpled ear folded up against her own. A woman could live her whole life and never be so close to a child, not even one's own. Not like that.

She bit hard and through, freeing the cord, and the baby began to slide fast into her hands. Dr. Cliffe tried to push her aside and she cursed him like she'd curse a mule. The child wasn't breathing, so she put him up to her shoulder and began to coax the breath from him, squeezing, patting, and humming.

I don't have a lick of magic and I don't need it.

The child was breathing and starting to pink up by the time Dr. Cliffe finally managed to get the baby from her, ready to pry and prod with his shiny new tools in the black satchel. The room had seemed so dark and empty before, just Mariah and mother and her baby, but now the doctor and some of the other children had crowded in. Not the husband, though, Mariah noted. He hadn't attended the other births either.

Mariah went to the mother, took that pale, gray face scattered with freckles in her hands, and whispered, *You've got a boy.* When she returned to the foot of the bed to assist the doctor with the towels and the rest of it, he glared.

The child lived because of her. It had been fate that had tried to kill him, and Mariah had taken fate in her own hands and run it off. *She* decided who would live and die. How did the doctor not understand that? That baby wasn't the first, not nearly, among those who owed their lives to her. She could still feel the child against her face, and that first flush of blood that had ever so slightly warmed her cheek.

CHAPTER 2

TOLE

July 2, 1867

There had been a heavy summer rain the night before, and the smell of early July rose in the air, a heady scent of sweet olive, daylilies, and the rich earth that bore them. The dirt smelled different in the South, George Tole thought, not like back east—not bad, but it didn't smell like home either. The summer had turned muggy and endless, with long bouts of daylight and dancing fireflies. Tole would listen to the children outside of his window, horsing around past their usual curfews, up to no good, probably, the way children of a certain age could be.

Tole didn't have a lot of reasons for leaving his house, but the summons from Mr. Elijah Dixon was undeniable. One of the children had brought it. He had knocked and then dropped the envelope before racing back to his friends. The note was short but clear. *Come see me. Elijah Dixon.* Mr. Dixon was an important man, a magistrate, maybe someday a judge, and had important friends. Tole had heard the name Elijah Dixon way back when he lived in New York, seen his name in the newspapers. He didn't know what to make of the summons. He considered whether maybe all that trouble had followed him to the back wilderness of Middle

Tennessee, but then he talked himself into believing that there was no way Mr. Elijah Dixon could know anything about that or care if he did.

Now Tole made his way down Fourth Avenue, weaving through horse-cart traffic and a parade of businessmen headed to work, newspapers snug in the crook of their arms, a whole block of black coats and bowler hats. You wouldn't know Tole was a freeman by the way he walked: a tall, dark Negro with a scar above his eye shuffling like a ghost, heavy-footed and head bowed, eyes fixed on the street. But he was as free as any man walking south toward South Margin Street that day. He never was anything but free.

He continued past the southernmost commercial block and into the residential streets, stopping only to lift his pant leg and scratch the small mosquito bites around his ankle. He kept on, turning onto South Margin, a quiet street of cherry brick houses. This was his favorite block, softened by trees, sourwood and sugarberry, river birch and American beech. The leaves seemed to burst with a new shade of green, revitalized by the previous night's rain.

Tole stood at the corner house on South Margin, a stately brick Victorian with a pitched slope for a roof and a cupola just above it. After looking it over he walked up the dozen steps, holding the black iron railing, and knocked on the door.

An older Negro woman, white-haired and proper, answered.

"Here to see Mr. Elijah Dixon," Tole said.

"He expecting you?"

"Uh, yes. I was to be here at ten o'clock. His wishes."

"Wait there."

The woman closed the door and Tole waited outside. When the woman returned, she asked him to walk back down the steps and around to the side of the house where he'd find a latched gate that would lead him to the backyard shed, where he was to wait. Tole did as he was told. Inside the shed he found some wooden pallet beds, a couple of wash buckets, a few pieces of rough furniture. He pulled a stool over and sat down.

When the door finally opened, Elijah Dixon stood in the doorway, a large, heavy man, well over six feet, with a drum-tight belly that hung like a sack over his belt buckle. Dixon was older than Tole by twenty years. Tole guessed he was close to sixty, but he didn't look much older than Tole himself, despite that auburn beard, marbled with gray and white, that had spread like wild grass over his jowls, onto his second chin, and down his neck.

The Dixons had lived in Franklin as long as anyone could remember. Elijah's father, old Lyceum Dixon, had made bricks and sawed boards back when Abram Maury was exploring his way through the territory. Elijah Dixon, the last of the patriarchs, flushed red in the sunlight behind his beard, and never wore shirts with collars because he fancied himself a laboring man and inheritor of the great strength of his forebears, though this had long since become only a kind of costume, a myth Dixon repeated about himself.

Tole knew that Elijah Dixon had turned the building of houses, sidewalks, bulwarks, and forts into a speculation operation heavily invested in railroads and the new furniture and textile factories back east. But he had also mastered the art of never appearing above himself, and since Dixons had always been thick-handed, hard-hammering beasts known for their ability to carry heavy things, Dixon wore the garb of the laborer, kept the brickworks in operation, and couldn't contain his smile when he passed by a new house or over a new sidewalk built of bricks stamped *Dixon*.

"George Tole," Dixon said in a loud, jovial voice. "I apologize for keeping you waiting."

"It's fine," Tole said, standing.

"Margaret get you anything? An iced tea?"

Tole cleared his throat, not sure how to answer, and before he could, Mr. Dixon was already hollering the order to Margaret, who was standing on the back porch. Tole nodded. *Thank you, sir.*

"Please sit," said Mr. Dixon. Tole sat.

"A bit of commotion this morning," Dixon said. "My wife's having another baby."

"Congratulations, sir."

Margaret came in and handed Tole the glass of iced tea, and one for Mr. Dixon as well. *She must have had it ready*, Tole thought.

"No lemon for me," said Mr. Dixon.

Tole sipped his tea and tried to swallow quietly.

"It's funny," Dixon went on. "I adore lemon meringue, a lemon cake, a lemon chess pie, and my wife makes the most delightful lemon squares you've ever tasted, but I can't stand the taste of an actual lemon. Isn't that strange? One of life's mysteries, I suppose."

"Yes sir."

"Speaking of wonderful things," Mr. Dixon said. "You have children of your own?"

Tole paused, unsure how to answer. "No. No sir, I don't."

"Swore I'd never have a family," Dixon said. "Thought I was too old to be a father. Didn't think politics and fatherhood went too well together. Thought I'd always be too busy to raise children proper. But my daddy was always away, always at the office, so maybe it doesn't matter. It changes you, being a father. Didn't think I'd have enough love in my heart for a fifth child. Then my wife told me, and there it was. You'd think four would be enough to keep us busy, wouldn't you?"

"You would think," Tole said.

"Yet every time we bring a new baby into this world, my heart makes room."

"That's real special," Tole said. He had learned long before to nod his head and agree when white men took to rambling on about whatever was on their mind. In those moments he would make his mind blank so he didn't say anything he'd regret.

"I'm hoping for a boy—Augusten. If it's been a girl, she'll be Lily Kate. We were originally going to let our oldest boy name it, but he's not the most trustworthy when it comes to baby names. He came to me and he said, 'Daddy, if it's a boy, I want to name it Jonathan, after Grandpa. And if it's a little girl, I want to name it Stinky.' So we thought to go with Lily Kate, after my wife's mother. Shouldn't be long until we find out."

Tole sipped the tea, waiting. Dixon looked him up and down, a crooked smile on his face. Tole knew the baby talk had been a test to see if Tole knew his place, which was to sit and listen quietly to whatever Dixon said. Tole passed.

"I didn't bring you all the way down here to go on about babies and lemon meringue," Dixon said. "I don't want to waste your time, I'm sure you got many things to do." Tole heard the sarcasm and let it pass. Another test passed.

"It's no bother, Mr. Dixon."

"Heard some stories about you," Dixon said.

"I wouldn't believe none if I were you."

"Heard you were pretty sharp with a rifle."

"I know how to use one properly, that's true." His previous life had indeed caught up with him, and to be honest, Tole had known the conversation would go this way. He'd naively hoped it would be about something else: how, perhaps, a freeman from New York could help Mr. Dixon out with some issue that required a freeman's experiences. But he knew, because it was the only thing white men ever wanted of him, it would be this: *You were pretty sharp with a rifle.* This was the only skill of Tole's anyone ever remembered.

"Heard you were better than proper with a rifle. Heard you killed eight Union boys all by yourself back in New York. Sound like something you did?"

14

Tole nodded. "I've heard that."

"Heard some other things, too. Heard you killed your first man for pay when you were just nineteen years old."

"I know who told you that. They ain't to be trusted." He guessed all men like Dixon knew how to find each other, and that the one in New York had found the one in Tennessee.

"Doesn't matter who told me," Mr. Dixon said. "Just what I heard."

Tole kept silent. He'd already said too much.

"Don't care about your past unless you think I should," Mr. Dixon said, in a way that made it sound like a threat. "I called you here because I heard you were the best."

"I may be the best at drinking whiskey until I piss my bed," Tole said. "That's about the only thing I know for sure. Also, I know I haven't shot a rifle in a long time." He was desperate to steer the conversation anywhere but to where he saw it was headed. He had given up that life.

Dixon smiled, big and toothy and utterly false. "There's this fellow across town, a real troublemaking son of a bitch, doesn't like the way I conduct my business. He thinks he can make a name for himself by ruining mine. Fellow goes by the name of Bliss, wears a hat with an orange feather. You know the one I'm talking about?"

"Can't say I do."

Tole waited out the pause that followed. When Dixon spoke, it was clear, unmistakable. "I need Bliss to not be a problem anymore."

"I don't think I understand," Tole said. He wished he didn't understand, more like.

Dixon smiled again, grinned, eyes cold as fog. "You know, Tole, I don't like violence. I'm a family man. Was one of the first men to call for the bloodshed to stop when the war was still raging through these streets. But sometimes, it's the only way."

"You mean the easiest way."

"Is it easy?" Dixon was so eager to know. It was obscene, even to a man like Tole.

Tole didn't know how he should answer. Truth was, he was the most proficient sharpshooter to come out of New York. He was more at home holding a rifle than he ever was holding a woman or a child, and he had learned, after much resistance, that this was his fate in this world. This was, indeed, all he was good at. And though he had traveled far to leave his past at the bottom of an empty bottle, Dixon's question excited him a little, and then a little more. There was a part of him that missed it, hungered for the cold rush of knowing where he fit in the world. He missed being good at something.

"Now look," Mr. Dixon said. "All I'm asking is for you to do something you've done a dozen times before. And you'll be rewarded. You've got my word on that. I've invited you into my home, and I hope you'll trust me to make good on my promise."

"The man you been talking to must not have told you that I gave that life up a long time ago. I was a different man back then. I've changed."

"'Course you've changed," Dixon said dryly. "You're older and drunker. But people like you don't change that much, Tole. You are who you are. And I'm asking you politely, one more time, to join me in this venture. I think we could do great things together."

Tole looked down at the table. "Just one job?"

"Just the one."

"Because I'll only do the one. No more."

"No more," Dixon repeated. "Do we have a deal?"

Tole nodded assent, his eyes tracing the table's wood grain.

"Good." A pause. "So this is how it's going to be done. There's a man who'll be giving a speech next Saturday morning. Around ten o'clock, in the middle of the courthouse square. I'm sure you've seen white men deliver these kinds of speeches before."

"Time or two. Politics and such."

"Very well then. I want you to find yourself some high-up place, a rooftop or an attic window, anywhere with a clear line of sight to the courthouse square. You'll want to have a straight shot to the podium. Understand?"

Tole nodded, amused that any man would think he needed advice about shooting.

"You'll see a man with a hat with an orange feather. That's Bliss. He's a bad man, Tole. He's the one I want you to dispose of. A real rabble-rouser. He leads men to make poor decisions, and we will not ever have peace with men like him around. He's more dangerous than he looks. You follow me?"

"Yes."

"When he gets up to speak, a few of my—my friends will cause a little disturbance."

"Disturbance?"

"A riot. Of sorts. They're going to crowd around, cause all kinds of havoc, and that's when you take your shot. In the chaos. No one will know what happened. You hear me?"

He did, and one more time Tole was trying and failing to figure out how to get out of the job when the door to the shed swung open and a black woman—skin a light creamy coffee color—stormed in, arms full. Sweat shone on her face. She didn't pause deferentially in Dixon's presence, but spoke to him as an equal. "Mr. Dixon, you have a new baby boy."

"Wonderful news," Dixon said, grinning with those big white teeth. "Wonderful. It's Augusten, then."

"You want to see him?" the woman asked patiently, shifting the bundle she held.

"Of course! Of course! Tole, you'll excuse me? We understand each other?"

Tole nodded. The moment to change his destiny had passed, erased by a baby. Dixon left. Tole sat down to gather himself, and while he did so he watched the midwife.

The woman was carrying linens and instruments that Tole didn't recognize. She set them down on a table, went out back and pumped a few spurts of water into the bucket, returned and began washing the instruments. Blood polluted the water, spiraling like spilled ink, until the bucket was a dull shade of dirty pink. Tole watched her wring out a towel and mop down her arms.

"You the one delivered the baby in there?" he asked.

"You a pretty observant fella," she said. "What gave it away?"

"Ain't no easy way I know of to get dry blood off your hands. Not unless you got some kinda alcohol."

She turned to him, intrigued. "What reason would you have for knowin' that?"

"There was a war, you know." He was full of sarcasm and yet this woman made him want to confess, too. "Found myself with blood like that on my hands more times than I'd like to count."

It was the truth, Tole thought, with one difference: the blood on her hands was the blood of life, the blood of labor and innocence, the result of bringing something perfect into the imperfect world. The only blood Tole knew was the blood of vengeance, of endings, and even though he knew the blood of a dead soldier and the blood of a birthing mother looked the same, he couldn't imagine it felt the same when it was on your hands.

"Too many men like you around these days," she said.

"What kind a men are those?"

"The killin' kind."

And then Tole recognized her. He'd seen her before, near his house. The laugh lines around her mouth, the brilliant gray of her eyes. He hadn't been able to place her before, and then it came to him. "You Mariah Reddick."

Mariah turned, the angle of the sun lighting the planes of her face. "We know each other?"

"I suppose we don't. I live near your boy."

"You know my son? You know Theopolis?"

"Yes'm."

"What's your name?"

"Name's Tole."

"Tole? That a Christian name?"

"My mama named me George, but I never liked it much. George Tole. Most people call me Tole."

"I like the name George myself. Sounds presidential."

Tole smiled. "I reckon it does. But lots of Negroes named George, you ever notice that? Lot of wishful thinking, I think. Anyway, not many folks goin' to confuse me for a president."

Tole watched Mariah scrub the blood off her hands, blood that left a faded copper stain on her palms and forearms. He took a beat-up flask he had tucked down in his boot and unscrewed it. He stood up from his stool. "Got a good amount of whiskey left in here. It'll surely clean the stains right off."

Mariah looked up at him, and Tole moved closer. The floorboards creaked under his weight. He reached out toward her hands. "May I?"

Mariah nodded, so Tole held her hands in his and poured a thin stream of the moonshine over the back of her hands, rubbed the cloth over the thick, protruding veins that jutted out, high as her knuckles, and then asked her to turn her hands over. He drizzled a bit more liquor onto her palms. The smell filled the air like a promise or a ghost between them. He rubbed her hands with his, and up her arms, his eyes careful to stay directed at the task, never straying to meet hers.

"There you are, ma'am," he said, letting her palms fall from his.

"I think I can finish up here." Mariah took the bloodstained towel from him. "You shouldn't be drinkin' that poison."

"Hooper made it."

"Hooper?" She laughed. "Then it ain't poison, but still kill you."

Tole took a short swig from the flask and tucked it back in his boot. "I'ma be on my way now. That baby in there's real lucky to be born into your hands."

She stared at him a moment, impassive. Then he could see a smile touch the corners of her eyes. He wondered what a full-blown smile would look like. Dazzling, he thought.

"Kind to say."

"You have a real good day, Missus Reddick. Get some rest now."

CHAPTER 3

MARIAH

July 6, 1867

Mariah awoke and lay in bed to listen to the branches of the poplar brushing the side of her little house. She worked too hard for too little—even if the money now was hers, and didn't just go to the McGavocks as it had when she'd been a slave. She took on every birth she could, but Dr. Cliffe had managed to cut into her business recently with his promises of scientific reproduction and rational birth. He gave lectures. She'd been to one, "Progress of the New Man," down at the public room of the Masonic Hall. The point of this lecture, from what she had understood, was to reveal the existence of things called germs, little critters too small to see, which caused every manner of illness, including stillbirth, and which could only be battled by advanced sterilization procedures that the doctor, coincidentally, had learned. Well, she'd been doing just fine without his invisible germs, and she could see her handiwork walking down the street tailing after their mothers.

Once she'd cleaned up and eaten a cold biscuit, Mariah went and stood on her porch a couple of feet above the muddy thoroughfare of Cameron Street: the queen of all she surveyed, she leaned on her front porch rail like she had herself prepared a few remarks to share with the gathered mosquitoes, the flies, the white men rattling past behind their mule teams. Pillowy bolls of the Middle Tennessee sky floated above a wide expanse of blue.

Franklin was a town that some time before had lost a limb or two, or some fingers and toes, and had not yet fully recovered. It still limped; it could still feel its phantom limbs. What had not been forgotten had been pulled down or plowed under. Carter's cotton gin had been destroyed under the rush of the rebel army only to rise up again afterward; hundreds were buried where they dropped, right where the foundations had been. The entrenchments that had arced in front of Franklin's south side had been filled in, but the soil's settling had left long and shallow concavities, twisting here and there through town like the trail of a great snake.

People, soldiers and not, had disappeared, no word from them again. Quite a few of the Negroes had lit out for other places north. White families left, too, having lost a business or a father, back to Mama's old home place where they crowded into too few rooms and fought over the family land. Others, like the fancy German carpenter and furniture maker, Lotz and his family, had tried to stay, but eventually fled for some new life in the West.

In some parts of town, houses still stood empty. The quiet on some streets could be unnerving. An empty dwelling always seemed on the verge of being filled again, each window just a moment away from being lit by lamplight. And each day that a house's eyes remained dark and dead, its people snatched up and delivered to new places, was a shock; a rebuke to those who stayed. And why did they stay? Habit, greed, faith, philosophy, poverty—who could know?

There had been no black blocks before the war because there had been very few black cabins. But now little neighborhoods had grown up around those few freemen's houses that had existed before the war. Blood Bucket was the best known of these, and white people had made way for it by moving across town as quickly as they were able. New houses and shacks grew up on the white west side of town, while black men and women moved into the old ones on the east side.

The new houses on the west side were lined out and straight-cornered, elegant and monumental, building geometrically to angled peaks that looked out over the town. These Greek Revivals *appeared*, suddenly, but the metamorphosed shacks and shotguns of the Bucket just seemed to *grow*. This seemed right to Mariah; it seemed beautiful.

Mariah had brought Franklin into the world, in a manner of speaking. Not the physical town, but a goodly number of those who dwelt in it, especially the young. There they were right over there, across the way in the courthouse square, white boys and girls trying to climb over the new platform built that morning for the political meeting. The colored carpenters shooed them away. She had birthed all those children, she had caught them coming out, she had been the first person they'd ever seen. She was the first to bathe them, the first to whisper to them, the first to look them in the eye before handing them off to their mothers. She believed this was the hidden beginning of their memories. Even if they couldn't explain to themselves why they were so respectful and a little afraid of the colored woman with the gray eyes, it was no puzzle to the woman herself.

Inside, she stoked the fire and poured water for coffee. *Her* fire and *her* coffee. Her pot. Her house. She hoped she never got used to saying those words and meaning them, knowing they were hers in a fundamental and absolute way, that they were better than gifts. They were not loans made by her mistress, but hers that she could burn to the ground if she felt like it. She could paint a face on the side of her house, she could sit up on the peak of the roof and spend the day singing to the sparrows. Why not? She *could*. This could make some people very angry, she knew. Would she rattle her freedom at them, sing it from that rooftop? She wouldn't, because she had never actually stopped being the wise woman, the responsible woman, the sock darner and fever tender. She couldn't sweep back time, however much she wished it.

An hour later Mariah's own flesh and blood, her son, sat on a hard gray slatted chair next to her, talking low and amused about politics, which she let him do. He was a cobbler by trade, set up his own shop a few streets away, but already he was thinking beyond owning his shop. Now he was thinking of owning the whole world, Mariah sometimes thought. As if slavery were something that a stroke of a pen could just wipe away, and the whole world could open up before you.

Mariah kept two potted plants on the railing of her small porch, on either side of the steps to the street. She kept two chairs on the porch, facing the street on opposite sides of the front door. Mariah always sat on the left, and any visitor would sit on the right. Her chair had worn down some on the back legs, and there was the slightest black mark on the clapboard wall just behind. Mariah liked to lean back on the chair and rest against the wall. She liked to lean just past the moment of balance, constantly testing that balance. Sometimes she rocked forward, and other times she eased back. When she was balanced she thought it felt like flying. Or at least floating.

Theopolis once told her that she looked like an old man when she rocked like that with her legs spread wide. Her son leaned forward in his chair, elbows on his knees, hands clasped in front of him, staring at whatever happened to be going by on the porch floor, often ants. Or he looked out down the street squinty-eyed like he could see from there to Perdition.

"You'll come then, Mama?"

"If you going to make a fool of yourself, I suppose I'll be there to watch it."

"Who do you think is going to run, Mama, if it's not me?"

"Some other not my son. But you go on, you do what best."

"Good thing I don't listen to you."

Her Theopolis was damned modern, thinking he was going to put himself in charge of that House of Representatives in Nashville, even just a little bit.

This terrified her.

Theopolis would be giving a speech today. In public, in the town square, alongside a man running for the U.S. Congress and other bigwigs. But how could she try to talk her son out of something as honorable as giving a speech? *Quit thinking like a slave.* She vowed she would not say anything more to Theopolis about it.

"If you listened to me you'd be in that San Francisco by now, you'd have already took your mama out there where I be a comfortable lady looking out that ocean. But here I am."

"You wouldn't leave this place."

"Might consider it, you don't know."

Theopolis snorted and drank his coffee.

Theopolis had told her it gave him comfort to think that he, a Negro, might soon be sitting in the legislature with his feet up on the rail and voting according to his own instincts and philosophies. *I have instincts and philosophies, Mama. You do, too.* He would have his own polished spittoon when he sat in that beautiful chamber. He would sit and spit alongside his heroes in the state's Reconstruction government.

Governor Brownlow, for instance—Theopolis had last year traveled clear to Nashville to see him, and could recite whole chunks of the speech the governor gave. Someday Governor Brownlow himself might turn to Representative Theopolis Reddick and ask him what he thought of a new law, or some problem that needed fixing. Governor Brownlow would ask him for his vote. Governor

Brownlow would reach out with his big, important hand and shake Theopolis's. This is what he had told his mother, and it was these very words that terrified her. Not the words, but the fact that he believed them.

It would all start today, whatever she thought. These big, important white men and Theopolis, her son, with his instincts and philosophies, would stand onstage trying to win votes side by side.

Theopolis loved his mama. He loved her so much he came to see her every morning for his coffee, but he did not *fear* her like she would have liked. If he had feared her, he wouldn't be giving any speeches that afternoon right there, across the way, where the white men with their bricked-in faces would be watching.

His love for her, which when he was a boy she had felt powerfully every time he had slotted his hand into hers, couldn't compete now. Who was she, his mama, but a foolish woman who could hardly read and write, who needed to be reminded she had her own ideas about politics? Who was she next to those men, whose words he hung on like they were all that mattered in the world? No, he would go and he would speak and she would stand by, as always, afraid of what would happen when he raised his voice.

No one could say that Mariah acted like a slave: she held her head up and met every white man's gaze with a clear, gray-eyed stare. But no matter how she acted, she knew one thing: *Negro folk did not speak.* They raised their voices in a chorus only to praise the Lord and pray for a better time to come. They did not stand before white folk and try to change their minds, try to understand them, try to make the white folk *see* them.

And now, this afternoon, Theopolis would be *seen*.

❦

She smelled liquor and tobacco smoke and biscuits, and thought all three had never smelled so sweet or so definite, so full of things she'd never noticed before. Even the dogs seemed to know that something was imminent, for they trotted along barking at nearly everything they saw and nipping each other's necks distractedly.

"What about Mrs. McGavock, Mama? She'll want to come. She'll be there, I'll bet."

"She got better things to do."

"What's better than to be in the middle of change? Nothing, that's what."

"Miss Carrie has her dead folk to tend to. And Mr. John's away, traveling."

"That ain't more important than today. I'd think they'd want to come hear me speak."

"Don't be a sassy boy."

The whole town seemed jittery—even the air and the leaves dancing on it. Mariah's neighbors plied the wood sidewalks to and fro, from the academy to the Presbyterian church to the courthouse and back again, everyone buzzing. The Colored League Negroes swaggered, boots clattering on the paving stones, stopping each other with a clap on the back, bending their heads together, joining their voices in an excited hum. Upon meeting or parting they would give a spirited chant for the Republican governor—"Huzzah for Brownlow!" It all seemed very unnatural to Mariah.

The Conservatives buzzed with a different energy, dark and angry, coiled up like snakes preparing to strike. Their eyes followed the Leaguers around town as if they were tracking them. They spoke in whispers. Some had been angry for a long time. Some were planters made poor and small by Reconstruction, their punishment for opposing the Republicans and fighting for the Confederacy. They had watched their land and slaves disappear, their houses deteriorate. Mariah could feel their anger stalking the streets, bristling against the eager anticipation of the League men.

You couldn't *not* feel it. The day was breaking open, and it was everywhere—the anger and excitement both. It would be good to be out of town this morning. Mariah thought about going up to Carnton since Miss Carrie had sent her another note, another request to return. It was time to end *that* nonsense. She would never go back for good like Miss Carrie wanted. She even shivered at the idea of going back just for the morning, but she never refused Miss Carrie. That would have to change. She strengthened her resolve. It was time, finally, to sever the ties.

The farrier's hammer clanked clearly, ringing out agreement, as if Mariah were standing right next to the anvil and not four blocks away.

Theopolis got up to go, straightening his black trousers and tucking in his best white shirt, which Mariah knew would be a filthy mess by the end of the day. *The boy has good intentions*, she thought, *he just needs a lick more common sense.* Theopolis had been soiling his shirts since he was a boy, though, and Mariah supposed she would be disappointed if he ever stopped.

"I don't want to sass you, Mama. I just want you to come see me speak. It ain't going to happen every day."

"I'll come if you quit talking about it."

He smiled and kissed her on her forehead. Mariah smoothed the back of his shirt as he walked away from her, down the steps, and off up the street.

A breath of windblown dandelion fluff came to rest on his hair, white against dark, as if anointing him.

Later, she wished she had at least got up, followed him off the porch, and pulled him close enough to brush the stray fluff away, or told him he was a good man, or told him she loved him more than any child she had ever brought into the world.

CHAPTER 4

TOLE

July 6, 1867

Tole wore a buttoned-down shirt he had pressed himself that morning, a vest, and a cotton cap pulled close to his ears. The fancy clothing felt restrictive and strange. He loitered near the midwife's tiny house on Cameron Street, passing time, smelling the breeze, feeling as if the world were better than it had been—the colors fiercer, sharper, darker. Far away a mockingbird shrilled in a tree, and another answered it, echoing.

Around him men were preparing for the rally. Colored Leaguers hurried past with their easy laughs and their drums. White men followed them with slower steps, glowering. Some Negroes shook their heads as they watched the Leaguers go by making the white men grumble and stomp their boots. They wanted no part of that and didn't appreciate the disturbance of the peace. Eventually everyone moved off toward the square, away from Tole. He stood and watched them go, in no hurry to go anywhere himself.

And then: there she was, sallying forth, skirt shining in the sun, carrying a basket under an arm. She didn't see him, or feigned not to, and turned in the other direction, marching out past the other clusters of houses along the high road. Her hips swayed as she walked.

"Missus Reddick," he called to her. She didn't respond, so he called again. This time she turned.

Tole approached. "Thought I might say hello."

"Hello," she said. "Forgive me for not remembering your name. I never forget faces, but names are more difficult these days."

"Tole. George Tole."

"Mr. Tole." Something about the way she said it sounded musical. He was George after his mama's brother who died as a child; and Tole after his father, who was dead of drink, or worse, these long years past. But now, here, hearing her speak it, the whole name sounded exotic and mysterious and worthy.

"You heading out of town?" he asked her.

"Carnton. The McGavock place."

"Where you were—" *Where you were a slave.* He knew he didn't have to finish the sentence.

"Yes," she said. "Heading back to return some things to Missus McGavock."

"I ain't never been over that way. I'm still learning my way around here."

"Well, I don't make a habit of walking these back roads with strangers, but since you know my son, you welcome to walk along with me if that's what you trying to say."

"Thank you," he said, falling into step with her. "But I want to carry your bag there."

"I can carry my own bag," Mariah said. "You just focus on walking."

He felt an unfamiliar tightening around his lips: it took him a moment, as he fell into step next to her, to recognize that he was smiling.

There were certain simple pleasures, he reflected, that had been denied him—or that he had denied himself, more like. Simple easy graces that could fall upon you unexpectedly, if you had the good fortune to recognize them for what they were, like an unlooked-for gift from someone you loved once. Who would have thought it a gift, walking down a humid summer lane in Middle Tennessee with a beautiful woman swinging a basket next to you? But if you were a killer and sometimes con man, a drunk and washed-up soldier who could sit with a rifle in a tree and pick off defenseless men from a quarter of a mile away, it would seem a gift indeed.

She seemed different from other women he had known—a bringer of life, with a confidence and assuredness he envied and wanted to possess. But now, for this moment, it was enough just to walk beside her. Right then, with the dust of the road kicking up at each step, even with piles of horse dung and ruts to avoid, right then he wasn't a drunk and a killer. He was a better man.

"You say you not from around here," Mariah said.

"Yes'm, New York's home for me. Was, anyhow. Came out here to Franklin just before this summer."

"What a summer it's been," Mariah said. "I don't think it'll ever end."

"There'll be an Indian summer, surely," Tole said. "Though I don't know what the Indians have to do with it. I guess they go ahead and blame them for everything they can, even the heat."

Mariah smiled. "Why you come to Franklin, of all the places?"

"Oh, this and that reason," Tole said.

Her eyes narrowed. "That ain't no kinda answer."

"I guess I just needed some new scenery," he said. "New faces to look at."

"What was wrong with the faces in New York?"

"The problem wasn't so much with their faces," he said. "The problem was with mine."

"Ain't nothing wrong with your face as far as I can tell," Mariah said.

Was she flattering or flirting with him? Surely neither. Or both? Or she was just being kind. And was kindness such a bad thing? The war, after all, was over. This situation with Mr. Dixon would soon be resolved. Perhaps Dixon would be grateful for a job well done, help find him work. The man was a magistrate, after all, and very wealthy. Talk was that one of his children was sickly, and Dixon doted on her like a crazy man. The man had some charity in his heart. Perhaps this was the new beginning that Tole had sought. "Believe it or not, I had my looks when I was a younger man. I wasn't always this old fool."

"Don't go talkin' about age, Mr. Tole."

"You don't look a day over twenty years old, Missus Reddick."

Tole could have sworn he saw the tinge of a blush in her cheeks, but he took the summer heat to be the cause and lowered his eyes to his feet.

"You're kind. A liar, but kind. You think you can charm your way out answering the question, though, you wrong."

"Not trying to charm my way out of anything."

"Sounds to me like you running from something," Mariah countered, slowing their pace to a stop as she met his gaze. "Except you don't seem like the kinda man who's scared of much. Makes me think the thing you running from is more frightening than any war or anybody's face."

He held her stare. "Maybe I'm running toward something now, not away."

They began walking again along the dirt road, wide-open farmland on either side of them: to the left, acres of corn; and to the right, sunflowers breaking into bloom. Mariah adjusted the bag on her shoulder. Tole kept his head bowed, looking down at his shoes, only daring to glance over at Mariah when he knew she wouldn't catch him.

They let silence fall over them, the soft shuffle of boots against the dirt, and soon they were halfway to Carnton.

"You have any kind of family, Mr. Tole?"

"You need to call me Tole, ma'am."

"Tole, then. Any kind of family?"

"Can't say I have much left anymore," he said. "I believe I have a great-uncle still kickin' around in Albany, but he might as well be as dead as all the others."

"No wife and children back in New York?"

And there it was, the question, so simple, one of the first questions people asked him, the one he had previously found impossible to answer. But now he found the words.

"I had a wife and a son, but they dead now."

Mariah's stride shifted imperceptibly, like a stagger. She said, softer, "Lord. Sorry to hear that."

"Happened a few years ago. It's all right."

"Doubt any parent's ever 'all right' once their child has passed on," she said, looking over at him.

"You're probably right. But I get by."

She didn't ask how it happened, as people usually did. Instead: "What was his name?" And Tole said, "My wife named him Miles, after her daddy," and Mariah said, "Well that's a real nice name."

The silence fell between them again—rough with unspoken questions, unanswered thoughts.

A few moments later he saw a pair of brick pillars, and a sign, damaged and weather-beaten: *Carnton*, painted in simple black script on a white board. She said, "This is Carnton, where I *was*, once. Like you said. Thank you for the walk."

"Good to walk with you, Missus Reddick."

"If I got to call you Tole, then you call me Mariah."

"Mariah," he repeated. And then, nervously, "If you want, I can wait a bit and walk you back to town."

Mariah laughed. "No, I'll find my way. Must've made the walk a few thousand times on my own."

And then Tole reached out his hand. Mariah placed hers inside his palm and they shared the warmth for a moment before Mariah turned and headed up the drive, around the bend. For a while Tole could see her shadow, and then not even that.

CHAPTER 5

MARIAH

July 6, 1867

Up the steps of Carnton and in Mariah went. The house was massive, once—when Carrie and Mariah had moved there, upon Carrie's marriage to Colonel John—very stylish, with wallpapers from France and England and fine Brussels carpets on the floors. Books looked down regally from bookcases in Colonel John's fine Gothic office. But then the war had roared in upon them, and the house had been commandeered as a hospital, and the blood had soaked through the floorboards. Some of the walls themselves seemed gnawed upon: the officers' sabers carelessly ramming across the wallpaper and the plaster. Much had been repaired, of course, but the old house now seemed smaller to Mariah, and dim. Colonel John had eschewed the new gaslight, and candles were never where you needed them. So now the rooms were dark and close.

Mariah moved down the central passage and into the family parlor, where against the windows the dark silhouette of Carrie McGavock waited, dressed all in black, her mourning veil intact. Carrie dressed every day as if funerals were a regular though lamented fact of one's day, like rain.

"Miss Carrie, I got your note and I just want to say—"

Carrie would not let Mariah finish her sentence. She held her hands awkwardly out from her sides just a few inches, as if she had not yet decided whether an embrace would be in order. Finally she smiled very sweetly and placed a hand on Mariah's right arm in an approximation of an embrace.

"Thank you for coming, Mariah, and since you are in your work clothes, perhaps you would accompany me to the cemetery? So much more pleasant to converse there, don't you think?"

Mariah had not worn her *work clothes*; what she had on was her finest, though covered in the dust that had been kicked up off the road. Carrie didn't leave room for an answer and was already out the door before Mariah could reply. With resignation and familiarity, Mariah turned and followed. How easy that was. She hardly had to think in order to tread behind her former mistress, out and across the gallery, down the steps, and down paths that led to a cemetery that stretched far into the distance.

I ain't staying, I am decided.

Carrie marched down the path with the Book of the Dead under her arm, arms swinging and chin up.

Here, in this cemetery of Carrie's, a stone's throw from her house, the Book of the Dead recorded the final resting places of hundreds of Confederate dead, marked by even rows and columns of whitewashed cedar boards, arranged according to state, each board identified only by a number and initials, no names, no ranks. Every dead man and boy rested in equal relation to the other, laid out just so and blanketed by a thick, fine-leaved grass.

"I have your letter here, Miss Carrie."

"Let us not talk about that yet, shall we? So much work to do."

"It's why I come."

"You need not have a reason to come see me, Mariah Reddick, not ever, and you needn't blame that little piece of paper. Now,

I count forty-three rows from South Texas to the row missing its monument..."

Because of her constant patrolling of the cemetery, the hem of Carrie's dress was often faded with a light layer of cemetery dirt. Mariah's mother would have called this *goofer dust*. Goofer might be used in some bad work against enemies if they were known, but enemies were sneaky and often they weren't known.

"Texas forty-three!" Carrie called. "Who is that?"

Mariah ran her finger down the columns drawn in Carrie's crabbed blue script. "Jeremiah Carter."

"Poor Jeremiah!"

⁂

As children they had explored the old place in Terrebonne Parish in Louisiana, owned and mastered by Carrie's father. Back then Mariah could think that the general principles of a slave's life did not apply to her, since she was companion of the *master's daughter*. She and Carrie braided hair and wrestled and climbed stunted oaks together, and Maude the cook would hand them both pieces of sugarcane, each piece no bigger than the other.

When Mariah went off with Carrie after her wedding, Mariah sat high up on the dowry cart, face forward, following the closed carriage that contained the newlyweds, and she had never been happier. It didn't occur to her until later that she was in the dowry cart because she was herself one of the gifts.

They had continued for almost twenty years, mistress and slave, companions who knew each other best in the world. And then came a disruption greater than the war: Mariah became a freewoman, and they had found no words to talk about that.

"You have a bed in town, in a house. Do you feel at home there?"

"Yes ma'am."

The oaks here cast cool shadows, and the leaves rustled over-head. Sunlight dappled Carrie's black dress. "But you return here when I ask you."

Because, thought Mariah, *you are incapable of taking care of yourself, Widow of the South.* "Yes."

"Does it feel like home here? I think it's starting to feel like home to me, after all these years. And do you know why?"

Mariah shook her head.

"The life of summer dresses and tea cakes was never for me. I've cast all that off. I need *nothing* from the outside world now."

Carrie had not said so much to Mariah, and certainly nothing so personal, in years. This was an invitation offered to a greater inti-macy by a lonely woman, Mariah knew. She knew Carrie that well, at least.

"Except," Carrie said, "you are the only person who has ever run this household, and I wonder if it can possibly go on without you."

Mariah understood this was Carrie's way of trying to take care of things. The lady of Carnton could not, for instance, go calling on the old Negress in her tiny house in Franklin. They could not meet for tea, could not sit beside each other in church. A woman such as Mariah Reddick, free she may be, was to be seen and not heard unless spoken to, like a child. She was not to assume she had a part in the rituals of civil society, which were open to her by invitation only. This was the truth of the world after the war, and Mariah knew all about it. But Carrie persisted in thinking that they were friends even so, and that left only employment as the means for acting out the gestures of friendship. In Carrie's world, they could have tea together so long as it was Mariah serving it. Had she herself, Mariah Reddick, ever been given the choice of rejecting Carrie McGavock's friendship? For almost forty years that had not been an option. Whether or not to serve Carrie McGavock had not been a question either.

Mariah leaned against the oak tree, a couple dozen feet from Carrie. She felt tiny slivers of bark fall down the neck of her dress.

"You come back, and we start again," Carrie said. "No contracts either, not like John has with the tenants, just your own will to stay. I have work here for you, but perhaps it won't seem so much like work. The work of helping me with this cemetery is special, spiritual work. You know there is more to this life and the spirit. Your mother knew, certainly."

Carrie had never spoken of Mariah's mother. Mariah wondered if she even knew the woman's name.

"Not sure what Mama knew."

"Oh, that isn't true! She had the sight. She could talk to the dead! You know that. We all knew that."

It was news to Mariah that this was something Carrie McGavock had known. "What you mean by that?"

"The dead! She had the power of the dead. She saw the dead, she communicated."

Carrie stood closer, so close Mariah could feel her breath on her cheeks. Her eyes were wet, crinkled half-shut by one of Carrie's sweet, world-forgiving smiles. Mariah knew that her mama's use of the arts had been nothing so exciting as Carrie imagined it now.

Carrie put her hand on Mariah's shoulder as if to steer her toward the house. There were no sounds of birds. Mariah strained to hear them, but nothing. Then, in the distance, she heard the sound of a mockingbird, very faint, and she was glad. The world had not stopped. She felt the light tap of a fly at the top of her head.

She had once ruled this place. The kitchen ran according to her direction, as did the cleaning of the house and the maintenance of the yard and grounds. A dozen others curried her favor, hoping to someday be appointed out of the field and into the house. Others feared being sent out into those same fields, and when she passed them by in the parlor she noticed how hard they seemed to polish the silver tea set, or how persnickety they became about dust among the rows of Sir Walter Scott's volumes on Colonel McGavock's shelves.

She had once had power, yes, but it had been borrowed power, the power of a slave for the moment raised up among other slaves. She could feel the essential falsity, which was like playacting, but nonetheless it had been appealing. Her memories held lots of people in them, and not just any people but people who thought of Mariah and wanted her time and her attention. Most of these had fled Franklin at the first chance. There were not so many people in Mariah's life anymore.

Mariah had been given free will by her Maker, that's what the Methodist preachers said, yet she had never before then been able to *act* freely. The world of possibility had not been hers. Every slave had been separated from the entirety of God's creation. Every other slave was alone even when they worked and ate together. *That* was loneliness.

Mariah took a step away from the house and shook her head. "Not today, Miss Carrie. I come back another day, and maybe we talk then again, but I ain't staying now. Got business."

"Business?"

"Theopolis is speaking this afternoon in town." She tried to say it casually, but could feel the cool thrill on her lips: the thrill of pride—and of fear, too.

"He's one of the speakers?" And then, simply: "Oh, Mariah." Sharing the pride as well as the trepidation. "You shouldn't be out here with me—when's the speech?"

"Not till this afternoon."

"Let me get Lester to run you back to town, so you have plenty of time."

"That would be very kind."

Carrie had already taken a couple of steps toward the house, having assumed that Mariah would follow. She stopped and turned. "But don't think I won't stop trying." She smiled, but down came the veil. Carrie turned back toward the house, floated across the grass again on the way to her fortress.

CHAPTER 6

TOLE

July 6, 1867

On returning to town, Tole got to work on Dixon's errand. He went by his little shack of a house and took his rifle, which he wrapped in a quilt and stuck in a kindling carrier, the kind one would not be surprised to see a Negro carrying through the town on bended back. He went scouting for a perch, but none of the first buildings were right, so Tole went farther, into the white section of town, stepping out of the way of the brand-new carriages that rolled and clattered over the streets. He wove between the proprietors out on the sidewalk offering free samples: molasses, cheese, swatches of cloth, printed cards. They didn't offer any to him.

Unimpressed by the possibilities, he continued into the residential streets, always keeping the courthouse in a direct line behind him. Here there were more interesting places, fewer flat roofs and more cupolas and pitched slopes and dormers and attics. An attic window in Dr. Cliffe's house had a direct line of sight to the courthouse and the stage. *That's the spot*, he thought.

He put the kindling carrier down, under a pecan tree and concealed by a privet hedge, and pushed his way through the

Cliffes' picket gate and into their backyard. But he heard voices from the house. He withdrew to the shadows across the street, waiting.

Up the hill, the white boys at the military institute marched across the drill yard keeping time, shouting at each other as if what they were doing was deadly serious and not some insignificant playacting, a pastime for fools and cowards. The Negroes hammered up the stage over in the square.

Dr. Cliffe stepped out with his wife, down the steps, her arm in his, her skin a soft Scotch-Irish pale. As they headed west, away from the soaring sun, into the shadows cast by blooming trees, Tole noticed the way her strawberry hair fell down her back, and how it matched the freckles that dotted the backs of her arms.

He waited a long ten minutes, worried that some routine slip of mind, something forgotten, would cause them to turn back. He waited, and when he felt they were good and gone, he crossed the street.

The weight of his government rifle pulled against his shoulder. On the stock he'd once carved *GT*, so that he could keep the other men in the company from claiming it—they who didn't spend near as much time polishing and cleaning theirs. They called his rifle ol' GT, and teased him about it, but they didn't ever pick it up as their own. Because of this he had known one thing at least, at all times: that his rifle would always fire. That had been no small achievement.

Tole slipped into the doctor's backyard as quietly as he could. The gate had been left unlatched. There, under the eaves, the attic window looked out across the street, above a few low buildings, and unobstructed into the square.

He quietly stowed his kindling carrier under the hedge, pulled out the rifle in its cloth, and moved quickly across the yard to the back door. It was unlocked, these being overly trusting people. He walked quietly down a narrow central hallway, which was broken by only one doorway. He guessed, correctly, that this was the door to the attic. He went through and up.

Hanging from one of the beams of the attic was a collection of men's hats, bowlers and slouch hats, tall stovepipes hardly ever worn. In one corner stood a dressmaker's dummy, a headless and legless curve of a monstrous half-woman.

He had no attic in his shack down in the Bucket. His neighbors painted their houses awful bright colors and were always tap-tap-tapping at the roof and the walls with their hammers, like they were all hell-bent on building up their own creation. He lived surrounded by a crowd of manic colored doers and builders, cobblers and carpenters. They tolerated him well enough for an outsider. He tolerated *them* well enough for a lot of folks who couldn't leave well enough alone.

Every once in a while he checked the crowd that had begun to gather in the square. What he was about to do, he'd been told, would be a great service. *We'll see about that.* Tole unlatched the attic window and pushed it open. Wind and voices blew in with the late morning sun. He unwrapped ol' GT from the blanket, raised the butt against his shoulder, sat down cross-legged with his elbows on his knees, and looked through the rear sight and stared at the front sight. He lowered the rifle, adjusted his position until he was aligned with the podium set up in the courthouse square. He breathed in deep and sighted in again.

Across the way, in the square, men gathered, buzzing like ants. Two crowds, really, the Colored League men hard by the stage and the Conservatives across the street, standing on the corner, under cover of a shop's front wall, facing the square. The crowd by the stage was almost all Negroes, former slaves now freedmen with their drums held close to their chests and banners clasped in some of their hands.

One skinny black man held his banner out toward the crowd at the corner like a dare: *The Radicals Build School Houses—The Conservatives Burn Them.*

Another, right at the head of the crowd, proudly held an American flag. Tole thought of the Union boys carrying the stars and stripes into battle, how the other boys had rallied around it, eyes raised to watch it wave. He remembered, too, how many of those Union boys later lay bleeding on the ground with that flag at their sides.

There weren't as many Conservatives at the corner—no more than thirty overall—but they all had a similar look to them. All those hard white faces. Pistols clipped to their belts or strapped to their chests. A smattering of Negroes stood among them. *Always somebody to disagree,* Tole thought.

As the time for the speeches got closer, he could tell that words were being lobbed between the groups, thrown like stones into separate pools, but he was too far away to hear what they said.

The men at the corner bristled as the speakers filed onto the stage. Tole thought he recognized one of them, high up above the crowd. He wasn't sure at first—the angle and the hat obscured the man's face—but once he turned, he knew for sure it was him: his neighbor, Theopolis Reddick. The cobbler. Tole wasn't sure why Theopolis was there. He assumed he would speak. Tole himself was never one for great oratory and had respect for any man who did, especially young Negroes, many of whom were taking advantage of the new opportunities opening up to them—becoming politicians, business owners, and who knew what other possibilities. *No slave ever did that,* Tole thought. The young had a courage that made him proud and envious. He'd been born free in New York City, but somehow the opportunities had never really presented themselves to him—and then the war came, and the possibilities had been defined by the notches of a rifle's sight.

Near Theopolis, but not speaking to him, were two white men—politicians, Tole could tell, important men from out of town.

Another white man came behind them, with another Negro by his side.

The mayor trailed at the very back, near the sheriff and his deputies, stalking around the stage like guard dogs, keeping the Colored League men back. Even from this distance Tole could hear the beat of drums and the cheers ringing out.

From the group of white men at the corner he heard nothing at all. Near them a pair of mockingbirds worked out their disagreements, which among birds meant a whole lot of fierceness, pecking and clawing, feet first. It was always over quick, which was one thing different about birds. Men never wanted to get things sorted out for good. They liked their blood feuds.

There must've been a few hundred folks gathered in the courthouse square by two o'clock: businessmen and homeless vagrants, disenfranchised Confederate boys and members of the Colored League, conservative loyalists and Republicans. It was a rally of sorts, Republicans and Conservatives, politicians shouting over each other, over jeers and riotous yelling. Tole sat up straight.

He hadn't anticipated a gathering this large, a killing this public. *Mr. Dixon must want to make an example outta this man*, he thought to himself. In the right corner, at the back of the stage, almost obscured by picket signs and tall hats, he saw a white man with a round face, his upper lip swallowed by a graying, upturned mustache, and a black top hat pulled down tight.

Tole's gaze would have shifted, seeking other pale faces in the crowd for his mark, had it not been for a flash of color that caught his eye on the mustached man's hat. There, at the top, sprouting from the base like some sort of extraordinary flower, curled a bright orange feather. *The man Mr. Dixon wants dead. Jesse Bliss.*

He repeated the name in his head, the next man he would kill: Jesse Bliss. One moment Bliss would be breathing, speaking, yearning; and the next Tole would squeeze a small metal lever and, like some type of terrible magic, a metal ball would puncture the front of Jesse Bliss's forehead and all of his breathing, speaking, and yearning—his hopes and his cheating at cards when he got drunk and his laughing too loud at his father-in-law's jokes, the things Tole imagined white men did with their time—all that would end. *Click.*

Tole made minute adjustments to the angle of the barrel, judging the direction and strength of the breeze by the soft billow of the nation's flag in his periphery. His hands stilled as he cocked the trigger and squinted, eyes trained on that orange feather as his heartbeat slowed. One more instant and—

Just then, Theopolis walked out onto the stage and stood behind the podium. A roar from the crowds. Tole heard, or thought he heard, men shouting, *Get back in the field where you belong.* But he was too far away to hear distinctly.

These boys gonna reignite a war right here, they ain't careful. The crowd seemed suddenly much more unruly as it condensed toward the front of the stage.

Theopolis, he could tell, was trying to yell over the crowd.

And then Tole's nightmare really began.

CHAPTER 7

MARIAH

July 6, 1867

A rumble, like the earth clearing its throat, came drifting over from the courthouse square. Down the wide expanse of Fourth Avenue, where she stood in the doorway of the dim little quilt shop, Mariah could see the fringe of the crowd clustered around the stage, though not the stage itself. She could see the great brick courthouse, with its grand cast-iron columns and long windows, its long smooth steps and the round clock face that stood out in the middle of the pediment, looming over the gathered figures like History itself. The courthouse made everything around it look smaller—the surrounding buildings, squatter and made from darker brick, that bordered the square; the pair of elm trees that framed its entryway; and the people, black and white, who stood in its shadow. For a moment she just looked toward the square and listened to the swelling sound.

"They got theyself started I guess," Minnie Bostick, the chimney sweep's wife, said from behind her table, arms crossed, short and wide-set, cheeks full and dark. Her eyes said, *What you doing here?*

Mariah didn't answer—neither the spoken nor unspoken.

"Someday I'm getting one of these here quilts, Minnie, but not to-day." *How she keep them quilts so clean with Mr. Bostick's dust all over everything? He as coal chalky as they come*, she thought. She walked on, letting Minnie eyeball the back of her head.

More cheers and groans wafted over from the courthouse square. Mariah wondered if Theopolis had given his speech, and whether the others had liked it. She took another two steps, toward the courthouse, yet safely far away.

At that very moment—at least, this was the way Mariah would always remember it—she heard the first screams and shouts from the courthouse square.

And then, unmistakably, gunfire.

She spun on her heel and ran toward the square.

CHAPTER 8

TOLE

July 6, 1867

At the base of the podium, the crowd surged. Tole could not see the cause—the press of bodies was too tight—a whirl of heads and arms reaching out.

A bottle crashed near the stage. Gunshots rang out from the corner, and from Sykes's grocery, too. The Colored League boys ran for cover, pulling pistols from bootstraps.

The white Conservatives were firing.

A Negro in rough blue homespun staggered and fell, shot in the back. Women were screaming. The Leaguers fled the square, some turning to return fire. The courthouse bell rang out. A few white boys went down, some trampled, some shot in the legs or shoulders. A stampede of whites and Negroes, gunfire and burning flags. A riot of shouts. Three white men stormed the stage. Another smashed a bottle. One man set fire to a washrag and threw it into the mob.

Jesse Bliss and his hat loomed bright and clear in the midst of the chaos.

Tole's mind tumbled over itself. He sighted back in. He calmed his heart and his breath. This was the only thing that gave him any power, that rifle and its ball seated in the chamber, his eye, his knowledge of wind and angles. He felt the stock smooth on his cheek. Beyond the straight line between that window and the stage, the world faded away and time stopped.

Bliss's men tried to get him down from the stage, but it was all happening too fast. Tole had only a few moments to take his shot. This was his only chance. He had nearly squeezed the trigger when his chance disappeared.

He lost sight of Bliss in the raucous ebb and flow of people. He swung the front sight post over the crowd, past a white man with a twisted, two-fingered hand raised to shield his face, past the burning washrag, past the men fighting on the stage, and on to the front left corner of the platform. There was Bliss. He sighted in on the man's face, and let his eyes focus one last time on the target before he entered that loneliness of eye and front sight post, when the world was reduced down to a small piece of metal and a slow draw of breath. He looked one last time at the target, to make sure it was indeed a man and that he could tell his head from his ass end.

A head, blond, with a heavy-brimmed dark hat, loomed up between Tole and Bliss. Then Bliss's hat disappeared in the mob. Reappeared.

Again and again Tole sighted, aimed, but couldn't get a clear shot.

The hat disappeared again.

Tole could see Theopolis Reddick, young and vibrant and waving his hands for calm and a stop to the disruption. *Good luck*, Tole thought. Mariah's son very obviously had no idea what to do.

As Tole searched through the chaos, the man with the missing fingers raised a bottle in his good hand and threw it toward the stage. This one shattered over the head of the young black man who'd been trying, desperately, to speak before the chaos erupted.

After the bottle hit him, Theopolis seemed to sway a moment, and then crumpled. Several other men—white men, all—leaned in over him. *They'll help him*, Tole thought, *they'll pick him up and carry him out to safety*. That Negro was an innocent, they would know that.

And then one big man with a reddish-auburn beard pulled back his arm and his shoulder and let loose a powerful roundhouse punch at Theopolis's face.

The mob swarmed in, kicking.

They had the boy surrounded. Tole could see one man choking him from behind while another leaned in with a club, aiming for his face. Tole could imagine the brittle crack of jaw and bone. They were beating the boy to death, Tole had seen it before. It wasn't just the violence, it was the looks on their faces. They couldn't stop themselves if they tried; they'd crossed a terrible line Tole knew very well.

Why kill him? Was it because of his politics or simply because he was a nigger in the wrong place and they had come to kill as many as they could? He wondered if even they knew. The crowd was so dense that Theopolis disappeared beneath flying fists and boots; for a moment all Tole could see was the pale blur of all those white faces closing in. He focused in on one of the faces, gaunt with a cleft lip, and the lip was smiling. Tole imagined the kicks to the ribs, the kidneys, hands reaching for the eyes, clawing.

There was a moment that George Tole would relive till the end of his days, a moment that he recognized even as it happened as a moment dividing all others, creating a world contained entirely in the words *before* and *after*. A redtail hawk wheeled overhead, and although George Tole was fixed upon the scene in the courthouse square, he also remembered the bird's flight, its slow, lazy circles, imprinted on him forever.

For the briefest moment the mob parted and Tole had a clear

line of sight to Theopolis, bloody and screaming and mangled. A man raised an axe.

If anyone had been listening, they would have heard a single shot ring out. In the clamor and the dust Theopolis quit moving. His arms lay twisted at his sides and blood flooded the stage. The white men slowly backed away.

Afterward—his whole life would now be, it seemed, an *afterward*—he fled to the river and thought of leaving ol' GT right there on the bank and wading in to die, to finally be bathed in the blood for good. Instead he headed home through the shaded grove and by back alleys, drinking in deep gulps until his flask was empty, trying to stop the trembling of his hands. He took GT with him, as if it were attached.

CHAPTER 9

MARIAH

July 6, 1867

Running didn't seem fast enough. Mariah wondered about the people passing her going the other direction. Had they not heard the screams? What other important business did they have, their faces painted with worry or dreaminess, hands in their pockets or held before them, black hats and feathered hats on heads cocked down in thought, all of them seeming to want *out* when she wanted *in*? Their world seemed wide and forbidding, entirely mysterious.

She felt pulled along by a cord attached to the center of her chest. Every few steps she imagined the worst; the cord drew tighter and her feet moved faster. She had been the worst sort of mother, she thought. She had even resented being a mother at all sometimes, and now she dreaded that there was some kind of divine settling of accounts at work and she still had that debt to reckon with. Had she been a mother? Had she been enough?

She was so angry he had chosen this path of his through politics where he would always live at the whim of whichever white man decided he could find use for a clever ex-slave, *a dancing bear*, who could read and write and speak well in front of crowds. *That is not fair*, she thought. She was not being fair to her own son, who might very well have had a plan that was beyond even her. Maybe she was the ignorant one. He was her son, but also a man and not only a reminder of her neglect when he was a baby, his days in the cabins going hungry in the company of women not his mother. He had known his father only barely, and then only when his father was dying. Theopolis was now a grown man. She loved him, she hated him. He was hers nevertheless, a boy and a man.

She ran up the blocks and then up Main Street. The crowd grew denser on the wood sidewalk, so she weaved around carts and others walking down the middle of the street. They called out to her, *You're too late*, but she wouldn't turn. On this side of town it was black faces, but as she got closer to the square the faces turned white and red, eyes flashing. She was a block away when she realized that, yes, she had heard screams, and that under those screams were the loud, vibrating drone of shouts, curses, and feet stamping.

In the square the bodies moved in every direction. The crowd pulsed and rotated at its center, and at its edges men flung themselves out of the storm, running in every direction. The center, which she glimpsed only briefly here and there as she pushed closer, appeared to be located at the front of the stage, a dark and pulsing thing.

Time stretched out and she pushed through. Men stepped on her feet and she on theirs. She smelled them, they smelled of peat and coal. She fit herself between them, and as she got closer she began to push without regard for whom she was pushing or what the consequences would be. She nearly knocked over the magistrate Dixon, a big blowsy fancy man. He gaped at her. It felt a million years ago since she'd stood in his house and told him that he was a father again. What she cared about was finding her son and seeing that he was all right. She only wanted to see. Didn't need to speak to him, didn't need to touch him, he didn't need to know she was there. She had to see it for herself and then she could disappear and Theopolis could have his life and she could have hers and she would be free again. She told herself this.

She came closer to the center. Men began to recognize her and make way. They said things to her about what had happened, but she didn't hear them, or refused to register the meaning. There was the preacher, standing in her way, both palms toward her, shaking his head, and then he was gone, yanked to the side by the carpenter whose words she did hear: *She should see this*. Then she was through and stood at the center.

The others had drawn in a rough circle around an empty space. Entirely men, they were black and they were white. They radiated puzzlement or anger or horror or fascination, and sometimes all these at once. Their faces burned her; she shied away. She looked down. At the far end of the circle from her, a white man lay dead upon his back, his arms neatly at his sides, a dark pool of blood growing quickly underneath his mangled head. And upon the trampled ground lay Theopolis, her only son, the body of her body, the flesh of her flesh, without whom she was merely something afloat in time.

All things stopped, or seemed to. Dr. Cliffe knelt beside Theopolis, whose shirt had been ripped open. The doctor must have sensed life, because he pressed clean rags against the chest of her boy. He kept one hand on his chest, holding down a cloth, while he grabbed more rags from his bag with the other. The fabric kept the blood back for a moment, but soon it rose up through the bandages and seeped between the doctor's fingers. Her boy's chest rose and fell, but each time it became harder to see him move. Theopolis's head lay back on the doctor's coat. His eyes were open but he was not blinking. Blood ran down his face and the sides of his head, into his ears. His head was misshapen, she thought, like someone had been sanding it down and reshaping it. Blood soaked into the dirt and formed a dark halo around him. Sound disappeared, and Mariah heard nothing except the roar in her own head.

The doctor recovered and began trying to wrap Theopolis's chest. She held her son's head in her hands.

Mariah couldn't remember holding Theopolis this way since the morning of his birth. He was covered in blood that morning, too, and he wailed in her arms. She sang to him in a soft voice as she brought him to her breast. And now she sang to him, the melody lost behind sobs and her breaking voice. She remembered giving birth to Theopolis, alone on a strawtick pallet. She cried out and gripped the edges of the bed and screamed into the sky. He was heavy when he was born, and she held him then as she did now, trembling, kissing him on his forehead, pressing his face into her chest.

The little doctor sweated and pulled and stanched, but nothing changed until Theopolis rolled his head over in his mother's hands, toward her own face. He still did not blink, he did not see her, but he was faced toward her when he disappeared for good, drawn back into depthless darkness.

That was what had happened, she would say forever afterward. He just *left*, his face said nothing more eloquent than *gone*. There he was, and then, in less than an instant, he wasn't.

A man stepped forward. *And here's the nigger's gun. Rogue nigger. Just started shooting!*

Mariah was not really hearing his words, not right then; but the words would echo in her ears for years afterward.

This nigger boy shot the grocer. Shot John Sykes dead.

The cobbler boy here shot him? No sir. That's not his gun.

You bet it's his gun. I the one who took it off him.

You a damn liar.

Somebody shut him up. He saying Theopolis Reddick started shooting. Where he get a gun from?

She watched as someone laid a pistol by Theopolis's hand. She ignored it, left it in place. It had nothing to do with her or with her son.

She didn't recognize this gun, old and worn and dark-handled. She doubted Theopolis had ever carried one in his life. Still, she could see the story unfolding. They would make Theopolis look like a killer when he was anything but. His head was heavy in her lap, paradoxically heavier now that the soul was gone. In truth, she preferred that story, *the rogue nigger*, to the one more likely, which was that he had been taken down from the stage and slaughtered like a winter hog.

Theopolis believed in this world, so much so that he would make for it some speeches and try to win its votes. Her own head felt heavy, too, and seemed in danger of collapsing in on itself from the pressure of sound, too much sound, everything so loud now, all of it directed inward through her ears to her brain.

It was some time before she realized that the sound in her ears was that of her own voice. She wailed and directed the sound at Theopolis's face, but the vibrations would not revive him.

CHAPTER 10

TOLE

July 6, 1867

Evening calmed the chaos. George Tole had returned to his house in the Bucket, where he listened to the sounds of the street. Children cried out and carts clattered quickly past, their owners eager to be done with their business and go inside, safe in their homes like Tole. But Tole didn't feel safe. The day's crowd had dispersed, but still the voices rang out inside his head—clear, brittle, overly sharp.

He hadn't expected to see so much mayhem. He saw a Negro boy shot dead, a white grocer, and dozens wounded. Had to be at least forty or so boys wounded from the gunshots and beatings.

Around him he studied his hobby, the one thing he had that he loved: the tiny houses and buildings he carved out of scrap wood. They were little figures, the men in high pants and the women in long braids, going about their tiny days under the supervision of their God, George Tole. He had spent months carving his own crazy-angled version of a town and city, Franklin and New York and environs, a hybrid creature. This work took up most of his floor space—on the ground and on low tables he'd built for it. Now he looked at it and wondered why he ever bothered. In its regularity it seemed a horror.

Through the window in the south wall, over his wood-and-clay version of the town square, he could see through several yards to the cobbler's shop. He tried to pray, but he'd lost the rhythm of prayer, the sound of it. His prayer was straight wishing and pleading and waiting for a sign. He prayed for time not only to stop, but also to circle back on itself before certain decisions had been made, permanent and eternal.

When he fled New York he thought he would forget, but there was no forgetting. Mariah Reddick would know this fact soon enough. He knew the guilt would catch her, the helplessness, the not knowing, the growing suspicion that it could have been anyone who had put that bullet in her son and, therefore, by the logic of the grieving, that it had been *everyone*.

He thought he should flee again. Sure as day there would be men after him, maybe not that day, but soon. Dixon would be nervous, at the very least, about letting a Negro have so much knowledge of what happened and how it had been botched. That alone would get Dixon's men lurking around with their knives and torches. Lord knew what story Dixon would invent, but Tole knew he would be blaming a Negro sure as hell. Or all the Negroes, perhaps.

But the urge to run was weak. The idea of running exhausted him.

All that long night he sat on that stool. He was not crazy. If he made it through the night without incident, he would stay. He would stay, and then he would try to discover what he was supposed to do next. He wanted control again, he wanted to understand the world and his place in it. The tiny town he had created made no sense anymore; he needed more knowledge to bring it back in line with the world.

While he waited for the things to happen, he took out a piece of old oak flooring no bigger than his palm and began to carve a house with an attic. In the attic, he painted two eyes peering out from that window up under the eaves.

———

It was not true, as others assumed, that what existed in Tole's house was an elaborate display of *carvings*. It was much more than carving. Some of the figures—horses and people and houses, small dark shacks, fences (split rail and picket), stone walls, rifles—were carved from wood, yes, but this was by no means the only way Tole made his figures. Some were of wire wrapped tightly around nails and shaped, others were newspaper cartoons cut out and pasted to scrap pieces of wood, some were marbles glued to clothespins, and some were silhouettes cut with tin snips from coffee cans. Tole had no particular instinct to use one thing over another; he used what he could find.

But every figure, at least every human figure, was delicately painted, every detail down to the piping on trousers and the particular agitation of curl in an old man's hair. But none of them had faces. Or, rather, they had color but no features. They were white and black, in every shade from chalk white through the ivories and tans to the browns and blue-blacks. Every figure had been given its own shade; no two seemed alike. Sometimes when he looked at them he saw each grain of sand on a river bar. It occurred to him that he had much, much more work to do on his creation.

Tole poured his coffee and turned upon his chair toward the part of the diorama that portrayed the town square (in maple twigs, tobacco twine, clay, broken glass, and a gross of hatpins), where it appeared some men in hats and dark suits (carved cork, old lemon drops he'd painted white, and red clay) had gathered. There was a stage there against one side of the square, and the little men had begun to gather in front.

Tole stood up and looked down. He put his hand on one of the houses and watched the little stage, staring, as if something might happen. But nothing ever happened, at least not while he was there, at least not while he was looking.

But the town was growing up around him. It was alive and always changing. It was not strictly Franklin town, and it wasn't strictly New York either. It was a collection of time, really, glimpses in time. Times that were clogging in his head and wouldn't get out, wouldn't be forgotten. Other men forgot things, especially the bad things, but Tole's head was full to bursting with such memories. In his head they were too real and vivid, so he made them into the kinds of things he could hold in his hand or toss across the room: things that were real and yet not real, insignificant things, things that could not take over his head. He painted the display, and then painted it again every few weeks, always changing it. And all the time more people crowded the display until they were piled one atop the other.

He knew his neighbors thought him an eccentric, prone to disappear for days, preoccupied with the little houses and buildings and wood horses that were filling up his place. Rumors of madness and so forth. "Oh, Tole got hisself a whole *town* up there. Hardly a place for a grown man to stand," he overheard one day. "He carve what he could walk out the door and see, for goodness' sake." He hardly cared what they thought.

He longed for his boy, Miles, his dead son, more than ever. Sometimes when he was working on his town he imagined that if Miles could rise again and come looking for his father through three hundred miles of dark terrible lands wracked by war and shivered by misery, he would stumble into his father's little shack at first grateful for fire and light again. Then he would see the miniature world his father had created and look up at his father as if he understood that the town and the world that had killed him had been whittled and glued and nailed and placed so carefully down that they could never really be forgotten, and that each house and rail and roof and chimney had been put there for him, for Miles, to overcome and exceed on a day that could never be.

CHAPTER 11

MARIAH

July 8, 1867

The warblers and finches and robins that lived in the oak trees of the cemetery had no sense of occasion, Mariah thought. Here they came, leaping from branch to branch, diving from tree to tree, all the time loudly oblivious to the young men buried just beneath them. Tiny bird shadows flashed across the raw black dirt. She thought she should feel enraged. She felt sure that a proper and good woman and mother would curse the birds, rend her dress, shout insults at God. But birds, as far as Mariah knew, had no particular sound for sorrow and mourning, no special chittery language for sadness. Not even these Tennessee birds, despite everything that they had seen.

She might say the same thing about herself. No words for any of this, and no tears. There was a white oak a couple of hills away that had been standing on the Carnton plantation since the time of George Washington, and that had cast shade on Andrew Jackson when he'd come visiting. Surely that living thing had witnessed horrors. She wondered if this could be seen in the branches, or in the way the grain bent and curled around the tree's center.

The ghosts of war and the past were everywhere, in the sighing of the leaves and in the taste of the evening air on her tongue. The war was over, but it was still being fought, still surrounded her. Men still screamed and bled and wept for their mothers and wives.

And that riot was just the latest of the killing—not the last.

People stood around her in their dark colors, hands hanging down and clasped before them. Mariah lowered her head, stood beside her best friends, the sisters April and May, both of them now owners of the Thirsty Bird tavern, both of them former slaves of Robert Buchanan out on Coleman Road. April had been a cook and May the housekeeper. The two girls often dreamed of becoming tavern keepers, though they'd never before set foot inside a tavern until they'd opened one themselves.

Minnie Bostick was there, too, and all the folks from the Thirsty Bird—the blind piano player, Hooper the ragman, the carpenter. Many white folks had shown up, and Mariah was gratified to see them, as if they owed her to come: the sawyer Thomas Hoosier and his family, who were always partial to Theopolis and used to give him sweets when they saw him in town; the postmistress and resident busybody Anna McArdles; William Johnson and Ben Bettson, who bought shoes from Theopolis; and many others besides.

Presiding quietly from the back stood Carrie McGavock, her old mistress, clad in black mourning, with her black veil, and her good black lace gloves that came all the way from Paris, long before the war, and which Carrie kept for special funerals such as this.

"Psalm 103," the preacher said. From where she stood Mariah couldn't see the top of the poplar coffin, now that it had been lowered. All she saw was the hole.

She stepped forward, stood at the edge of the grave, and looked down. The coffin had been joined nicely, but it was still just an unfinished poplar box, canted slightly from one side to the other on the uneven bottom of the grave. It wouldn't last long against the worms and beetles. She shook her head as if to shake the thought out of her ears. She wanted never to think of that again. There was a knot in the wood, a nearly perfect circle just above where Mariah imagined Theopolis's face lay. An eyehole? A portal. If she could squeeze through that knot she could visit the next world. *His days are as grass; as a flower of the field, so he flourisheth. For the wind passeth over it, and it is gone*, she heard the preacher saying. *That's an ignorant thing to say out loud*, Mariah thought.

She remembered the pale yellow rose in her right hand. Who gave her that? Carrie. It seemed a long time ago, when she arrived in Hooper's cart and Carrie helped her step down. *For you*, Carrie said while handing over the flower on its long stem. But no, it was *not* for her. She stood on the edge of the grave and accepted that this was what it had come to, that this was how it would be. She didn't much care about being alone; she cared that this life of her son would end so badly, so commonly: in a wooden box at the bottom of a hole.

Mariah tossed the flower in as if casting aside dirty laundry. With a gentle thump, almost a whisper, it covered the portal knot. It looked very pretty there on the lid. Mariah took three steps to the pile of dirt that the gravediggers stood next to, leaning on their shovels. She shoved her hand wrist deep into that pile and the gravediggers stepped back. She came away with a fist full of brown clay that spilled out between her fingers. She stepped back to the edge of the grave and threw the dirt in as hard as she could. It made an awful drumming sound, the sound of something knocking to come in. The flower had been thrown off center and befouled.

Good. That is how it is and ever was.

No, she did *not* accept that. She *would not* accept that. How it is and how it ever was? That's talk that kills.

She would do something.

And what would she do? What *could* she do?

Time slowed. She stepped back as others stepped forward to toss their own fistfuls of dirt. Mariah felt a little wobbly and sought out the oak tree to lean against. She felt the rough knobbiness of it on her spine, and it caught the back of her black veil, borrowed from Carrie. Carrie had a whole collection of such things.

Around her the crowd whispered and shifted. She thought, *Did you do it? Did all of you do it? You all did.* She let her mind take off on its own, and then reeled it back. What if they had? All the killers, now shuffling forward to the grave and back again, past her, nodding their heads and clasping her hands, saying words she would never remember. What would justice look like when it was brought down on their heads? She shook her head. No, not these men and women, not April and May and the rest, they weren't guilty. All mourners *do* look a little guilty about something, but not about that.

These people also looked angry and hurt. Afraid. They had lost Theopolis, too, she thought. Not like she had, not like a mother, but they had lost him, too. Many of the Colored Leaguers were there, they who had marched with him and drummed with him, dreamed with him, talked with him and agreed with him about politics—and then had watched him die.

They had all heard the whispers of the Conservatives, telling them they might be next. Telling them they should be next. These people weren't killers, she thought, looking around. Some of them were puffed up with their anger, chests thrust out and chins raised as if they were preparing themselves for a fight. But most of them, with their hunched shoulders and their scared eyes, looked more like prey than anything, like mice standing in the shadow of a trap.

Carrie detached herself from the other white folks on their mission of charity to the poor Negro funeral, and now she moved toward Mariah slowly, tentatively. Mariah wouldn't look her in the eye, couldn't stand to do it. *What of the guilty*, she wanted to shout at her. *What about the white men?* Was there any doubt that they had killed her boy? None. So what did justice look like on them? She didn't know.

Carrie stood beside her now, not saying anything, staring toward the grave. Mariah didn't know what justice for Carrie's kind *was*, and the thought of this made her tear up. Carrie offered a handkerchief, which Mariah took because she felt in a mood to take everything. Would a white man be beaten in his guilt? Would he be leaned against a post, back bare, and take his stripes from the leather? Would his rations be reduced, would he be made to sleep in a hole? Would he be sold as incorrigible? Would he be hanged?

She dabbed her eyes with Carrie's handkerchief, which smelled like rosehips. The mourners filed past her and began to leave, wandering down the little road to town, past the lines of the Confederate dead.

For the first time she noticed George Tole, broad and impassive. Had it been only a few days ago that she'd met him at the Dixons'? She caught his eye for a moment before he turned away and followed the others. She remembered, after she'd met Dixon, that Theopolis had described the elaborate carvings and gewgaws that filled Tole's little house. Mariah saw a black man who had kept his freedom his whole life, who might know what this kind of justice, the justice she imagined for the guilty, would look like. He had a hard face, dark. Such a man might know. Others might know, too; probably everyone else knew but Mariah Reddick. She felt so lost. Then Tole was gone down the road and Hooper and the gravediggers had begun to shovel in the dirt.

Carrie gently tugged at her elbow. "We should go to the house, Mariah." The house, Carnton, loomed open-eyed above them. "There's food in the dining room." Mariah had eschewed a funeral gathering. Now she wished she hadn't as Carrie went on, "Please eat with me. Together." This last clarification was, Mariah guessed, meant to be meaningful and gracious. She knew what that table would look like: set with the mismatched coin-silver and the worn-out Old Paris plates that Mariah had washed nearly every day of her previous life. Back then she had been fond of the McGavocks' eccentric tableware that she had never been asked to eat on. Had she ever used it, though, she would have wondered why she couldn't do so every day, and would have come to hate it. She knew herself well enough to know that. It occurred to her then that Carrie might have thought the same thing about introducing her slave to the china and, for her own reasons, had made sure it didn't happen. Instead, she had appreciated its cracked and imperfect beauty from a distance.

"Not very hungry."

The gravediggers hitched up the cart and drove off between the back gallery of the house and the cemetery. The cart bristled with shovels and picks. They nodded their heads as they passed. Down at the end of the lane, they picked up that man Tole, who looked back once before they disappeared between the last ring of fences.

Every piece of the McGavock property had been marked with borders of either white board horse fencing, reminders of the blooded horses that once grazed within their confines, or by drystack rock fences built from clearing fields. A few years before the war, Colonel McGavock had received a coin-silver cup at the county fair for the best half mile of drystacked rock fencing in the county. Though he had never laid a rock of it himself, he had taken great pride in that cup, just as he took great pride in his fences, back then.

Rings circled within rings, fences marked paths. *Here you are to stay, and here you are to walk.* Out in the open, which is to say, out in the life she lived in town, there weren't so many fences marking the danger areas. Here at Carnton, though, Mariah could understand the full utility of the fences she had hardly noticed before. They kept things out. But standing at the very center of the property, smelling the new dirt on Theopolis's grave, she wondered if the fences, the rings within rings, weren't also meant for those who were contained within, so that they might know the extent of the earth to which they were entitled to roam without care, no more and no less. It made her anxious, all those fences, and she nearly wept at the idea of being held back. But she could hardly think of what else to do, and at this felt relief, and then shame.

Carrie glided across the way to the house. Mariah drifted back a few paces. Carrie held several white carnations in her hand, which Mariah knew could be made into a perfume to bring luck to gamblers. Her feet trod five-fingered grass, which could be made into a bath for uncrossing those who had been cursed, who had roots thrown at them. Over by the corner of the house, blowing in the wind, was sheep weed, which could be made into a tea to restore sanity. Everything was a material of conjure if looked at properly and with the imagination of spirit, the sort of imagination that had comforted her mother.

Mariah returned to Theopolis's grave. Carrie stopped and waited patiently, not watching. Mariah wondered if Carrie knew what she had it in her mind to do. Carrie was no stranger to the conjuring of spirits.

At the grave, Mariah stooped down and scraped up a handful of dirt from the mound atop Theopolis. A handful of goofer dust. She did not know how to use it, but her mother would have taken it, and just having it in her hand calmed her. She wrapped it in the handkerchief she'd borrowed from Carrie, knotted it neatly, and dropped it in the secret pocket of her skirts. Carrie said nothing. If she had asked, Mariah would have said that she needed something to help her against the men who had taken her boy, but what she really needed, far more than dust, was *names*. She wanted the names of those responsible, whether or not there was justice in the world.

At the steps up to the house, Carrie spoke again. "You know you can stay here as long as you like."

Mariah nodded and watched a tiny green beetle climb up the back of Carrie's long black dress, worn for Mariah's dead son. *My dead son* was the name of a patch of ground now, a patch of the Carnton estate.

And what should Mariah call herself now? *Mother*? There was no word for the woman left alone by the death of her own child. She had been a widow and had been honored as a widow, but no one honored the woman who buried her child.

To her left she saw something moving across her field of view. A man she recognized, though he seemed barely a shadow. He carried something heavy on his back and, at that distance, seemed to disappear into the tall grass. She thought she recognized his head, or maybe the rhythm of his walk. *This one, he of the old world,* she thought, her other world, the one before she ever could have considered sitting down at the table with Carrie McGavock. In that world there had been the McGavock children, needing their noses wiped and their lessons laid out for them on rainy afternoons. There had been little Theopolis, in the cabin, making armies of straw men tied with twine and marched across the boards Mariah tried to keep swept in the cabin. There had been the bed in her cabin, a small thing barely bigger than a pallet.

And most of all there had been no reason to think much about anything beyond the fences and the walls, the path between that cabin and those parlors.

———

Later in the afternoon Carrie and Mariah sat together inside, in the family parlor, the two of them sharing some finger sandwiches the cook had made, turnips and some cauliflower, a small bowl of chilled okra soup. Mariah hadn't been eating, and Carrie remarked on this twice.

Mariah remembered, almost with amusement, that it had been she—Mariah—who, all those years before, had forced Carrie to sit down and eat, to nibble on a carrot or a radish or a bite of bread. *Have this piece of cheese, Miss Carrie. Worth taking just a bite. Here.*

Now, sitting here in the same room where she demanded that

her mistress have a ham sandwich, Mariah was more stubborn. She forked her vegetables around her plate. The family parlor felt different, emptier than before, with those mismatched plates and stained cloth napkins. Mariah never would have tolerated stained napkins, wrinkled and tattered, but Carrie didn't even seem to notice. The rooms seemed darker than before, gloomier, the summer sun failing to break through grimy windows and tattered curtains—had Carnton always been so filthy? Surely not. When Mariah was there, Carnton shone.

Not her house anymore. Not her life.

She surveyed the wreckage of the mashed turnips, and bit her lip to keep from crying out.

A suffocating kind of silence had arisen now between them, former mistress and former slave: the gentle tapping of a coin-silver fork to porcelain plate, the clink of glass to table, each inadvertent noise a reminder of how little they spoke, and how little, really, they had to say to each other. They defined themselves by what they were not: they were not friends, they were not mistress and slave, or employer and employee. They were two people washed up together on a farther shore with nothing in common but the air they breathed, and perhaps they even breathed different air.

And yet there was a kind of familiar peace about being back; a peace she hadn't expected, a peace she resented. She hated that Carnton still felt like home, even in the slightest way. Carnton. What a horrible name for a house. She'd heard somewhere that it meant tomb—how could the McGavocks, Mr. John's grandfather and great-grandfather, and all the line of all the McGavocks back to the past that Mariah could scarcely imagine, want to entomb their children?

Carrie's throat made a slight clicking sound as she swallowed. "I'll be sure to have a proper tombstone made for him. A bigger one. With his name and all the dates."

"Not your place."

"Of course not. But it's my cemetery."

"What does it matter?"

Carrie sipped her water, and a sliver of a smile wrinkled her cheek. "Do you remember when he was little, probably four years old, and he'd hide beneath—"

"Stop it."

Carrie's smile froze.

"I don't want to talk about him."

"He was a special boy, Mariah."

"You don't know nothing." Mariah could hear the anger in her own voice.

"I do," Carrie replied. "If anyone would know, Mariah, it's me."

Mariah didn't respond. Carrie was probably right. Carrie had lived with grief and rage so long herself that she probably forgot as it followed her from room to room, like a midday shadow.

Was this how Mariah was doomed to live? Filled with grief and a rage so inarticulate and so elemental that she would come to rely upon it, like a cane or an extra toe, to give her balance? Would it come to a point, for Mariah, too, where the darkness was so much a part of her that she could not bear to live without it? A time when she would revel in the long straight rows of the Confederate dead, dead for their lost and stupid cause?

"Have you decided what you're going to do with his belongings?"

"You like thinking about them things that don't matter."

Carrie raised her eyes from her plate.

"They can burn it for all I care," Mariah continued.

"Don't do that," Carrie said.

"Do what?"

"Pretend he never existed."

Mariah stood up, the wooden legs of her chair scraping along the floor. "You don't get to tell me what to do. Not no more, Miss Carrie."

"I've noticed something since he's been dead. You can't even bring yourself to say his name. You say, 'My son,' or 'My boy,' but you can't say 'Theopolis,' can you?"

Mariah stood frozen. She pursed her lips.

"Say it," Carrie said.

"You go to hell."

Carrie stood. "The regret will haunt you worse than any ghost if you don't make peace."

"I ain't like you."

"No, you aren't. I know what kind of woman you are. I watched you raise that boy to become a man. A good, sweet, loving man who cared about the world and thought he could make a difference in it. But it doesn't matter what you've survived or how strong you act. This is different. Remember that time you got bit by the copperhead?"

Mariah nodded her head yes.

"It was just on your finger but I remember how your hand swelled. Your whole arm swelled up. You couldn't stop crying. Remember?"

"That don't matter."

"How old were we then? Seven? Eight? But I remember how awful it was for you. I remember how scared I was, and I wasn't the one who was bit. Remember how you wept because the pain was so bad?"

Mariah nodded again.

"Now you know, the pain of that bite doesn't come close to the pain in your chest, does it?"

Mariah spoke through quivering lips: "No, it don't."

"It's all right to miss him, Mariah."

Mariah looked away.

"Look at me." Carrie took Mariah's hand, her palms still rough and calloused. "It's all right. And it's all right to remember him. And it's all right to laugh when a memory comes in the middle of the day of the silly little boy that used to run around this house. And if that laughter turns to tears, that's all right, too."

"Why you saying this like I don't know?"

"Because you need to hear it and you don't know it. Because you're too brave and too strong for your own good. Sometimes you have to give in, be weak. That's the only way you'll survive it. You don't always have to be so strong."

"I should be like you? Dress in black. Live with the dead every day. That's what I got to do?"

"No, Mariah."

"Good. I ain't doing it. I won't carry around the dead forever like you do."

"We all carry the dead. We all do it. Some of us ignore the ghosts that follow us. Some of us turn and face them, look them in the eye. And when you finally turn around, you'll realize they're not here to haunt you, my dear."

Warm summer blew through the open window. The heavy damask curtains—how long had it been since they'd had a good washing?—billowed and fell back against the windowpane. Soon it would be night, and Mariah would watch the moonlight ripple through deep purple sky, and she'd remember those nights when Theopolis was a young boy, the two of them lying on their backs, staring toward the heavens, and Theopolis would count the stars, and use his tiny finger to connect them all. He always had such an imagination. Night was the quietest hour, when a single cricket's chirp could keep time like a second hand, and she'd wait for sleep to come. Some nights, she'd hear a stirring in the summer kitchen just steps from her cabin, something like the wind, rattling the old windows, or maybe the soft patter of a bird walking on the roof. The sounds weren't anything supernatural, nothing she couldn't blame on the weather, but that didn't mean she didn't wish it. Mariah never much believed in ghosts, but now, during those nighttime hours, would she wish for them?

Tears burned in her eyes, but she tightened her jaw. She was not weak. She would not appear weak. Not even in front of Carrie. Especially not in front of Carrie.

"I miss him," Mariah said.

Tears burned down both cheeks. How had this happened? She vowed she would not weep, and then she had. She spoke, not to Carrie but to the window and out the window and to the universe.

"When I'm dreaming, he's there, Theopolis, my baby, and we're somewhere together, I don't know the place, ain't no place I ever been, but he's there, smiling, and I know I'm dreaming. I just know it. And I beg myself, 'Please don't wake up, not yet.' And he turns to me and he says, 'No, Mama, you ain't dreaming. This world here is the real one. That other world is just a bad dream.' And I feel this kind of relief. I can't explain it. And then I wake up, and I stare up at the ceiling, and it takes me a moment to figure out which world is real, and which is a dream. Then I remember he gone. And I close my eyes tight as I can and I try to get back to the other world where he's still walking around and where I can touch him and kiss his face. But I can't never get back."

Carrie held Mariah's hand tightly in hers. When she had reached over to take Mariah's hand, Mariah almost pulled it free, but couldn't summon the strength.

"It's going to take time, Mariah."

"How long?"

"Until you stop dreaming of him? Maybe never."

Mariah smeared her tears away.

"That's not such a bad thing," Carrie told her.

"You dream of the dead, Miss Carrie?"

Carrie looked down. "Every night," she said.

Would it be so bad, right now, to dream of the dead every night? Mariah thought not.

And suddenly there it was, cold and stark before her: the road she would travel, back to her small house in town. The days stretching out, endless and free, before her. She'd heard someone talking about a woman in Franklin who'd lost her only child to consumption, and the loneliness, the emptiness she felt. This was what her days and nights would be. The burden seemed immense.

She resolved that for a moment—only a moment—she would pause. She would hold her head high and not pick up that burden. Not quite yet. She would let the memory of her only son live around her. She would live where he lived. That was something she could do with freedom now, couldn't she?

"Ma'am?"

Carrie turned.

"If you still wanting me to stay, I'd just as soon stay," Mariah said.

Carrie clasped her hands in front of her. She smiled gratefully. "I will send someone to fetch your things from town."

"For just a little while."

"Of course. Just a little while."

Chapter 12

Tole

July 9, 1867

A dog followed Tole on the way to Elijah Dixon's office.

Dixon was the sort of man who could be everywhere at once. He was one of *them*. The sort of white man who was always watching and taking note. Tole had known such men in New York, and you could see the fact of their power in their faces, which never flinched or betrayed what boiled underneath. They wielded enough power to animate men and mobs, though not always enough to control events once they were set in motion. Sometimes messes had to be cleaned up, and Tole assumed he was one of those messes now. He carried a small pistol in his pocket, just in case.

Dixon hadn't needed to spell it out for Tole, it was clear: *Put a bullet through the bastard.* Tole would be cutting off the head of the snake, and Tole had expected to be shown a great monster of a man taking the podium, someone like the men he'd known back in the Five Points, hulking and top-hatted and dead to everything but getting theirs, and to hell with the Negroes if they got in the way.

But when Jesse Bliss stood on the stage with his feathered hat,

Tole had momentarily thought to pack it up and slink away. He had thought: *No more killing.* He had thought: *I can be better than this.* He had thought: *I can be like everyone else.*

And then Theopolis Reddick had come into the crowd, and the bottle had smashed over Theopolis's face, and the blood ran down his ear and neck.

He had known Theopolis, knew more about him than he did most people just by virtue of living a few houses over. Theopolis talked loud when he'd been drinking a little, could sing hymns down low in his throat, and he walked a little bowlegged. He smiled often, sometimes to himself when he was walking up the street to his mother's.

His mother, Mariah, reminded Tole of his own Charlotte. It was just a fact, both were light-eyed and worry-lined and fierce.

Dixon stood on the landing in the sunlight that set the air and dust on fire, swirling here and there ahead of Tole as he mounted the stairs. Then Dixon turned and reentered his office, leaving the door open, which Tole shut behind him.

Dixon sat at his desk, and Tole stood on the other side of the room under a bird's-eye map of New Orleans. He kept Dixon between him and the window, and his back to the corner, just in case the men Dixon had sent to follow him were planning something with gunfire.

Dixon looked at him dumbly and innocently, like he halfway expected Tole to compliment him. Maybe he wanted to know what Tole thought of the bourbon so magnanimously poured out in a tin cup and handed to him with such ceremony. "Of course, Mr. Tole, I will need your cooperation in the coming days."

Dixon could not make his move now, could he? Rumors had spread of an investigation brought by men from Nashville, from the Freedmen's Bureau or perhaps the U.S. Army, on the subject of the riot and the deaths of the men, Theopolis and the grocer.

The day before, a group of Federal men had come to town,

fanned out, and taken depositions of anybody who might have seen what happened, or had something to say about it. Tole had heard they would take their findings back to Nashville and decide on next steps, quite possibly a full-on investigation.

Dixon couldn't have *another* killing and another Negro get lynched if investigators were on their way, so Tole reckoned he was safe for a while, maybe a week. But as long as he was alive he assumed Dixon would think of him as a danger, someone who could run his mouth. Tole made these calculations nearly instantly. He had been suckled and raised on such practical reasoning in New York, which had at times seemed not just a real city, but also an exquisitely calibrated scaffolding of plots and hierarchies and postponed revenges. But it turned out that Franklin was unlike New York in some ways he hadn't predicted.

"I aim to cooperate and always have, Mr. Dixon."

"We had an agreement in place, Mr. Tole, and as far as I can tell, you failed to hold up your end. My directions were as clear as my intentions, but instead of a clean job, I have a mess. I have just now received official communication to the effect that the U.S. Army will be here in a month—exactly one month after the killings— to hold a tribunal on those killings, and all the while, that bastard you were supposed to kill is sitting with his feet up, still breathing. That is what educated men call irony."

Tole looked at the floor. He seemed to always be looking at the floor, as if he were scared to make eye contact with the man in front of him. He didn't like the way Dixon said *educated*, as if it were an accusation aimed at him.

"All those stories I'd heard about you being a marksman. They were all just folklore, weren't they?"

"Those were different times. I was a different man. I told you."

"You lose your nerve? All that booze got your hands shakin'? Can't aim right anymore? You know what a broke-down nigger means to me? I know you do."

This one will kill me when he gets the chance, is what Tole heard.

"But I am in a generous mood, and so I don't intend to hold that against you. Not much, anyway."

They sat silently together for a minute or two, Dixon watching Tole's face.

"You ain't afraid of me talking?"

Dixon laughed, and reached out to fill up Tole's tin cup. "No, I'm not afraid of you talking, Mr. Tole."

"Because I know a lot." Tole sounded to himself like he was still a boy a million years before, boasting and puzzling his way.

"Right, of course, you're from *New York*. I suppose they listen to niggers there, right? To what they say they know?"

Tole nodded, knowing exactly where the man's point was headed.

"Your knowledge is not a *danger* to me, it is merely inconvenient. If you talked, I would have to have a few extra conversations I don't have time to have, I'd have to make extra assurances to the right people, but what you know is not a danger to me. If I thought you would talk I might have you killed, but not because you're a threat, but simply an annoyance. I don't like to be annoyed."

"You hired me to kill a man."

"The story everyone will believe is that a mean nigger jumped into the crowd and shot a white man dead before getting killed by a mob."

"The people in that crowd know that ain't true."

"Maybe. But what are you going to tell them? *I was up in an attic with a rifle pointed at the square because the magistrate of Franklin told me to kill one of them politicians, but I botched the job?* And the magistrate will say that he did *not* tell that nigger, who happens to be crazy and a trained assassin, to kill anyone. And they'll leave my office and you'll be dead in five minutes."

Tole thought that maybe this had been the whole point of the meeting, for Dixon to let him know how *little* he mattered to anyone, and how much he depended on Dixon's favor. He mattered so little there, in Franklin, that it wasn't worth killing him or even roughing him up to keep his silence. He was nothing, hardly a human, with no standing and no thoughts or knowledge.

Tole's heart beat fast and his face went hot. He realized that he had been expecting to be punished for what he did, or at least to feel some heat. Without that, the guilt he had felt since the day of Theopolis's death was now compounded by shame. He deserved pain, consequences.

"So," Dixon continued, "just for convenience's sake, if they ask you, you were anywhere *but* up there in that attic, and you don't know anything about me or the man in the hat or any of it. We'll just keep this simple and clean."

"Of course." Tole's instinct for survival was an abomination.

He waited expectantly for the threat, and it came in the form of a new proposition: "There's one more thing, Mr. Tole. I'm going to need you to finish the job I hired you to do."

"Sir?"

"You're going to go put a bullet in that man's head. It's real simple."

"Can't do that."

"You're going to."

Tole was quiet. He thought of his sleepless, dreamless nights, when the drink wasn't enough to put him down, and he'd lie awake trying to remember all the men he had killed. He was never able to finish the list. He'd count his kills as a means of drifting away. He believed it was two dozen or so, but he could never be sure. He knew it was enough that he never wanted to do it again. *Enough*, he would tell himself, his voice slurring as he rolled around his small bed, half-conscious. *Enough killing. Never again!* But killing was like drinking. Every time, he promised himself it was his last. *Just this last one and I'll be finished*, he'd say.

Or what? Tole stared out, unblinking, unmoving. What could

Dixon, realistically, threaten him with? Death? It had been a long time since the mention of dying had caused his heart to beat any faster. Prison? He wasn't scared of it. In his mind, he stood and said, *Mr. Dixon, you go ahead and kill me if that's what you want to do. I don't give a damn.*

But there was another truth, too, which Tole had been trying to drink away these last few nights: that he just might have a reason to stay around, living and moving, and this was something he hadn't had for a long time. He hadn't been expecting a reason to live. But he couldn't get the image out of his mind of the gray-eyed midwife holding her dead son in her arms.

Too often Tole acted without thought of the immediate consequences; too often he acted just to act, to move forward in the world, because any action is better than standing still like a dummy, like a brainless scarecrow. He followed his first instinct. For George Tole, at that moment, the future unspooled like a ragged thread, all options equally dark, equally bitter. *The right play would be to get the hell out, head west, and not turn back*, his instinct said.

Except.

Except, perhaps, if he stayed here in this miserable town with its backbiting neighbors and terrible plots: if he stayed, just for a while longer, perhaps he could make a difference to *her.*

He nodded. "All right, sir."

"What do you mean, all right?"

"I'll do what you asked. I'll finish the job. Kill your man."

Dixon seemed satisfied, for the moment. He leaned back in his chair, which creaked. He sipped the bourbon and licked his lips. Never took his eyes off Tole, though. He leaned farther back in the chair, contemplating his guest behind slitted eyes, before bringing the chair crashing forward again and dismissing Tole with a wave of his hand.

CHAPTER 13

MARIAH

July 10, 1867

Mariah told Miss Carrie she would be heading back into Franklin to see about some business. *What business? If there's a baby to be born, the families will come to you. Stay here, where it's safe,* Carrie might have once asked, but now she swallowed her tongue.

Mariah walked into town and through it, taking the side streets around the courthouse square, avoiding the place where the stage, now gone, had stood. She traveled beyond that, into the Blood Bucket, just as she had left it. The neighborhood shifted as she moved east, the world slowly dilapidated around her, from the pristine cherry brick houses to boarded-up shacks that housed two or three black families at a time. She stood on the edge of her old neighborhood, just a few blocks from where Theopolis had lived, and a couple more blocks from her own house, but nothing about it felt like home. Not anymore. From the windows wafted the scents of fatback and ashcakes. They all still ate slave food.

Around her, men and women moved about in anxious groups. She could hear bits of their talk as they went by.

I heard they was coming for Mr. House. Tonight.

They getting their rifles together down at Colby and Vaughan's stable.

Ben Bostick still hiding, you hear? Won't even see Doc Cliffe 'bout his head.

They ain't done with it...They ain't done with it yet.

Mariah arrived at the Thirsty Bird and found April and May in their cane-back chairs against the wall, whispering to each other. Mariah was sure they were gossiping about the military men's depositions from the other day.

Now April and May grinned and called out insults to Mariah, which was their greatest expression of affection. May was short, broad-shouldered, and sleepy-eyed, and April was her opposite: long-legged and sloe-eyed. She had a small head, and her hair flowed back into a loose knot. How had her face managed to emerge unblemished, unscarred, from all of their history? None of the rest of them had made it through without marks; even their basic features, eyes and noses and ears, had got twisted up and mashed down by time. But not April's.

"Guess they don't got none of Hooper's cure out there at the big house, Miss Mariah?"

"Better cures than that," Mariah said. She was happy to see April and sat down close to her on a stool.

May, who hardly talked, brought Mariah a short drink of the thick Hooper liquor. She winked when she did it, and took her seat on the other side of April again.

Mariah took a long sip at the sticky jar. Across the room, at the end of a long table, April and May had set liquor and loaves of bread. This was their idea of a saloon, and why not? Mariah thought. She leaned over and put a little coin in May's hand. It occurred to her to stand up and announce that, in fact, she had earned this money herself and not taken it from the white lady who was her former owner. She knew no one would care, and so she stayed quiet. There was a lot of shouting, anyway, and she wasn't sure she'd be heard over the din.

The last couple of days, April told Mariah, their tavern had been half-full with black saloon-goers, riled up about the shootings, talking too loudly, too drunkenly, about Theopolis being shot. Each Negro had their own theory.

But so much of the talk was political: these freedmen could *vote*. The very idea was enough to get them drunk. Many were vocal about supporting Brownlow. A few of them were Conservatives, and they would try to shout the others down, saying that the Republicans needed to tone down their support for the Reconstruction government so that they could live alongside the whites, and get and keep their jobs working for them.

It was easy for Mariah to ignore such talk—she was focused on something else.

She looked out at the rest in the room: the fiddler was plunking at his fiddle like it was a guitar and mooning at April; a couple danced with one arm around the other and a jar in the other hand; a treecutter and a turpentiner sat on chairs in the corner closest to the window; and a scattering of others, mostly country people she'd seen before but whose names did not immediately penetrate the growing fog of Hooper's liquor. These men talked to each other animatedly, their hands sweeping through the air with the force of their words. The saloon, usually light with laughter and friendly conversation, felt heavy with their anger and their fear. *Brownlow*, Mariah heard them say, again and again. *Bliss. Dixon. Brownlow. Theopolis. Dixon. Brownlow. Brownlow, Brownlow, Brownlow*. She wished they would be quiet.

April put her hand on Mariah's shoulder. "They gone to come and set a hearing for the killings. Maybe you knew that."

Mariah leaned forward again. "Who they?"

"Nashville people. They coming soon. August 6. Just a few weeks away now. Freedmen's office too. And the U.S. Army itself is coming back."

"The whole Army?"

"Don't know. Talk is a hundred or so. There to keep the peace for the Nashville folk."

"White folk from Nashville? I got my fill of them for right now."

"Well, who you think, Mariah? Who you think they send? Least they send someone."

"Someone ain't always better than no one." Mariah thought for a moment, wrinkled her eyes with her squinting. "What they looking for?"

"Want to know who killed your boy and the grocer, and they wanna talk to all them others who got hurt. They say more'n thirty people got a bullet in 'em that day, black and white folks."

"They don't care about none of that." That day Mariah had lost any faith she might have had in the idea that there was even one person in Nashville who cared how her boy had died, or that he had never owned a pistol in his life, and had very clearly been murdered without a thing to defend himself with except for a speech he had scrawled on some crumpled butcher paper. Not a gun or a knife or a stick or a rock.

Theopolis had stood beside her when they filled in the grave of his father, her one and only husband. He put his little arm around her waist, reaching about halfway. She had tried to leave him behind, but he insisted and set about preparing himself. He washed his face and cleaned his shoes, and when she leaned over him the top of his head smelled like cooking fires and sunlight. They were two alone, the last of their kind, and she had loved him. Right then, she had wanted him beside her at all times, forever, underfoot or no.

Now she was the very last of the Reddicks, their little family. *I am the only one left to make things right. I am the last one before we all disappear from the face of the earth.*

"Hey April."

"Yes darling."

"What do you know about that man, Tole?"

"Not much, though he come in pretty often."

"You find out anything about him, you be kind and let me know."

"Mariah Reddick is sweet on a man!" April cackled, the romantic notion getting the best of her.

But when Mariah looked over at May, she was squinting at her in that way that she had, which meant, *I know something going on, Sister Mariah, and it gone get you in trouble.*

Mariah sat for a time with these people she had known most of her life, letting their warmth and sincerity wash over her and trying to shut out their anger.

"I so sorry 'bout your boy passing. He was real special. Those damned Conservatives gonna pay for what they did to him, you hear?"

"Decent man, your boy was. More decent bones in his body than every one of those white devils put together."

"Fine cobbler. Nobody made shoes as fine as he did. Even them that got their hands on him, they was wearing his shoes. *They* knew his was fine."

They surrounded her, the former property of Frank Colby and Jim Vaughan and Jasper Morton, field hands and grooms and stable boys, laundresses and seamstresses and cooks and ragpickers, and they talked and they laughed and they remembered.

"Special man," Pleasant repeated. She was the former maid of Logan Neely, who'd owned her mother, and owned her and her brothers, when they were born.

"You younger than he was," Mariah told her. "What you know about how special he was? You just repeating what the others sayin'."

"I old enough to know a decent man."

"I remember the morning you was born. I was the one pulled you outta your mama. You were stubborn as a damn mule...You woulda thought we was pulling you away from Eden, the way you didn't wanna come out. Musta been something about her belly that made you wanna stay. Maybe it was Eden. And when you came out, you were the fattest baby I ever seen."

"I wasn't no fat baby."

"Oh you was. You was so fat. Meaty legs and full cheeks like corncakes. And a big ol' belly. And you was precious."

"All babies precious."

A round of nods and agreement.

Then Mariah said, "Spent damn near my whole life here. And I reckon I brought most of these folks into this world in some way or another, same way I did you. And now somebody take my own child out the world, and I wonder what I been doing all this time, filling up the world with people."

Mariah paused, thinking, *I made up my own lullabies and I sang 'em in the softest voice I could muster until he'd stop kickin'. And I pushed him out in a tub of blood and bathwater, and he came into this world with a full head of hair, and he looked just like me. I never thought I was much to look at, but damned if he wasn't the most beautiful baby I'd ever seen. And I didn't feel like no nigger when I held him.*

What they took, what they always took from Negroes, was knowledge. *They were scared what we would do with it*, Mariah thought. *And we was too tired and beaten and…hell, we was scared too. Scared to get knowledge, to know why things are as they are.* If there was anything that made her feel like a nigger, it was that state of un-knowing. It was one of the ways the Negro had been walked upon for so many years. *Don't tell the Negro nothing and after a while the Negro quits expecting there to be explanations: for why they getting lashes, or why they getting sold to Mississippi, or why they got to live* here *while the white people live* there. The Negro had learned to praise Jesus instead. The Negro might even forget to look for someone to explain why her son been killed. *No more*, Mariah thought. *No more, or I might as well put the shackles back on myself.*

Mariah turned to April and May. "It just now come to be that I should be here asking for your help, you two and Minnie and Patsy and Maggie and Pleasant and all of 'em. You tell 'em all I came by to see you, and if they hear anything about what happened there in the square, seen anything, heard some white old fool whisperin' from down the bar. Anything. You tell 'em come find me. You hear? Tell 'em to tell the white folk what they want, but I want to know the truth."

They heard what she meant, how her words sounded in a world where the fate of a black man was of as much concern to the white man as that of his favorite horse.

This time she would not go forward quietly, Mariah thought. And thus it began: the first conversation, the first stirring. Mariah would fight to *know*. And with knowing, change the world.

Over Carnton lay a low, starless sky. The trees were like dark clouds against the sky before they disappeared entirely into the coming night. Mariah's walk back to Carnton had been quiet.

Now she sat at the window, letting the reflection from the window glass magnify the oil lamp as she hemmed and rehemmed table linens, an unending task within a household that seemed threadbare at every turn. Mending was a break in the list of Carnton's daily chores. Today had been wash day, which had meant that clothes had been boiled in the old work yard, behind the wing of the house. Washing and ironing were constant, as was setting the menu and overseeing the preparations for supper. She had taken on the duties of mistress years ago, after the McGavock children had died and Carrie McGavock had lost all interest in the daily life of a working household. The difference now was that there were only three folks on staff—including Becky Ann, but she was a young and inexperienced cook, generally irritating to Mariah. What had Miss Carrie been thinking, hiring her?

Then again, who else was there? Most of the former slaves had either run off during the Union's military occupation of Franklin, or had simply walked off since the end of the war. The McGavocks were trying to adjust by hiring freedmen, but most didn't want to be servants anymore.

But Mariah could take comfort in such tasks: fixing the cracked windowpanes and finding a local man to replace rotting floorboards, cleaning last winter's leaves from the corners of the stairs, and on and on the list went. She'd even found bats hanging upstairs in the room of one of Carrie's three dead children. Carrie had not been spared that pain, Mariah grudgingly admitted.

There was still a cook and a staff of two to clean the place, but nothing seemed right. Carrie, focused on the cemetery, cared nothing for the house. Her husband, John, away now in Memphis, was buying fruit trees, thinking that a great orchard would save them. *Who'd tend the trees and pick the fruit?* Mariah wanted to ask him, but of course this wasn't her concern, and he wasn't around to hear her anyway.

Mariah was overwhelmed in disbelief at what she saw when she returned to Carnton. It had felt as if she'd inherited the place years ago, before the war, while Carrie was consumed with grief at the loss of three of her five children. Somehow it had seemed understandable then, but Carrie's focus and obsession with the soldiers killed on the battlefield—killed on Carnton's front fields, many of them—now seemed too much to Mariah.

Did Carrie believe that Mariah would return forever and fill the vacuum that Carrie had left while she patrolled the cemetery and her cult of the dead? Mariah felt elated to know the answer to that question—that she was just regrouping, gathering her strength. When she was ready, she would go.

Out the back window, a silhouette made its way through the trees. A woman stepped out of the fallen shadows and into the half-moon's light.

Mariah stayed still, watching.

The woman moved closer, wide-set hips and big-busted, and Mariah recognized her—Henrietta, who worked for Mr. Hill, a big-time banker from Georgia who had come to Franklin so his wife could be closer to her sister. Henrietta did his cooking and his sewing, his house cleaning and his shoe shining, even watched the two young girls when Mr. and Mrs. Hill headed up north to Chicago for business and the theater.

Henrietta had a round cherub face and black tar skin, and the other ladies, so many years ago, called her "Old Girl." They'd pat her on the back after a long day of work and say, "It's gone be okay, Old Girl," as if she were a horse that needed to be put down. *Poor thing came all this way to see me,* Mariah thought. She stepped onto the veranda and lit a lamp.

"Henrietta, sweet thing, you have any idea what time it is?"

Henrietta walked into the lamplight, out of breath. "Oh, Mariah, it good to see your face." She walked the few steps up to the house and the two hugged.

"I thought you was a big fox rustling around in the trees there. You gone get yourself shot walking around this time of night."

"Either that walk gettin' longer or I'm gettin' older."

"What older? You was old when I was a girl, and now I'm gettin' on in years, you still old."

Henrietta smiled, and then stopped smiling. "I come to tell you Ise sorry 'bout your boy."

"Thank you."

Mariah led her off the porch, down past the two brick two-story cabins, once slave quarters, one of which she still lived in. Inside Mariah's room, Henrietta spoke with her eyes closed. "You oughta be real proud of Theopolis."

"It wasn't havin' pride that was the problem. No sense, maybe."

"They say you wasn't there that morning, didn't come to see him speak."

"That's right. I even asked him not to do it. But you know how he was. Stubborn damn fool."

"Just like his mama."

Mariah did not smile.

"I don't know much of what happened," Henrietta said. "Wish I did. But I've been listening to Mr. Hill in the dining room. His dinner guests like to talk about it over supper."

Mariah held her breath.

"He say Theopolis leapt into the crowd and cut three throats before he was brought down low like he was."

"You believe that?"

"No ma'am, I don't."

"What else you heard?"

"That it was three white men that killed him. Conservatives."

"What their names?"

"Can't say I've heard any names."

"Some boys from Nashville came down this way yesterday to take the testimony of any folks who might know about the killings that day."

"Yes ma'am. The whole town's been talking about it."

"You know if Mr. Hill was one?"

"He was. No way for me to know what he said. Even if he saw somethin', he ain't the type to get himself in trouble."

Mariah thought. "You remember some years ago, there was a girl came all the way from North Carolina, outside of Raleigh, I think it was, and she worked for some lawyer I think, cleaned the small brick building in the shadow of the courthouse on the corner of the square. That sound familiar to you?"

"You talkin' about Della, ma'am. Man up there named Mr. Burch. He a lawyer, you right about that."

"That's the one. Della. Heard her daddy died of the hiccups. You think there's any truth to that?"

Henrietta laughed. "Oh Mariah, you makin' that up."

"I ain't."

"Why you askin' about Della?"

"I have this memory of her, hangin' out her garments in the sun one morning, six in the morning, somethin' like that, and she was goin' on about how she enjoyed moppin' the floors and shining the silver in that building. She said it was 'cause that office had the best view of the main square. Best view in the whole town, she said. And sometimes she'd look out the window at the men down below and make up stories for them, for where they were walkin'. She liked tellin' that story. I always got the feelin' she enjoyed it way up wherever, lookin' down on people."

"Della not that way. She been through a lot."

"You tell her to come see me, would you?"

"I'll tell her, ma'am." And Henrietta would do it, sure enough, because the other thing about Mariah was that folks were afraid of her. Mariah took some pride in that.

Soon once or twice a day someone would appear walking on the road, or riding in a cart, or sneaking through the backwoods in their domestic uniform or their work dungarees. Carrie told Mariah she was touched by the grief of her friends and acquaintances who came bearing all those condolences. They did bear condolences, always. *Mariah I am sorry, Mariah he was a good boy, Mariah no man deserve that, Mariah you strong, Mariah you were a good mama to him, Mariah he made the most beautiful shoes.* The long, slow march of servants to and from Carnton was full of grief, but also full of slyness and even a kind of pride. They had information to give her.

Mariah met with them in the kitchen out of earshot of Carrie. Sometimes she shooed off the cook, but the times when they had visitors were the times those two got along best, so often Mariah let her stay. The girl would serve up some tea, and Mariah would face her visitors across the small wooden table where the kitchen help ate, praying that they would have something of use for her, something that would not only explain who killed her son, but why, and possibly even what she could do about it.

She quickly learned the virtue of patience, as most of her conversations went something like this:

"I heard something, Mariah."

"Yes?"

"He was killed by white men. In the square. White men. Did you know that?"

Or this:

"I heard that Theopolis had a thousand dollars in French coins sewed into the lining of his coat, and they was after that when they dragged him down."

Or this:

"I heard Theopolis leapt into the crowd and pulled a man's heart out through his chest before he was brought down low like he was. He were a battlin' man."

But sometimes even when the information was of limited use, the wild imagined stories of bored servants sitting in pantries and on chopping stumps, they held pieces of something that Mariah began to stitch together.

"I heard Theopolis's haint haunts Elijah Dixon's house."

"There was a bloody axe I took, someone tossed it under the stage. Not sure what it got to do with nothing, but thought you should see it."

"I seen with my own eyes two white men fighting over whether Theo should speak that day. Those Conservatives, you best believe they didn't want him talking. All those speeches were getting them real mad. They don't even want us colored folks votin', so they sure as hell don't want us speakin'."

"The grocer closed early that day, said he might be closed a couple days. I know because I went to get the missus some of that licorice that just come in. He was carrying an axe handle and said he had to go get it its head, that it was missing a head."

"The doctor's house was as hot as blazes when we got back home, the door and a window were open, and some things had been pushed around in the attic. Nothing were stolen, but there was the shape of a man in the dust under the window. I know what I think, and I said it to them plain as day, but the doctor don't believe in ghosts."

Mariah was grateful for the information and rewarded her visitors with butter or flour or some good thread she'd been hoarding in a stash for many years. She thanked them, everyone, even those whose information was less than useful. She saw them to the door and watched them disappear back down the road. She invited them all back.

I want to know everything. She tried to fit the puzzle pieces together, every stray bit of nonsense that nevertheless contained some bit of the plausible. But without knowing how the pieces all fit together, she could do little with them except dream of ghosts and French coins falling from the sky.

CHAPTER 14

TOLE

July 10, 1867

Tole's shaking hands woke him that morning. He sat up in bed and poured himself a shot of whiskey, syrupy thick and honey-colored. He threw his head back, one gulp, before lying back down. It was usually a shot of bourbon that would get him out of bed in the mornings; this morning it was two shots. He would need steady hands to do this job, he knew that much.

Today was the day.

Tole's plan for Jesse Bliss was simple enough: Bliss would take his mother to the Presbyterian church on Main Street for prayer meeting. The service was usually over by 6 p.m. by Tole's count, and then Bliss and his frail mother, both dressed solemnly in black, she in white gloves and he in his orange-feathered hat with a pistol of his own strapped to his ankle, would walk the few blocks to his family's home, where Bliss's wife, a Campbellite, would be waiting to greet them. Then he'd leave the women to their tea and head down to Main Street, where he would spend the rest of his evening looking in at the shops.

Dixon told Tole to get Bliss alone, somewhere quiet, an empty street or some deserted alleyway. "Get up nice and close and kill the bastard," Dixon said, his words echoing through Tole's head. "Quick shot. Don't take chances."

There was always a certain amount of space between Tole and the men he killed. Even in the war, he made sure to never get too close. Something about the distance made it easier for him to accept what he would do. He thought to himself, *You get too close and you're not just killing the man, you're taking his soul.* There was an empty attic space just above a brothel where he decided he could hide. He would have a clean shot at Bliss from up there. The maidens and the hookers and the wastrels had an arrangement with the local police, and there'd be no law poking around. Nobody would see Tole enter or leave. He would be little more than a ghost.

Blackbirds found sun-dappled branches to gather on as Tole walked through town with his usual pained gait, down an alley and into the back door of the whorehouse, up three flights of steps to the attic.

Tole knew that if he didn't agree to kill Jesse Bliss, he would be dead himself in a matter of days. And while he didn't mind dying, there were just a few things he needed to see to before they put him in the ground. A few things he needed to make right.

He reckoned he had half an hour before Bliss would stroll down Indigo Street. Outside the attic window he heard chatter and street noise, the repetitive clatter of rolling horse carts and the rhythmic knock of women's heels. He pushed open the window that looked out onto Walnut Street, letting waves of heat slither their way into the small space.

Finally Bliss's barrel-shaped body marched down Main Street, two men strolling behind him.

It was time.

Tole peered through the sight, but at first couldn't find Bliss. He looked up—there was Bliss, unconcerned, peering at the haberdasher's display.

Tole's hands shook. They never shook. Well, they never shook this *bad*.

He looked through the sights again and he saw the mob beating Theopolis again, he heard the gunshots, saw the blood spilling in the courthouse square. It was all right there, spread out before him. He closed his eyes and opened them again, pressing his cheek to the stock. He knew he couldn't kill this man, that he couldn't bring himself to do it, and as sharp a shooter as he'd been, he no longer trusted himself to wound the man without killing him. Even a bullet to the meaty part of the thigh could rupture an artery, or turn in ways you'd never expect and end up in the pelvis, where surely a painful death would follow.

Only one option seemed open.

Tole set ol' GT on the floorboards, reached into his back pocket for a piece of paper and a pencil, scribbled a note. Down the stairs he went, past the hookers and the businessmen, out the door, and around to Main Street.

He walked up to Bliss and stood beside him. He dropped the piece of paper. "You Mr. Jesse Bliss?"

Bliss looked at him, startled. "Who the hell are you?"

"I think you dropped a piece of paper there, sir," Tole said, and walked quickly away, turning down the nearest alley. There was a white bar at the end of the alley where the old, one-armed proprietor knew Tole to have been a soldier. Sometimes he would let him drink if there weren't any white men to object.

A moment later Bliss came in, clutching the folded piece of paper, on it the shaky-handed scribbles of a child, Tole's handwriting: *Follow me. I can save your life.*

The bar was dark, blanketed with shadows, some rainwater still puddled in the crevices, and Bliss's wood-bottomed shoes knocked loudly as he approached Tole, who leaned against the closet door.

Bliss whispered, "What's this all about?"

Tole gestured for him to sit, but Bliss refused. "I prefer to stand for now. I asked you a question: who are you, and what is it you want?" He removed his feathered hat. The daylight lit his pale face and he seemed to glow from the neck up, except for the dark beard that lined his round chin and the dull brown, hooded eyes.

"My name is George Tole. You be dead if it wasn't for me, Mr. Bliss."

"Dead? And how do you know this?"

"'Cause I the man supposed to kill you."

Bliss said nothing, just stared. Tole could watch his mind working, wondering if this might be some kind of trap. An ambush by a poor nigger luring him down an alley into a dark bar under the excuse of saving his life, only to mug him, rob him, cut his throat. Bliss slowly reached for the pistol on his leg.

"You ain't gonna need no pistol. I'm unarmed. Left my rifle behind. You wanna kill me, you can. But I'm here because I didn't want to kill you, not because I couldn't, so I'd hate for you to force my hand."

Bliss straightened. "All right then. Let's say I believe what you're saying. You say you're supposed to kill me?"

"Yes sir. Was s'posed to shoot you in the head just four days back, at the speeches in the courthouse square."

"But it was John Sykes and that other boy, the Negro shoemaker, who got killed that morning."

"That's right," Tole said. "The Negro shoemaker was named Reddick."

"Reddick, that's it. Theopolis, I believe."

It gratified Tole that Bliss should remember Theopolis's name. He wondered if Bliss knew Theopolis as a politician or as the man who made his shoes.

"That's the morning," Tole said.

"So I was the target?"

"If it wasn't for Theopolis taking the stage first, you wouldn't be sittin' here, sure as day."

"And so now you come to finish the job?"

"Yes sir."

"Who's payin' you, boy?"

"Man named Elijah Dixon pay me."

"Son of a bitch," Bliss said. "He hired *you*? No wonder it was a disaster."

"He heard some rumors said I was pretty good with a rifle."

"That true?"

Tole took a pause and rubbed his hands over his eyes. "All men good at somethin'. Some good at talkin', some at makin' laws, some at makin' whiskey. I was good at killin'. You ask me what I wanted to be, I'd say an artist, maybe. Some kinda job where you use your hands to make things beautiful. But that's not the way it is. I a killer, and I been good at it."

"So why you tellin' me this? Why not put a bullet in my head? You don't need the money?"

"I reckon I killed enough innocent men in my day. Maybe you innocent, maybe you not. I'll let God decide. And someday you'll be face-to-face with him, but I don't wanna be the one to send you. I done enough of that."

"So Dixon wants me dead. They had asked me, during my deposition the other day, if I had any reason to believe I was a target, and I said no. I should've known. I just can't *believe* he would hire a nigger to do the job, except it's perfect. If everything goes wrong, he's got you to blame, some crazy Negro with a gun. And it sure did go wrong, didn't it?"

"Sure did."

A pause. Bliss removed his hat and set it on the bar, damp with stale beer and littered with peanut shells.

"You take this with you. You tell that son bitch Dixon you found me and killed me dead, just like he asked."

"You think he'll believe me? Just like that?"

"Don't matter. I just need to buy myself some time. A week, maybe two."

Bliss was standing from his barstool when Tole stopped him. "One question, sir. Why he want you dead?"

"No idea. But I'm going to find out." Bliss eyed him. "You know how to read?"

"'Course. Grew up in New York City."

"City boy, are you? All right then. That's good." Bliss pulled out the scrap of paper on which Tole had written his note. "Set your address down here for me. Might be some time, a week or so, but you should expect a letter. Soon as I figure out what's going on. I'm going to figure it out, and you know what? I'm not going to let the son of a bitch get away with it."

"You best disappear now. Them boys gone be lookin' for you. They find out we lyin', we both dead."

"You did a good thing, warnin' me 'bout all this."

"Maybe." Tole nodded. "We'll just have to see how good it is." Bliss pushed his feathered hat a little closer to Tole and walked out the front door of the saloon.

Tole stayed until night fell, held the hat on his lap, and blessed himself for the first time since his boy died. He had to go see Elijah Dixon and tell him he killed Jesse Bliss out by the Harpeth River, and left his body to make its way out toward New Orleans many miles and twists of river away.

CHAPTER 15

TOLE

July 12, 1867

A few sparse blades of grass had begun to sprout on the grave of Theopolis Reddick the day George Tole hopped onto the back of a southbound wagon and rode it all the way out of town, past the cornfields and the sunflowers, into the forests, and all along the trail he had walked with Mariah. He rode on the back of that wagon all the way to Carnton, each bump like lightning up through his tailbone. He recalled his pleasant memories of the path and the walk with her. When he saw the painted sign and, rising beyond the trees, Carnton's roof, he yelled to the driver, "This here'll do," and he stepped off and into the summer-hardened dirt.

Through the gate, onto the dirt road, up to the front of the antebellum house. Now he stood before it: two stories of brick and white pillars, war-battered and crawling with spirits, the sides now covered in vines, the front porch left in crumbled bits, an attic window boarded up; a broken shell of a home. All around him, bleak and naked tree branches. He walked around back to the picket fence and, inside, the patches of verdant green in the cemetery, the rows of whitewashed cedar slabs, already showing their age,

103

that seemed to go on for miles, out of sight and beyond the slight dip of the land.

He wandered through the grave markers, some covered with withered flowers, most just letters and numbers. *No use trying to picture their faces. Nothing but bone and hair and fingernails left now.*

Down the rows he went, between the dead soldiers, sons and fathers, brothers and friends, most every one of them good soldiers, and in being good soldiers they had become killers, just like him. And there, lost among the forgotten, there might be a cedar plank with a number just like the others, a young boy who had played at soldier. Tole had known a boy like that once, on a distant battlefield, and had shot him down. He tried not to visualize that boy's death. *Maybe that's how God wanted it.* Tole didn't have much of anything to say to God. Not lately. Lately he'd been thinking the sky was as empty as it looked. Was the boy's daddy still alive? Did he make the trek to his boy's grave, kneel there in the dying light in the dying of the year, whisper prayers or words of comfort to a wooden plank? Maybe Daddy had never been by to visit. That would be a damned shame, but Tole would understand.

A white woman, dressed real proper, all in black, stepped out onto the back veranda and began to make her way toward him. Tole removed his hat and approached her.

"Sorry to be moseyin' about, ma'am."

"And who might you be?" the woman asked.

"Name's George Tole. I'm a friend of Missus Reddick."

"I see. A friend from Franklin, I suppose?"

"Indeed, ma'am. I was the neighbor of her boy."

"He was a good man."

Tole nodded and shifted his eyes toward the dirt.

"I'm Mrs. McGavock, of course."

Of course.

Mrs. McGavock went on. "You think you might know one of these men buried here?"

"Oh, no ma'am. I'm from back east. New York. I was just struck by the sight of it."

"You here to see Mrs. Reddick, then?"

"Yes ma'am. I was just roaming around the neighborhood and thought I'd stop by."

"Roaming, you say?"

"Yes ma'am. I like to pace and clear my head. Found myself over by your cemetery, and realized that this was where Missus Reddick was living now."

Mrs. McGavock gave him a sad smile and nodded. "Come this way, I'll let Mariah know you're here."

Tole followed Mrs. McGavock up the wide back steps to the porch, where he waited, looking back out onto the cemetery. *Imagine*, he thought, *having a cemetery in your backyard.* Planting it and taking care of it the way others would tend their gardens.

"Mr. Tole." Mariah's voice. He turned. She was there, gray eyes glinting.

"Hello, again," Tole said.

"What in the world you doin' back this way?"

Mrs. McGavock, behind her, answered for him: "He was just roaming around the neighborhood."

"Roaming?"

"Yes ma'am. My apologies for stopping by unannounced."

"No need for an apology," Mrs. McGavock said. "We don't get many visitors."

"Why don't you come inside, Mr. Tole?" Mariah said.

———

Inside, the house was muted with shadows, with small pools of morning light only serving to accentuate the darkness. Tole immediately had the sense of neglect and grandeur, bound together with sorrow—as if the old house had lost something indefinable, some color of light that Tole could not quite see, but could taste like blood on his tongue. Mrs. McGavock disappeared up the stairs, leaving them alone. He'd heard stories of this house, the blood that threatened to overwhelm the place. The wallpaper had once been bold with stripes and panels and foreign scenes of places that Tole couldn't even dream at, but now only seemed faded, battered. The carpets on the floor were grimy and worn. But what a house it had been, Tole thought. He imagined light and laughter from a farther room.

Someone had told him that the house had been a Confederate hospital during the war; that the blood from the sawn-off arms and legs had dripped between the floorboards upstairs, staining the walls below. Not true, perhaps, but what ghosts lurked here? What songs of sacrifice and despair?

"Coffee?"

"Not if it's any trouble now. No need to go makin' any."

"No trouble at all." She disappeared for a moment, then returned with a pitcher and two cups. She poured, and Tole sipped with the timidity of a small child. He seemed uncomfortable.

"Can't say I was ever any good at makin' friends. Not even in grade school."

"You went to school? You may be the only colored man I ever knew who went to a school."

"Lots of Negro folk go to school in the North."

"Learning how to be judges and businessmen, eh?"

"Book learning. Latin and mathematics."

"You like it?"

"Wasn't much for it. Was always wanting to take my rifle out and shoot at things. Thought I'd be a crack shot. Maybe join one of those traveling shows, see the country."

"Still can do that."

"Still could," he agreed easily.

"So why you come here?"

"Saw it during the war. Seemed like a man could like it here."
She eyed him skeptically.

He looked at her. "I like this town. Like the people in it.
They're friendly and they seem to mean it. Your boy, for instance.
He made me feel like I could belong, always waving hello, tipping
his hat at me. I liked seeing him."

Her eyes glazed over with memory as the sides of her mouth
turned up. "He had a way about him. Made folks feel at ease. He
were real gentle."

Tole looked down as if he had intruded on a private moment,
a foreign presence in the space meant for just a woman and her
thoughts. "My apologies for raising the subject. You probably tired
of thinkin' about all that."

This broke her reverie, and she looked up at him. "I guess
talkin' about him makes me feel a lot of ways. Almost a week
gone by. I find myself awake in the middle of the night, and I
think to myself, 'Almost a week already?' And then I think, 'Has
it only been a week?' How can it feel so long ago when it feels
like I was just talkin' to him, fixin' the collar on his shirt the way
I would, and he'd give me that look—that look that could singe
your eyebrows right off your face. Same one he'd give me when
I'd walk into town with him and kiss him on the head in front of
his friends."

This made Tole laugh.

"You had one of those, too, I reckon?" Mariah asked.

"Oh, my boy never quite made it to that age. He passed on just
shy of his eighth birthday."

Mariah shook her head and said, "I don't know why God do
what he do sometimes. How he die?"

Tole struggled to say, "Dysentery."

Mariah spoke softly. "Terrible thing."

"I remember Miles's first birthday after he died. Don't think I
made it outta bed that day. No reason to see the daylight, the way

I was feelin'. Can't say that feelin' you got in your chest ever goes away, but it gets a little lighter."

"Can I tell you something, Mr. Tole?"

"Yes."

"A few nights ago, I found myself thinkin' about Theopolis, and I didn't cry. It was the first time I didn't. And that done broke my heart most of all. How could I?"

Tole set his cup on the table. "I think I understand. I ain't much for advice. Never been any good with words the way some men are. But I know, sometimes the tears just don't come. When the time comes to start healin', you oughta let yourself."

Mrs. McGavock's light footfalls came back down the steps. Tole stood as she entered the room. "Mrs. Reddick, I'll be on my way."

Mariah nodded. Like a queen, Tole thought.

"Ma'am, pleasure to have met you." He reached out his hand and Mrs. McGavock placed the tips of her satin gloves in the palm of his calloused hands. A breach of all the rules of etiquette, he knew, but did it anyway.

Mrs. McGavock did not seem to notice. "A pleasure."

Tole turned to go, and Mrs. McGavock said, "I noticed some of the grave markers are wearing poorly. Down in the Mississippi section."

Mariah spoke, eagerly: "Remember how deep the snow was?"

"The snow fell so heavy we couldn't barely see the boards after long. Like a blanket of white laid over everything." Mrs. McGavock was looking straight at Tole. He looked over, and Mariah was doing the same thing.

"This whole plantation done suffered some terrible blows," Mariah said.

"I'm not sure we'll ever be able to fix all the damage," Mrs. McGavock said. "That's the thing about war and winter. But we keep on, fix what we can. But we do so little." Both women looked at him curiously, and he finally understood the question. He formed an answer as best he could.

"If it's any help, my daddy was a carver," he said. "His daddy, too. I wasn't never one by trade, but I picked up a trick or two watchin' him all those years."

"Oh, that would be too much trouble, Mr. Tole, I couldn't begin to ask you to do such a thing."

Mariah just nodded her head, like he was saying the right things.

"No ma'am, it's not. I sure don't mind feelin' useful now and again."

"All right then," Carrie said, as she did whenever she embarked on a new project. "We would welcome the assistance. And the boulders out by the west boundary, you think you could move them to the south pasture?" She seemed to have a list of things to do, Tole noticed.

"That'd be no problem. Happy to."

"I'm afraid I don't have much to offer you, Mr. Tole. But we pay a fair wage."

"Ain't no need for that. I'm happy just to do it."

"That's mighty decent of you, but you will be paid and that's that. Mariah, why don't you show Mr. Tole here the grounds. Get him acquainted. See to it he has the proper gloves."

Mariah rolled her eyes so Carrie could see her, and led Tole out the back through the kitchen.

CHAPTER 16

MARIAH

July 13, 1867

Della Swanson came to visit Mariah on a Saturday. It was just after dusk when she arrived at Carnton on foot, walked around back and down the hill to Mariah's cottage, and knocked so timidly on the door, so gently, that Mariah thought at first it was the scuttle of a mouse at the door, and then a wren, perhaps, pecking. She opened the door to find her standing with her hands folded in front of her tattered work smock, those almond-shaped eyes with the reddish-brown hue of polished oak, and her skin brown as fallen leaves. Della was a pretty girl. Mariah figured she must be coming up on twenty-five by now, or somewhere close to it, but Della herself probably didn't know her own age. Mariah no longer bothered to keep count, or track, of the ages of all the children she had brought into the world.

Mariah smiled, facial muscles tight, unaccustomed to the movement. "Welcome, baby, come on in, you must be tired." She closed the door behind her.

Della was shy, the type to nod and say, "Yes," in a soft voice that was more a chirp than any kind of whisper, lips pursed thin and tight, eyes lowered. She was easily awed and intimidated by white men and their wives, the powerful folk from the courthouse square, the dinner guests and visiting politicians who made their way in and out of Mr. Burch's home.

Mariah asked her to take a seat and sat right beside her, turned her chair so she could see her eyes, and waited.

"Henrietta come see me," Della said. "She say, 'You gotta go see Mariah,' so I come first thing."

"Appreciate that."

"You wanna ask me about your boy? Don't know nothin' about what happened, Mariah. I sure am sorry to hear he dead. They shot my brother Simon, too, out in West Virginia."

"Who done? A Union boy?"

"I think maybe it was. Nobody know for sure. They was battlin' outside of Wheeling and they shot him twice in the chest. He had a friend, some boy from Georgia, rode into town and let Mama know. Said they shot him up close. Said the hole so big you could reach your arm through him and touch th'other side."

"Good God, child. I didn't know. I'll pray for his soul. And your mama's."

"She don't do much but sit on the porch and watch the people go by. Don't talk much."

"She alone?"

"Yes ma'am. My daddy die the year before. She all alone out there."

Mariah set her hand over Della's. *This girl understands*, she thought.

"I know you scared, sweet thing. But you ain't in no kind of trouble. If you didn't see nothing, don't know nothing, then please head on back into town without one worry. But you do know something, heard something, and you think telling me is gonna get you whipped, then you stop thinking that right now. I ain't gonna let no man hurt you, child. Not going to tell no man nothing. I cry for my boy the way your mama cry for hers, and I got it in my head that finding out who killed him will take the pain away."

"You think it will? Really?"

"Pastor Willis said that getting some kind of vengeance won't heal a grieving heart. He say I have to forgive the man who did this. And I told him, before God, that I would. I told him it might take until I'm wrinkled and dying, but I promised him I would. But I can't forgive the man who killed my boy until I know who that man is, you hear? Too many women be sitting on their porches watching the people go by the way your mama does. You listen here: I'm not sitting on no porch. I'm going to find out who shot my boy and I'm going to get justice for him. And then I'll see about forgiveness.

"Now, I know you clean those windows in Mr. Burch's office, and I know those windows look out onto the courthouse square. I know you get there bright and early. And I know you like to watch the people down below walking on by. So if you're going to tell me you didn't hear no gunshot, you didn't hear no ruckus, you didn't hear my boy scream, then you go ahead. Look me in the eye and tell me you don't know nothing, and I'll believe you. Hand on the Bible, I will. But you gonna have to look up from your feet, look me in the eye, and tell me it."

Della looked up, her eyes pooling with tears, and she struggled to swallow, to look at the woman before her.

"Mariah, I don't clean no windows on the top floor. I just say that so people think I'm one of the special ones, you know? But that ain't the way it is. It was just somethin' that sounded nice, so I pretend it's the truth. But Mr. Burch, he don't let me in his office. He like to keep me at his home a couple miles from town. He say, 'A pretty little nigger like you shouldn't have to work so hard.' So I mostly stay out back, make sure the house in good order."

The two women stared at one another, Della's words hanging between them. Mariah could feel herself becoming angry, and swallowed it down.

"But just because I ain't there to see it don't mean I ain't heard nothing, Mariah."

Mariah regained her composure. "Mr. Burch ain't hardly been eating lately, you see, and I know because I serves him and his missus," Della said. "He just pick and pick. And one night I cleared the table and he and the missus sat at the table a long time, so long their coffee got cold. But they waved me away when I come to fill it."

"Yes, and so?"

"And so when I come in with the fresh pot and they waved me off, I did hear one thing Mr. Burch said. He said, 'Ain't to be them two, not a grocer and a nigger. Who give a goddamn about them?' That's what he said and that's all I know and all I want to know."

Della sat trembling but resolved. She had set her face, and Mariah could tell she had come to say what she was going to say and no more. Mariah admired the girl's courage.

A long silence, and then Mariah said, "All right then, child. I'll leave you be. You go get back to Franklin before it gets much later. Don't want you gettin' yourself in no trouble now."

Della nodded gratefully and turned to leave. But she stopped at the door. She was quiet awhile, like she was arguing with herself. Then she turned.

"There's that saloon on Main Street, where Mr. Burch likes to go some nights. He says they got the best whiskey in town. Says there's always a fat man there at the bar, man named Smithson."

"Smithson? Ain't that the boy who works at the newspaper?"

"Ain't much of a boy nowadays. He all grown. But yes ma'am, he work at the newspaper. Mr. Burch says he knows all the secrets this town done locked away."

"I knows him."

"Mr. Burch says he usually has his Negro with him. Some country girl he bought awhile back. Nessie's her name. Can't say it'll help you none, but she might've definitely heard a thing or two about your boy." Mariah noticed how she raised her voice on *definitely*.

———

Two days later, in the evening, Mariah found herself back in Franklin, a few blocks south of the courthouse square on Almond Street, back again in the Thirsty Bird.

She started to make her way toward the bar, but a man kicked over a chair in her path, jumping to his feet with a force. He was a big man, heavy; one of the Caruthers brothers, with his muscles tight and strong from pushing a plow. Mariah caught May's anxious eye across the bar and stepped out of the big man's way. He had no interest in her, but in a little man across the table from him. He moved quick and caught the little man by the collar. Soon the little man's feet dangled off the floor.

"What you say to me?" Caruthers shouted, so close to the little man's face he blinked against the words.

"Nothing." The little man's voice shook. "I didn't say nothing."

"You a damn Conservative coward, and I best not see you here no more. That's what *I* saying."

The little man shook loose and skittered away from him, toward the door. "You damn black son of a bitch," he spat at Caruthers, who was now at a safe distance. His voice still shook a bit, with anger or fear, Mariah couldn't quite tell. "You be dead before the end of the day, hear me? You lucky I don't do it here and now."

Caruthers moved forward as if to catch him again and the little man jumped back through the door, quick as a rabbit trying to dodge a fox. The door swung shut behind him. Caruthers, grumbling something under his breath, moved toward the back of the bar and was absorbed into a circle of men Mariah recognized from around town.

For a moment, it was dead quiet.

Then April called over to a man sitting alone in a corner. "Working on the sermon, then, Preacher?" The air settled down around them, like she had breathed the tension right out of it.

Preacher, a round-shouldered man with a tonsure of grizzled white hair, snorted and took a long sip at the sticky jar he kept cradled in his hands. He sat at the end of a long table on which April and May had set the usual liquor and loaves of bread. Unlike Pastor Willis, the comfortable and well-dressed leader of the Negro Methodist church, Mariah knew this preacher only vaguely—she'd heard that he preached in small hamlets in Middle Tennessee, but he'd never given a sermon that she'd heard.

She saw him watching her through the side of his eye. She was intrigued. He traveled the back roads, he knew the travelers, the beggars, the flotsam that washed up like driftwood after the immense flood of war had washed them away. Did he know who'd killed her boy?

Or perhaps John Scrugg knew something. Scrugg, an immensely tall and bent old smith who worked out of the back of his old shack on the other side of the river, lived close to the road north to Nashville, and from that perch he watched the comings and goings of traffic, shoed the horses of travelers, and paid attention to the news of the world. John detached himself from the group around Caruthers and walked over to the serving table, where he poured himself a taste, dropped some coin in the hat, and turned to survey the group. Surely he, too, might know who these men were?

And then she saw Nessie, a scrawny woman with twiglike arms, sitting in the back on the other side of the room—she who Della said might *definitely* know something.

Mariah bought a cup of ale and sat down next to her. Nessie moved farther over on the bench to make room. They chatted idly, Mariah acknowledging Nessie's expressions of sympathy for Theopolis, and then began.

"I want to ask you a few questions, and I hope you'll show me the respect I deserve by givin' me the truth. You hear?" Mariah wondered how long she could count on the respect of being older and smarter and fiercer than most. At some point she'd have to be trickier about her approach, but just then she was in a hurry.

"Yes ma'am."

"How long you been workin' for Mr. Smithson?"

"Ise afraid I don't know exactly, ma'am. Could be a couple three years by now. I worked on a farm in Laurel Hill since I was real little. With my sister. The two of us."

"Mississippi?"

Nessie nodded again.

"We was sold to a farmer down there, we worked good for him a long time. Not sure how long. Then some men from Tennessee come down, say they need a few niggers up here, so he rented us out and sent us up to work at a place called Wheatlands."

"I know the Wheatlands. What they have you do there? Oats and sweet potatoes."

"Can't stand a sweet potato now, that's the truth."

"And Mr. Smithson. He buy you from the Wheatlands?"

"Yes ma'am. But then the war got done not six months later."

"And he payin' you now?"

"Some. Don't know how much is a lot, but I got money now."

"He works at the *Daily Gazette*, that right?"

"Yes."

"You know what I'm about, don't you? Tryin' to find out what happened to my boy."

"I heard ladies talkin' about it, yes."

"Tryin' real hard. And ain't nobody seen nothin' real, only heard this and that. And now I'm here because they say your man, Mr. Smithson, he sees and hears everything in this town. That true?"

Nessie wrapped her arms around herself and looked around, uncertain.

"Nessie, girl, you listen to me. If you heard that man say some-thin' about who did this, I'ma make you tell me."

"Oh, ma'am, I can't help you."

"Why not?"

"I'm telling you same as I told that lawyer. I don't know nothin'."

"What lawyer?"

"One of thems come from Nashville asking they questions."

"You tellin' me you never heard that Smithson say nothin'? Not even when you in his bed?"

"You don't know me, you don't know what I do."

"Damn liar!"

People were looking at them. Nessie was no scared girl, though. And she didn't seem to want to fight, either. She tried to calm Mariah and lowered her voice. "I heard only things he say when he drunk."

Mariah leaned closer to Nessie, their noses nearly touching, Nessie's breath warm against her cheek. "You tell me right now."

"He said it was some nigger who shot him."

Mariah exhaled and stepped backward, paused for a moment, and then broke into a fit of laughter. "A nigger?"

"Yes, Mariah. That's what he said."

"You tellin' me a group of white men attacked my only son and beat him within an inch of his life, but it was a Negro who put the bullet in him?"

"I know it don't sound right, Mariah. That's just what I heard him say. He was drunk."

"You stupid girl." Mariah knew it wasn't true, that Nessie was as smart as anyone, but she wanted to say it anyway. It made her feel worse as soon as she said it, especially when Nessie wouldn't be provoked.

"I'm sorry, Mariah. He a drunken fool. He just write what they pay him to write. He ain't no different than none of them. I don't got no idea what he know for true, and what he know for tales and rumor."

"A Negro," Mariah said, disgusted. "Them white men would love that. They'd build a statue in the courthouse square for him. You think it's true?"

Nessie considered it. "It could be. Might not be. It ain't like we Negroes agree on much." She looked over at Caruthers. "Maybe someone had their reasons, I don't know."

A pause, an inhalation, an exhalation. Mariah looked about her—at the Preacher, at John Scrugg, at the others. Someone would know something. One of them *would*. She would not stay a slave to the abuse of that white world no more. She would at least know it, it would not be a mystery.

CHAPTER 17

TOLE

July 15, 1867

The next few days, Tole and Mariah developed a routine. Tole went out to Carnton to work around the cemetery by late morning dressed in tattered overalls and work boots crusted with field dirt, and Mariah would have the day's work planned out for him. In the early evening, when swirls of pink and sapphire would marble the sky with billows of broken cloud, Mariah would holler for him, tell him supper was on the table, and Tole would go first to the shed to wash up some, and then go inside to the kitchen and sit in front of a hot bowl of stew.

"Musta been somethin', livin' in this house during the war." Tole slurped his soup, held his spoon like a young child. Mariah sat beside him with a bowl of her own.

"You seen your fair share of war. Don't know the difference."

"Did indeed. Thing is, I was out there killin'. You was here bringin' em back to life."

"Mostly they died, too. But slow. Or they lost they legs. Maybe you done that to them."

She'd remembered being on her knees with old sheets and linens, mopping up puddles—lakes, oceans, it seemed—of blood.

She remembered the piles of limbs outside and below the bedroom window where the surgeons did their work.

She couldn't remember every man's name who died, and she often thought of this. Was it William who had asked for water, William from Georgia? Or was that Hank, from Alabama? It sometimes seemed desperately important that she remember. There was one essential thing different from their two experiences, Tole's and Mariah's: Tole's enemy had been Confederates, but Mariah's enemy had been death. Though some of them would have liked to see her and her posterity in chains forever, and all of them fought on the side that would have ensured that, she remembered fighting the deaths and pain of the Confederate men, who whispered their gratitude to her. Death, despair, giving up—that was the enemy. She hardly saw the color of their uniforms, which were all different shades anyway. She was not sure she would be so generous now.

Mariah sat back in her chair. "You ever wonder what your life would've been like if it wasn't for that war, Mr. Tole?"

"I wonder, yes." Tole took a pause, a slurp of soup, and said, "Sad for me to admit this, but awful as it was, the war gave me purpose."

"That sounds ugly."

"I was good at it. Never been real good at nothing before. Hell of a thing for a man to be good at, but it's true."

"What about before the war? You ain't gone tell me you grew up wanting to be a soldier."

"You mean when I was a child?"

He had the weathered face of a man twice his age, etched like a hunting knife into soft birchwood, lines and crevices that splintered like shattered glass, and the droopy eyes of a drinker. He could hardly remember being a child. By her reaction, it appeared Mariah couldn't hardly think of him as a child either.

"What's so funny?"

"Nothin', Mr. Tole. You go on. Answer the question."

"Childhood seems so long ago these days. I can barely remember running around uptown with my older brother. He and I used to talk about joining the circus."

Mariah's mouth twitched.

"Don't go laughin' now. Ain't nothing funny about that. Them boys work real hard."

"Oh, I know it. I was just picturing you balancing yourself on one foot on some beast of an elephant. They'd call you *Zanzibar the Zulu King* or some such."

"All right, make fun."

"I'm not makin' fun, Mr. Tole. I think it's nice when boys dream."

"I wanted to be a clown, myself."

"Oh Lord help me."

"One night my daddy caught my brother painting my face white and he whipped me."

"He don't like clowns."

"Nah. He thought I was making my face white so I could look like the white kids."

"Were you?"

"Maybe I just wanted to look like a clown, how about that? Ain't that good enough?"

"George Tole, the circus clown. You done made my day with that one." Mariah sipped her water.

Tole smiled and used his spoon to push his vegetables around the reddish-brown broth. "All right then," he said. "What about you? You ever have dreams as a little girl?"

Mariah was quiet for a moment, then said, "No," with an unblinking honesty. It was just a fact to her.

"No? Just like that."

"It was different for me, Mr. Tole. You was free. I wasn't raised like that. I lived on the plantation in Louisiana with Miss Carrie.

I was hers. Her plaything, though sometimes I thought we was friends. And when I grew up, I was the girl who kept her clothes neat and brought her breakfast in bed. And when I grew older still, and Miss Carrie suffered them children dying, I was the one who ran this house."

"And all that time, you never let yourself daydream? You never wondered what was beyond those trees?"

Mariah shook her head. "Didn't do much good to dream. Never seemed much point in it. Life wasn't bad."

"I don't understand."

"The McGavocks treated their slaves better than most. We didn't get whipped or beaten or taken advantage of as much."

"Yeah, so?"

"Miss Carrie never laid a finger on me. I was never hurt. Not ever. Other slaves on other places, they wanted to escape worse than I did. They wanted to be free right then. But me, I could imagine staying at Carnton forever. I never thought there'd be a day where I'd be free, that was the problem...It was a different kinda slavery, the kind that steals your desire and hides the world. I spent my whole life serving other people, and I didn't think much was wrong about that. It just was. Some women stare out the window their whole lives wondering what's out there. They know there's something else they was missin'. I didn't look out the window—too busy."

Tole felt angry, hearing this. These were terrible words to hear from a woman so intelligent, and he hated slavery even more in that moment. "What about now?" he finally asked, barely able to say the words. "Now that you free. You have any dreams now?"

Mariah pondered the question for a moment. "You promise you won't laugh?"

"Long as you don't say you wanna join the circus."

Mariah chuckled. "I think I'd make a fine doctor."

Tole nodded. "I can picture it."

"Yeah? You ain't just sayin' that?"

"Not just saying that, no sir. You as strong a woman as any I ever met. I remember seein' you that day with Missus Dixon's blood all over your hands. Besides that, you have a special way with people. You know when to be hard, know when to be soft."

"I always thought medicine was the only magic I'd ever need."

She stopped talking and tucked her lips in. Her eyes turned glassy and she widened.

Tole could tell she was keeping herself from crying. Maybe she was thinking of the war.

"Healing people makes me feel like I matter."

Tole considered this. "I reckon that's a true thing, it does matter."

The two of them finished their soup and stared off through the window, grimy with cook smoke.

"Soup was good," Tole said. "Thank you."

Mariah picked up her bowl and his and brought them to the washing area. "It's no bother. Used to make it for my husband, but he died. Couldn't heal him neither." She looked back at him as she washed the dishes with soap and a washcloth.

"You ever miss being married, Missus Reddick?"

Mariah dried her hands on the towel. "Suppose I miss it some nights. If it were up to me, it would always be daylight," she said. "How about you?"

"Oh, I weren't much of a husband."

"That ain't what I asked."

"I miss having somebody around. Feel like I've gotten a little too used to it being so quiet all the time."

Mariah nodded in agreement.

"I bet you were real good at it," Tole said. "Being married."

"I was young. Not sure I believe there's such a thing as being good at it. You just gotta try your best to be decent. I think maybe we learned that a little too late."

"Where you meet him?"

"McGavocks bought him over in Montgomery. Brought him back to train their blood horses. That's what John McGavock did, before the war—raised horses. They're all gone now, of course. Now he's trying for fruit trees."

"He a good man?"

"Bolen? He was. He was a difficult man, but I could depend on him."

"Did you love him?"

Mariah smiled sadly. "I don't know. Some days I guess I did. Some days I coulda strangled him, too, 'specially in the beginning. But we had some happy times. He knew how to make me laugh. He got under my skin like nobody else. He used to whistle in the morning time, sometimes before the sun. I might have stabbed him some of those mornings. But we was happy enough. We was always working, and always knew they could split us whatever time they want, we weren't officially married in a church or nothing. We was as happy as they let us be. It's some kind of marriage, I reckon, but not the kind for white ladies."

Tole nodded and bowed his head shyly.

"I never expected much in the way of kindness. But I remember I musta told him a hundred times how much I loved white lilies."

"White lilies?"

"They been my favorite flower since I was a little girl and I always wanted a man to bring me white lilies. I always thought, someday, he gone take the hint, and he gone bring me some. But he never did."

"I know how that goes," Tole said. "There so many things I think back on, things I shoulda done."

"I remember I'd hear stories of women bein' in love. They'd tell me about that feelin' in their stomach when their man would come around. Said it felt like a million butterflies, and I'd say I knew that feeling real well, but the truth was, I ain't never had it. You ever had that feelin', Mr. Tole?

Tole looked up at Mariah and said, "Yes ma'am."

That evening, Tole worked well into the blackness of night, the cemetery lit by a soft dusting of light from the half-moon. Finally he pulled a pile of brush from one corner of the cemetery, dragged it into the fallow field to be burned, and decided he'd had enough for one day. He glanced off across the trees and the fields to where Franklin lay sleeping.

When he turned around, Mariah was standing there staring right up into his eyes, her brow crumpled and angry. "She leave you after your boy passed on?"

Tole nodded, as if the conversation had been going through his mind as well. "Not right away. Think maybe she should've. She was a better woman than that. She tried to forgive me for his death and how it was after he died, but after a while it was too late. I wasn't much of a husband to her. I wasn't much of anything."

"You was a sorry man." She said it because it was true, and she said it direct because that was her way. It didn't make him mad.

"Can't think of a single night I didn't wake up on the floor somewhere," he agreed. "Stinkin' like booze. And then I'd get home and yell at her the way my daddy used to do me and my brother. Pound on the doors when she'd lock herself in the bedroom. Punched holes in the walls. Never lay a hand on her, but only because she left before I could get that bad. One day, I woke up and found a note on the bed. She said she'd gone to stay with her sister upstate. I didn't even care, just went back to drinkin'. It was probably a week or so before I realized she was gone for good."

"It's the Devil in it."

"And then he get in you."

"Why she need to forgive you for your boy dying?" Mariah still stared up into his eyes, frowning, searching. The moonlight was cold upon them. Far away the crickets sawed, out of tune. A single candle lit up one of Carnton's windows upstairs, and Tole could see the curtains moving slowly in the breeze, like water, like grief.

"When I tell you little Miles die of dysentery, I didn't tell everything, neither. He die because of me. Because I leave my whiskey where he could reach it. Eight years old. He was sick, already dying, and then he took a big gulp of my whiskey. Maybe more, no one was paying attention, we was sleeping. After a while he began choking up blood. Charlotte woke up first, tried to help him, waked me up, too. She was shaking me and crying and hollerin', but I was too goddamn drunk to even stand. But still I tried, Mrs. Reddick. I tried to get him to stop choking. He was already weak. His big brown eyes turn red and he had blood in his tears. And I screamed, 'Somebody help him, please,' but nobody come."

Quiet grew between them. What more was there to say? A lot, Tole thought, but not then. She had been tense and on guard at first, but he could sense her relaxing, unclenching. After a while: "Where he buried?"

"Don't know."

"You don't know?"

"Wasn't in no fit state to remember."

"How drunk were you?"

He didn't answer. More quiet. An owl called out, mournful, from down in the Alabama section of the cemetery. Mariah walked right up to him; he could feel her heat. "Reckon not knowing that is the worst kind of torture."

She knows, Tole thought.

She inspected him, and he became conscious of how he appeared—his clothes, once the best of the best, had worn through here and there at the elbows and knees, and had gone gray from dust. His shoes flapped at the toe. He had no socks. He could feel her taking stock, and felt unworthy.

"You been here how long?"

"Since just after noon."

"I mean in town."

"Six months."

"And the work you do here the only work you got?"

Tole nodded. "Not found any of my kind of work," he said, which was a lie. He'd found *too* much of his kind of work. Any amount was too much.

"And what is your kind of work, Mr. Tole?"

What to call it? He had been a man called to fix unfixable situations.

"Handyman." All of Franklin was falling down, people were desperate for skilled workers, and he, a "handyman," couldn't find a job except one given to him from charity? But what could he tell her? *I'm a drunk? I'm living off my soldier's pension and drinking myself to death, here in this broken southern town in the middle of nowhere, where even God can't find me? And my trade is death?* "Handyman" sounded vastly more respectable.

Mariah nodded. She had softened toward him, he thought. Her eyes were so gray, they might blow away like smoke. She smiled kindly, which was more than he knew he deserved. He had tricked her, misled her, run a game on her. He wanted to deny it, to denounce this part of himself. But this woman! He would do anything to right the scales for her, to make things right. He knew this instantly, even though he also knew that righting the scales would make things very dangerous for George Tole.

"You know Hooper?" she asked.

"The liquor man?"

"He's a ragman and a liquor man. He also delivers firewood, and I think he got chopping to do. When he come to see you, you know that I sent him. That be two jobs, then."

"Thank you. Appreciate it."

She turned and began along the path back to the house. There wasn't another soul in sight, and Tole wondered how she could stand the quiet, so much quiet. He wondered if she was lonely.

"You can come up to visit the graves, or whatever you do up here, whenever you want. I ain't stopping you, Mr. Tole."

As she got farther away, she seemed to disappear into the tall grass, and Tole was sorry to see her go.

CHAPTER 18

MARIAH

July 17, 1867

It was raining when Mariah found Hooper's chimney by the smoke she saw tailing up out of the woods far off, down the stream. Hooper had built the chimney himself from river rock and old abandoned stone fences. It tipped here and there but never fell, and it always contained the warm fire the whiskey man used to make the heat that drove his chemistries.

Townsmen told many stories about the liquor man: that his was a recipe brought directly over from the old country by pirates; that his secret ingredient was the tears of abolitionists; that each jar contained six months of work; that he had been stolen and set free by the outlaws of Cave-in-Rock on the Ohio because none of them could defeat him in a wrestling match; that he never drank his own product; that his own liquor man was the Devil hisself; that he never slept; and that his only real pleasure was the tending of fire. Only Hooper knew what part of it was true. If they kept buying his jars, what trouble could he ever have? He aimed to avoid trouble first and foremost, always. He took very few risks.

Mariah entered the clearing that was Hooper's workshop and living room, mud packed and hard, ringed by scrub oak and hickory.

"What you want, Mariah?" He sounded uncomfortable, like he already knew what she wanted but had to go through the ritual of asking, the back-and-forth.

His voice came from behind one of the burlap sacks that hung low from tree branches, embroidered and drawn upon like tapestries. Hooper had many private rooms in his clearing set off by these hanging sacks, and a lean-to at the south end of the clearing in which to sleep. The sacks flapped in the storm wind, barely a breeze now but getting stronger, and it seemed to Mariah that the clearing itself was moving, flapping, shaking. She went to the hearth before answering.

"That you, mister?"

"Who else would it be, girl?"

"Abraham Lincoln for all I know."

"Mr. Lincoln dead, everyone know that."

The fire spat and smoked behind her, heating the copper kettle. She sat on an oak stump Hooper used for wood splitting. On the stone hearth sat a near-full jar of that thick, syrupy stuff the whiskey man made every day of his life. Mariah dipped her pinky, took a suck.

Hooper came around the edge of his burlap and stepped into the center of the clearing. In his full glory, it became instantly clear why he could remain alone out there in the woods, unmolested by man or law. Far from Carnton's porch, in the seat of his power, he seemed tall as a horse and practically as wide. He was dark brown, and his beard, which he had been trimming with a Bowie knife, was gray-flecked and thick, not so much grown on his chin as sculpted there. He was powerful- and hard-looking, but something about him seemed pieced together to Mariah, none of the parts seeming to quite fit into the whole. He had been beaten severely at least once in his life, probably many times; there were scars at each corner of his eye, and his nose had become flattened and canted to the left. His eyes were almost black and very wide. In him she recognized both the power and the wreckage she associated almost always with black men—especially in her memory of the three brothers she had not seen or heard from since she was twelve.

White liquid dripped from the lip of Hooper's still, which sat squat on a platform of stone next to the chimney.

"I heard they killed your boy."

They. He knew. What did he know? She nearly leapt up to claw his face off until he told her. They all knew, of course. *They, they, they*. He sat down across from her and stared unblinking. The wind picked up and blew tiny dirt swirls across the cleared patch, from her side to his.

"I liked your boy, Mariah, and I reckon all this don't sit well with you." His vest, made from deerskin like the roof of his lean-to, opened wide in the wind and flapped around.

"Everybody liked my boy. Didn't matter much, did it?"

"He was a good customer. Don't know where he got the money, but he always paid."

"He made shoes, that's where he got the money." She looked down at Hooper's own shoes, which were sprung at the sole and had been wrapped with twine and rag. "Might have thought about buying some from him yourself."

Now he stood up again, like something ancient unbending itself, all creaks and cracks. He walked over and stoked the fire to roaring, and turned back. "When I heard you moved back to Carnton to live with Missus McGavock, I knew right away why you done it. That town, every town, got a thirst for blood and don't care who you are or what you want from this life—you best be living their way and according to their rules so long as you live among 'em. And their rules what done Theo."

131

He took a deep breath. "I did want to talk to you, Mariah Reddick."

"I know. It's part of why I come."

"I suppose you read my mind, houdou witch."

"Don't take much to read you."

Hooper slapped his knee. "Good! I'm glad! I ain't gone sneak through this life." He looked down at the ground again. Mariah wondered if the words were going to kill him and if he was afraid of dying.

"I guess you know that I get around that town a lot, though I hate it."

"Part of your business, I reckon."

"That's true. And people drink in front of me, and when they drink in front of me they say things."

"Who they?"

"*They*. And you know who I mean."

Mariah nodded her head.

"I don't want them coming out here," he hissed. He was scared.

"All right."

He became a little more comfortable then, and looked her in the eye. "I know you got your little spies, and I'm sure they fulla horseshit, because I hear them talking in the back rooms and in the hallways when I make my deliveries. But you got the right idea, having them listening. If you really *do* want to know what happened to your boy."

"I do want to know," Mariah said. "Do you think you know?"

"No."

"Then why am I here? What the hell is all this about, Hooper?"

"I don't know the what or the why. But I do know two things. First, remember the lady whose baby they say you delivered the day before? I weren't there, so I don't know."

"Evangeline Dixon. Yes, I do."

"You have to talk to her."

"Why?"

"Ask *her*. I ain't speaking for her. But why the hell do you think? I ain't talking for my health."

"Fine then. I talk to her."

"And I know one more thing. Some of them men who were in that mob, some of them who was beating on your son, said they didn't see no guns on the stage."

"They say Theopolis had a pistol and shot the grocer. Mr. Sykes."

"You think that's true?"

"I know it's not."

"Smart woman." Hooper blew out one more sigh from puffed cheeks. He stood up as if to escort her out, so Mariah also stood and gathered her skirts in her left fist to avoid the mud. "Other people know it's not true, too," Hooper said. "And I heard that there are some who was beating on Theopolis who want to know who was doing the shooting. You find out who some of them men were, and maybe you find out what they know."

"Do you know who they are?"

But Hooper just stared at her. A little lightness had come into the sky behind him, and in silhouette he seemed to Mariah a massive thing casting its shadow over her. He loomed, he rocked and nodded his head, working up to something. "Your boy got caught in the middle of a group of men who don't like niggers, or don't like things changing. They 'specially don't like niggers like your boy, ones with brains, ones who could make a difference in this world. There lot of men who don't like anything about any of that."

He became small just then, or perhaps it was the rain that still ran down the leaves and dripped upon his head, flattening and darkening him. He sagged, she thought. The giant man was scared, and this fear made her nearly vomit. *What am I doing? I can't do this.*

133

"But you can get even if you clever about it, Mariah Reddick," he said.

Clever. *Even.* Later she would say the words over and over in her head as she walked back to Carnton in the rain. *Clever.* She could try. *Clever* would be getting the ragman, Hooper, her friend of many years, to be her spymaster. He moved in and out of every house in town picking up junk and delivering firewood, and she guessed that most of the people whose houses he visited didn't notice him and couldn't even remember his name. He was a *ghost.* That seemed appropriate; that would be useful.

And then she wondered if she would need to be clever with the woman whose baby she had saved the day before she lost her own. She thought not. She thought, instead, that such a woman would owe her the truth.

Before she left Hooper, Mariah had one last request.

"Hooper," she asked, "you been by my boy's house since he was killed?"

"No ma'am."

"I been meaning to go in there and clean it out, but I can't seem to bring myself to get it done. I don't know if I'd be able to throw any of it away, or give it away, like needs to be done."

"I didn't take you for sentimental, Mariah."

Mariah laughed, mostly to herself. "You know, when I was a young girl, five, six years old, before my mama would head off to the fields, she'd send me up to the big house for Bible study. She'd make my lunch out of whatever food there was laying around, scraps from this and that, and she'd wrap it tight in this brown parchment paper. Foolish little thing I was, I'd fold the paper up and save it. I remember Miss Carrie asking me once why I saved it the way I did, and I tried to explain to her, my mama had touched the paper, and I couldn't just throw away my mama's handwork. I haven't thought about that in years."

"Mariah, you need me to clean out your son's house, all you gotta do is ask."

"All right," she said. "I'm asking. And there's a man I'd like you to help with it. Name of George Tole. Lives right near Theopolis's house. He might want some of the things. If he does, let him have them. Pay him fair."

CHAPTER 19

MARIAH

July 19, 1867

The trip to Elijah Dixon's house should not have made Mariah so nervous. She had been summoned, after all, and not for her inquiries into the murder. It was Evangeline who wanted her.

As a midwife, she had made many such visits to newborns during the first few weeks of their lives. Most of the time there was some challenge that their mamas were at wit's end about, and Mariah would do what she could to fix things. There were colicky babies, babies that had become thin, babies that wouldn't sleep, babies that slept too much, babies that slept so soundly they seemed dead, babies that couldn't cry. There were also the fevered babies, the cold babies, and the babies that seemed perfectly healthy but had been brought into the world by women who couldn't stand their smell, their noise, their constant hunger, their breathing. These last were the babies that would have the hardest time of it, Mariah knew.

On the occasion that she found a child who just seemed to need to go on and cross death's river, she had no words to turn it back. Those children, motionless in their fevers by fireplaces, scaly-skinned, twisted up in bedclothes and unmoved by the sweet smoke and the smelly poultices she applied to their chests so lightly—those children taught her more than she ever could do for them. This is what she thought during those hours by the cradle listening to the wheels turning down the dirt ruts in front of the parents' house, when she was listening to the world move on by as if there were not a child dying in the house: *What does this child know?* She thought such children had some kind of foreknowledge, some sight that was more than human. Or, rather, such a child had an immortal's sense of time, which was no such sense. Such a baby was a pure thing, breathing shallowly, unmoved and isolated from the muddy, fleshy, and cruel state of being human that other humans would hold on to and kill to maintain. There was wisdom in such a child.

Evangeline Dixon came to the door bloodless and pale, gripping her skirt in one hand and balancing little Augusten precariously on her other hip, as if she hardly wanted to hold him. Behind her Mariah could hear the sounds of the other children playing—four others, she recalled.

There was nothing wrong with the child that Mariah could see. Augusten was pink like a piglet and nearly as fat. But Evangeline had not been thriving. She seemed thin, colicky, and the little purple pouches beneath her eyes seemed to indicate a young woman who had been trying to cry herself to sleep at night without success.

They walked around to the back, where they both took seats, Evangeline on the sofa and Mariah, hands full of the boy, on the settee. Evangeline twirled the hair at the nape of her neck until her fingertip turned bright red. "I need..." But she wouldn't finish her sentence. She shook her head, she closed her eyes, she flipped them open and locked in on Mariah's own, like she was waiting for the Negro midwife to come up with the words to describe a wealthy white lady's horror.

Evangeline had always been kind to her, and Mariah would have called her sweet and quiet in the past, given their long history together. She guessed that Evangeline, in her childhood, had spent days pressing flowers and reading ladies' poetry and staring out windows at floating leaves and dandelion seeds. That's the kind of white woman she seemed to be, but this was not the woman who now sat on the sofa. She was preoccupied, fidgety, uncertain. Mariah noticed the sweat marks on Evangeline's blouse, between her breasts and down her sides.

"I feel guilty, Mariah."

"What you feel guilty about, ma'am?"

"That I don't want to be a mother again, that I'm sorry I brought yet another child into this awful world. I have too many children who will suffer."

"It ain't so awful."

Evangeline stared at her. "How can you of all people say such a thing, Mariah Reddick?"

How indeed? But Mariah knew what she was supposed to say to women who wanted to go back in time before they'd birthed their children, to before they'd let their men touch them, to the time before they had any responsibility to take care of another human being.

"I still believe in it, but I admit it's been hard, Miss Evangeline."

"I'm terribly sorry." Evangeline burst into tears with a gasp. Mariah would have gone over to comfort her, but she had her hands full with Augusten, who was clawing at her breast.

"What are you sorry about? You ain't done nothing. You givin' birth to a beautiful little boy is all."

"You saved his life."

Mariah didn't say anything to that. She let the words hang out in the air between them, lending the room more gravity, more weight. A child's life had been saved, that was true.

"I do love him," Evangeline said.

"'Course you do."

"I don't love myself, though."

Mariah was taken aback. "He just need you to love him. You can love yourself later."

"But how can he love a mother who can't hardly stand to look at herself in the mirror?" Evangeline shook her head and slapped her thigh, hard, like she was trying to fling something out of her mind. She bent her head over for a moment, and then raised it. She looked directly into Mariah's eyes, unblinking.

"You came because God sent you, didn't he, Mariah?"

"Don't know nothing about that, but God is in everything. I do believe that." Had Evangeline forgotten the note she'd sent? Maybe. Mariah would play along. If this was what it would take to get her to say what Mariah could sense she was about to say, then she'd profess to be the Archangel Gabriel himself.

"God wants me to talk to you."

Mariah stayed silent, waiting.

"I can't keep this from you. I should keep it from you, because white business is not supposed to be Negro business, or so I've always been told. But you saved his life"—she pointed at her baby cradled on Mariah's lap—"and that changes things. You saved his life with your *teeth*. You were fierce that day, Mariah. I remember looking up into your face and knowing as fully as I've ever known anything that you would take care of me and my baby, and that you would yourself banish death from this house. And you did."

This talk made Mariah uncomfortable. She knew how the white ladies of Franklin thought of her. The mothers, the others in town. She had houdou, they thought. That's what they called it when they thought she couldn't hear them. She could see it in their faces: the awe. They handed her their births and their babies in the deep conviction that they were handing them over to a witch with power greater than their own. What she would do for them, what incantations and strange rituals she'd conduct, they'd rather not know; they were just in thrall to the idea of houdou, and more accepting of it than Mariah herself would ever have been.

Evangeline took a deep breath. "I know you've been asking around about what happened that day to your Theopolis. I heard it from the cook. When I heard this I knew I had to talk to you, but I didn't have the courage to go see you. And now you're here, as if you knew this. You are an amazing woman."

"You sent me a note."

"But you didn't have to come."

"Do you have something to tell me, Miss Evangeline?"

"I'm not a bad woman, Mariah. I want to be a good person. I want to be a good mother, and I can't as long as I'm being eaten up inside."

"Let it out then."

Evangeline blew the air out, sucked it back in, arranged her skirts around her. "There are men in Nashville who arranged to have that rally attacked. They wanted one of the people on that stage to be killed. It was about politics, but I'm not certain the exact reason. But I do know this, that your boy wasn't the one they wanted killed. And they're angry about it."

Mariah stood up with Augusten in her arms, strode over to the sofa, handed the child to his mother, and sat back down on the settee. She placed her hands in her lap in front of her and blinked the tears back. She had already heard part of this, from Della. "And how do you know this?"

"Because my husband knows, and I overheard him talking to some men out back in his shed. Elijah is a good man, Mariah, and he told them they had been damned fools and should have stayed out of Franklin. He told them they had managed to kill the one good cobbler in town."

The one good cobbler.

"He doesn't know that I heard. I wished I hadn't, but now that you're here I'm glad I did."

140

Mariah realized that this path she had embarked upon, her quest for truth, would contain moments like this that she could hardly stand. She would suffer pain along the way, and relive her son's death in a dozen different ways. She would have to accept this, or stop asking questions. She considered going back to Carnton and never leaving again, but shook her head. She would go on.

"Do you know who the men were? The men who were talking to your husband?"

"I don't think so. Although many looked familiar. One has a few fingers missing from one hand, I think. But Elijah has never introduced me."

So it was true: Theopolis hadn't been the target, his death had been a cruel accident or mistake. But then she remembered those other men standing around her as he died on the ground in her arms, she remembered their faces. Maybe they didn't come looking to kill her son, but they didn't seem to mind that he had died.

"I don't want Elijah finding out that I know anything, and he especially can't ever know that I told you anything. About him or those men."

"Is he one of them? Your husband?"

"One of the group? I don't think so. I only came in at the end. It sounded to me like they came to him with a question or a problem or some such, and he was trying to advise them."

"Why didn't he just turn them in?"

"I don't know. Really, I don't."

"Probably some of those Conservative white boys," Mariah said.

"It didn't sound like that. These men sounded—well, rougher somehow."

Mariah paused, thinking. "What else you remember?"

"That's it, I'm afraid. But I wanted you to know. I felt like I owed it to you."

All Mariah wanted was to walk away from this place and be alone and walk some more. She couldn't remember what she said when she left or if she said anything at all to Miss Evangeline. She just wanted away from the place. But Franklin was a small town, and there wasn't much room for being lost and unnoticed. She could feel eyes on her, as if people could see what she now knew. The walls and roofs knew it, too, and the squirrel running along ahead of her knew about it. Every white face she saw could see what she possessed, and condemned her for trying to find out the truth. She thought she ought to be scared, but she wasn't much scared at all. She looked at herself in the plate glass of the stores along Main Street and saw a taller woman than she remembered. She was Mariah Reddick; she had birthed their children and tended their war wounded. She was owed. And perhaps Theopolis had been right, it was time for Negroes to get their due, and it might as well start with her, sitting in the Dixons' house, listening to the white woman.

Mariah walked for a little while toward the Blood Bucket. In the window of the ladies' garment store she saw some of Theopolis's shoes, toes shining. She moved quickly past. *I am Mariah Reddick; I birthed the children of this town and tended their war wounded. I have nothing to fear.*

But she imagined the shoes following her down the street.

Chapter 20

Tole

July 20, 1867

The next morning, Tole carried his water jug out, chipped enamel cool and comforting in his hands. At his stoop, he poured some into his left hand and splashed it on his face. He rubbed his eyes and the water dripped down his open collar.

The opened letter on the table had been delivered in the night.

July 18

Tole,

You may write to me at this address. I am not there, but it will reach me. Your discretion is required in this matter. That means have it delivered by someone you trust.

Dixon and I don't particularly see eye to eye when it comes to politics. My allegiance is with the Republicans and Reconstruction, and we're in charge. Dixon would rather kill a Republican than listen to him.

I suppose because I am grateful to have my life, you should know the reason you were to kill me. Railroad companies are buying up good land for lumber and bribing everyone they can to subsidize them, especially our new governments. This is happening everywhere in the South. Some of my fellow Republicans, it appears, are not as committed to the party as they are to taking a share of the proceeds. I want to see a re-constructed South whose people aren't ravaged by sky-high taxes and displaced because their homes lie in the way of rail-road tracks. My fellow radicals and I want a united country again. We trust no one.

I came to Franklin because I had seen this corruption else-where and had a theory about Dixon. Judging by the fact that, probably on behalf of one of his Nashville masters, he hired you to kill me, I believe I am right.

You will hear more from me, and I will require your services again, soon. I am grateful that you spared my life.

Thank you, again, for sparing my life. Dixon will be brought to heel, and when he is, you will not need to concern yourself with me again.

Jesse Bliss

Tole read the letter twice, not wanting to miss anything. It amused him that Bliss thought he had to threaten him into help-ing, when in fact he could think of hardly anything better to do than to rattle Elijah Dixon and, as the man said, *bring him to heel*.

Unearthing a piece of paper and a pen, he sat down to write out a reply in his shaky, childish scrawl.

Dear Mr Bliss,

Im real glad to hear you safe and workin to get Dixon. I dont no what else he has planned to do here but it cant be any good I think. I will help you any way I can.

GT

When he was done, Tole folded both the letter and his response and tucked them away in his back pocket. Just then, a neighbor passed him by, on her way to get fresh water at the pump they all shared out by the road. Her name was Bett, and from three houses behind him he would often hear her cry out late at night, cries of lust and sadness and love. It made him lonely just looking at her.

"They coming week after next I hear, Mr. Tole." Bett stopped at his porch, dark-eyed and wild-haired above her properly pressed camellia-green dress and white apron, arranged and cinched. She wore old leather slippers Tole recognized as Theopolis's handiwork.

"Who they?"

"Some big men from Nashville, coming to have an investigation of them killings. Guess they ain't satisfied with all that questioning folks all over town. Guess they coming to look into it more. Everybody been talkin' about it. They gone be here in a couple weeks, they sayin'. Bringing the whole U.S. Army with them, I hear."

He could guess what those *big men from Nashville* would want, and it wasn't necessarily the truth. They would want order. He wondered how this fit into Bliss's plans, or whether he knew about it.

He splashed more water on his face, until his collar was thoroughly wet. The birds laughed at him and gathered together. He wiped his face and neck and stood up straight. Before the sun came up, it split the sky with banners of purple and orange and yellow, as if it were sending out scouts to check, to give the all-clear. The rooftops lit up, some glowed, and then shadows appeared. He was surprised that Bett was still standing there.

"You gone be in the courtroom then?"

"Why you ask that?" He said it sharper than he'd meant, and that was sloppy. This was what came of talking to people. Secrets get revealed in a word.

"Just wondering."

You are not a very good liar, Bett. Tole knew he was a figure of great suspicion and curiosity among his neighbors. An outsider.

Bett went off to get her water, passing the ragman in his cart coming the other way. Tole was surprised when the ragman pulled up right at his porch.

"Morning." Hooper stood up in his cart so he was almost eye level with Tole standing on the porch.

"Morning." Tole waited.

"Mariah Reddick requested I see you 'cause you need work, and since I got nothing against a man who can work, I got some."

"You friends with Mariah?"

"Ain't friends with no one. But she's tolerable enough for a house Negro."

"That she is," Tole agreed, eyeing Hooper. "What you need?"

"I got some house cleaning needs doing, and then some wood chopping, and plenty of work for a few weeks at least," Hooper said.

"How much you paying?"

Hooper named a price well below what Tole would have wanted. He nodded and waved Hooper into the house.

When Hooper stepped inside, he stopped short like he'd walked into a wall. He whistled and removed his cloth cap, as if he'd just walked into church. Tole tried to see his creation through the eyes of this new man seeing it for the first time. He goggled at it a little himself. The thing he had made still had the power to surprise him. He looked at it and couldn't remember making half of it.

What had once been a town a week or two before had become a dense, sprawling version of a world constructed simultaneously in the physical (here are the buildings, here are the people, here is a man with a rifle in the attic of the doctor's house) and the metaphysical context (here are the angels watching over them, here are the demons leading them down primrose paths, here are the souls caught in their migration, uncertain of heaven above and hell below). Heaven had been hung from the low ceiling of the house by hundreds of pieces of twine and string, each supporting an angel or a soul.

There weren't many souls drifting upward toward the ceiling, which had recently been painted blue. Below the tables and platforms that bore up the model of the town, Tole had painted everything red in thick, sloppy strokes. On the legs of the tables, crossing here and there, he had attached a lattice of wood strips and platforms, which both stabilized the display and provided ample room to present the full horror of hell. Considerably more souls hung below, drifting past demons and devils, tortured by tiny grinning tommyknockers.

The display now spilled from the tables onto the floor, where Tole had been carving half-size animals that appeared to be stampeding out his back door and down into the small backyard. These had been made from scrap wood and old sewing spools for eyes—raccoons and possums, goggle-eyed wolves and rats. They looked to be fleeing. *It's the animals what always know what's happening first,* is what Tole had intended by this. *They know to save themselves.* At the end of the hallway he had built a small house on fire, and two tiny figures standing on its steep roof.

Tole looked over at Hooper, not at all surprised to find a man struck dumb by his creation. He crossed and recrossed his arms, and let slip a trace of a smile at the corner of his mouth before recovering his composure.

"It's always the damnedest people who get they hands on some part of the great truth, ain't it?" Hooper said.

"Sounds like an insult, ragman."

"I mean, this thing is *true.*"

"No you don't."

Hooper nodded and took a seat on a stool, still staring at it. "This is a day, right, Mr. Tole?"

"Part of a bunch of days, at least right there where the streets at. The rest, above and below it, that's time out of time. Time don't mean nothing above and below."

"And that day is…"

"One part is they giving they speeches on the square that day, you know. Got black after that day, and nothing fit together after that."

Tole tried to be patient, but he couldn't help being eager to get to work. He'd thought about what working with the ragman would mean, and it would mean being able to move around the town smooth and without causing a disturbance. It meant becoming one of the locals who faded into the background. This was what he needed to complete his plan, because now everywhere he went he felt the eyes of white men on him, *the strange Negro*, tracking his movements and taking down his activities. He felt white eyes on him always; they were more aware of him than they were of each other. They listened to him and watched him. He wanted to be invisible, not chased by their gaze.

Hooper had a question. "Who on top of this house here?" He pointed north and west of the town square, where a man made of twisted baling wire and cloth scraps, with a tiny, bright red cork head, lay prone on the roof of a two-story house just about where one might find Doc Cliffe's house, if this were all real and Doc Cliffe's house were made of scrap pieces of an old *Superior Grimes Golden Apples* crate.

Hooper's question made him feel dried out and shrunk. Exposed. He should never have put that man there. He wondered if the big man would do him harm if he ever found out who that was and what he had done.

"Don't know," Tole said. "Just put him there."

Hooper looked back at the house. "What's he got there?" He pointed at something thin and dark in the hands of the wire man.

"If you got work, let's get started," Tole said.

"But it makes sense, don't it, Mr. Tole?"

"What?"

"That there was a fellow with a rifle. Make a lot of sense, that would."

"Don't know nothing about that."

Hooper looked queerly at Tole, his head cocked. "It do make sense, *Tole*."

Tole slumped over and leaned his backside into one of the only empty corners in his house. He was about to kick the big man out of his house when Hooper looked over at him with kind eyes.

"Let's get us a drink, Mr. Tole. I got a jug in the cart." And before Tole could say anything, Hooper was out the door and down the path to the cart, where he reached under the bench seat and pulled out a large jug. He hooked an index finger through the hemp loop that he'd made into a handle and draped it over his right shoulder. He walked light, the step of a man with a mission he was happy to have. He climbed the porch.

"Here we are, Tole," he said, and handed it over.

There is a state of mind men can reach together, on porches and not entirely in possession of all their faculties, that approaches a sort of comfortable, warm telepathy, Tole thought after drinking a goodly amount. It became less necessary to speak aloud because each of them knew what the other was thinking. Nothing on the street escaped their attention because each of their sets of eyes reported the news to one mind. That's how it felt.

After an hour or so, Hooper stood up and beckoned for Tole to follow. "Let's get started on that job."

"What we doing, then?"

And Hooper nodded in the direction of Theopolis's house. "His mama asked me to clear that out."

Tole followed, dreading every step.

In Theopolis's small house, most of the shoes were gone, but the forms still hung on the wall. Feet of every imaginable size and shape had their double there on the wall in matched pairs strung through the heel with twine and looped over nails. Tole knew they were only the working tools of a working man, but they nonetheless seemed macabre to him, and he looked away. They were like a wall of headstones.

Hooper soon had him moving furniture. They carried out two workbenches, a table, a bed, two bent-oak chairs, several wooden stands on which the foot forms could be attached, several large, knee-high stacks of leather—cow and calf, pig—and five books, including one Bible.

They carried out the foot forms last, piling them atop the furniture and in all the empty spaces they could find. Hooper said a lot of it they'd be able to sell for Mariah, and that the rest would get scrapped or burned. "That woman deserves to know her boy's things been taken care of. Ain't good for her to think that he still got any other place in the world but that grave where she can go to see him," he said. "We laying him to rest for good."

Tole looked back at Hooper. "You know his mama pretty well, don'tcha?"

"We go back a ways. Why you ask?"

"No reason."

"There's always a reason."

"I just been getting to know her a little, is all. She ain't like nobody I ever met before."

Hooper dragged a wooden table closer to the front door. "Mariah a special lady. She stronger than any living person I know. Too strong, you ask me."

"What's that mean?"

"It mean, she don't know when she need help. She don't know when she in trouble. She don't know when it's time to give up."

Tole helped Hooper lift the table and the two of them hoisted it, turned it to sneak it through the doorframe and out down the steps onto the street with the rest.

"She don't think of herself much, it's true."

"What's it to you?" Hooper said, suspicious.

"Nothin'. Just seems odd that a woman like her, beautiful and smart and strong, spends her whole life helping other people."

"She still think like a slave. You don't tell her I said that, or I'll pull your lungs out. But she like to think she fierce and independent, but she don't know how to be free."

Tole became quiet. "Let's go get the rest of it," he said, and Hooper followed him back in. The two men continued moving the rest of the furniture until Theopolis's house was near empty.

"Makes me a little sad to think about it," Tole said.

"What's that?"

"What you said about Mariah."

"Still don't see why you care. You got more than friendly feelings for her?"

Tole shrugged. "I just met her."

"It don't matter how long you've known a woman. I seen people fall in love in five minutes. Usually my liquor has something to do with that, but sometimes it happens all by itself."

Tole laughed. "Without your help, eh?"

"Sometimes."

Tole was quiet a moment, and then started, "Does she..."

"Do she what?"

"Do she take up with men?"

Hooper laughed his loud laugh that turned into a coughing fit. "Taking up with men ain't exactly what Mariah do for fun. She was married way back, but he died. She been worrying about raising Theopolis and taking care of Miss Carrie and her living children, and she seen more than her share of no-count men. Since she been free, she ain't jumped right into nothing."

"You think she'd ever marry again?"

Hooper grinned at him, but then his face became somber. "Don't know. Not right now, though. She want some kind of justice for Theopolis, that's all she think about. That's what I mean about her being too strong. She could use a good man by her. But she don't think she need it. She think she fine, she can do all this on her own. And she ain't fine."

Tole took a swig of water from the jug and used some to wipe down his brow, the back of his neck. "Sure she could have just about any man she wanted," he said.

Hooper shrugged. "She intimidates most men. Scares 'em off. Scared me off years ago, told me to keep my hands to myself, and I done so ever since."

"That's a shame," Tole said, not meaning it at all.

"She don't scare you, though?"

"No," Tole said. "She don't scare me. She the only one who make this town feel like home, you wanna know the truth."

<hr/>

When they were through, Tole waited for Hooper at the door and the two walked back to Tole's porch, where the liquor lay where they had left it. When they sat down again, Tole noticed that Hooper had a pair of brown leather boots in his hand. They were soft leather and polished; Tole could see the dimples in the curves and along the toe line.

"Saw these stashed under the bed. They look your size." Hooper held them out and looked down at Tole's own shoes, which showed his toes.

"I ain't wearing a dead man's shoes. Ain't stealing either." Tole didn't want the shoes of the boy he'd killed, and he couldn't say no to them either.

"Oh, I don't think they his shoes. I found his shoes, and they was worn out like yours, but they a real different size. Bigger."

"Why he got these under his bed then?"

"Maybe he just thought they was good. Maybe he was proud of 'em. Why you sleep on the ground with a crazy town built all over you?"

Tole had no good answer to that.

"They ain't his, so quit acting like you scared a ghosts. And anyway, yours are falling apart. Can't have a bum working with me, so you're takin' 'em whether you wear 'em or not."

Hooper tossed the pair over toward Tole, and they landed with a thunk, straight up, right next to his seat. "Quit walking around town like a poor Negro," he said. "You give us all a bad name. Put them damn shoes on next time you out."

No one would ever know the complexity of the gesture Tole made when he bent over to pick up those shoes, and when he slipped off his old ones and laced up the new. An eon's worth of worry about death, and one's obligations to the dead, passed through his head. *What are the dead? They aren't the living.* That seemed to be what Hooper was saying. And maybe that was true. The dead were gone, and those shoes had nothing to do with Theopolis anymore. He laced them up tight, and they fit well. No part of the dead man could be found in the objects piled high in that cart, and there was nothing in there that required anything of Tole, nothing that could speak to him anymore. It was only the living that mattered now. The dead wore death lightly, but under its weight the living could crumple. Hooper said this was a good thing they'd done for Mariah, and he believed him. He was glad. That was a start.

"Looks good on you," Hooper said.

"Feels good," said Tole.

They sat in silence for a long minute, sipping moonshine, nothing but the sounds of their swallows between them.

"Strange thing being in a dead man's house, ain't it?" Hooper asked.

Tole barely nodded his head.

"Always imagined myself dying an old man in my bed, somewhere, I don't know, maybe in a cottage near the Smoky Mountains. Been up that way?"

"Not yet."

"Oh, it's a damn pretty picture up there." Hooper pondered something. "You think about that ever?"

"Dyin'?"

"Dyin', sure. Death."

"Too much, I reckon."

"Hard not to, these days."

"You make it sound like it ain't nothing to be scared of," Tole said.

"I knew a man died at ninety years old. He tell me he spent his whole life worryin' about death, and when it finally started to come, he said all the worryin' drifted away. He said by the time death come around, he was layin' there in bed, barely able to breathe around the pneumonia, and he told me that he said to death, 'You? That's it? That's all you got?' He died a couple days after he told me that."

Tole chuckled a bit. "He sound like a character."

"Oh, he was. He killed many men for their gold, and only ever liked one Negro, and that was me."

The two men let the silence wash over them.

"When I was in the war," Tole said, "me and some boys, we used to talk about dyin'. We used to talk about food from back home. This boy named Raymond Allbey, he from Philadelphia I think it was, he used to talk about this pork his mama used to make. He said if he knew he were dyin', he'd crawl back to Pennsylvania just to get him one last bite of his mama's pork."

"How 'bout you?"

"For me it was a little café back in New York. Little old lady there make the best beans, they were smooth as cream."

"Any man who crawl home for beans ain't right."

"I'm tellin' you. You ever in New York, you let me know."

"For me, it'd be a slice of warm pecan pie from Nattie's. You know Nattie?"

Tole shook his head no.

"Oh, everybody 'round here know Nattie. She a sweet old thing. And damn can she bake a fine pie. I don't know what she do to it, but it so good you wouldn't mind dyin' afterward."

Tole smiled and sipped his drink and winced as he swallowed.

"Listen, tomorrow I got more work," Hooper said. "Chopping wood and hauling junk."

"I'll take all the work you got. But can I borrow the cart some-times?"

"For what?"

"Sometimes I got errands, sometimes I got my own *junk* that needs hauling. For friends."

"You got friends?"

Tole didn't reply.

"Sure, you can use the cart, but I get a cut of what you make."

"I do it for free."

"Then you a stupid Negro, but that's your business." Hooper eyed him with a squint. "You just promise to tell me what you up to with it."

"Maybe I will."

And then they shook on it and toasted their partnership.

CHAPTER 21

MARIAH

July 22, 1867

Thanks to Evangeline, Mariah had an idea about the identity of at least one of the gang who'd slaughtered her son, so one late morning, after her morning tasks at Carnton were for the moment accomplished, she walked into Franklin and out again, heading north to where the Crutcher family eked out a rough existence. The man of the house, Mariah knew, was missing the last three fingers of his hand. She hoped her excuse for going out there would be convincing to them. They were, as Evangeline had put it, very rough.

She had not been welcome at the birth of Lizzie Crutcher's daughter six months before, but she had been necessary. Lizzie and her husband—was he her husband? Mariah didn't actually know—had not wanted her there. Bill Crutcher, one of the number of lumbermen who called the town home, had only grudgingly returned from the deep woods to attend the birth. He was not happy to see a Negro in his house when he got there.

"We ain't need the houdou woman. Now get the hell out."

Lizzie, who had called for her, was not much more welcoming, but she was in great pain and alone, except for the hulk in her corner who, when he wasn't drinking, was cursing the nigger magic woman and her foul, dirty hands that would no doubt turn his child stupid. *This child gone be stupid whatever I do, Crutcher*, Mariah had thought. The cabin was cold, the chinking between the logs entirely crumbled away in spots so she could see the trees waving in the bright winter light, which streamed through the holes and gave Mariah more to see by than she would normally have expected from a backwoods cabin with no windows.

"Nigger, why? God, nigger, why this hurt? What the hell you doing? Do. Jesus. *Do something, nigger!*" Lizzie cursed her, but underneath the curses Mariah could hear her desperation, how she needed her. She talked hard, but mostly for the ears of the man in the corner who wouldn't lift a finger.

The child lay across its path to the world, as if she knew what she was getting into and wanted no part of it. *Nigger, fix it!* This was the white woman's first child, and she didn't yet know that there were some mothering pains that couldn't be fixed, that just had to be suffered. Mariah felt Lizzie's stomach with her strong fingers, and got her hand slapped for it. The lumberman stood up. "Don't be takin' no liberties with a white woman, witch," he said, before sitting back down. This was the world in which this white child would be raised and taught. Someday the child would taunt her and spit at her, Mariah was sure.

The black of the world had settled there in that room and had sucked up everything warm and welcoming. There was no sign of any decorations or handwork, no touch of a woman's hand, no fire in the tiny stone hearth. Good things had been erased, if they had ever existed. Even so, Mariah was fixed on delivering that baby.

She put her hands on Lizzie again, this time feeling for the baby's head and bottom, which she slowly pushed and pulled. Lizzie gasped but said nothing this time. The lumberman laid his head against the wall and closed his eyes, as if to sleep. Mariah pushed and pulled and the baby turned a little. *Get it out*, Lizzie hissed, but Mariah reached up and held her hand and told her it would come in a few minutes but not yet, not right that minute, that Lizzie had to hold tight to that child and keep her until all was ready. But Lizzie pushed anyway, moving with the pain, wanting to be rid of it. Mariah moved fast.

She made Lizzie stand up. Lizzie gripped Mariah's hand so hard she nearly broke it. Her blonde braid, dirty with clay dust and dripping wet at the end, hung in front of her. Her freckles glowed red. She cursed Mariah and lay back down, so Mariah took matters into her own hands. She reached up inside and turned the baby, ignoring Lizzie's protests. Then a head began to emerge, which brought its own more intense pain—a pain that a mother knows is the beginning of the end of pain.

Lizzie pushed and pushed again and the baby slipped out into the world, healthy and confused and afraid. She cried and Lizzie cried. The lumberman stirred long enough to take the baby from Mariah, inspect its privates, shrug, hand the baby back to Mariah. "Boy next time," was all he said before slipping out the door and back into the woods.

Mariah cleaned the child and watched for the rest of the birth, which finally came. The bleeding should have stopped then, but it didn't. She handed the little girl to Lizzie, who snatched her daughter away. *Get your time with her now*, Mariah thought, *because you dying*.

Why save such a woman? That was a question Mariah could only ask afterward, when the answer had become beside the point and meaningless. Mariah did what her mother and her mother's mother and every other woman like her did.

With one hand she pressed down hard on the part of Lizzie's stomach where she knew her womb needed to shrink, and with her other hand she pressed the place where she knew the blood was flowing through. Lizzie screamed at her and the baby cried. Lizzie tried to kick and push and punch, she tried to move off the table. Her green eyes flashed hate, her teeth bared beneath her pudgy nose.

"You're murdering me!"

There wasn't anyone to hear them, Mariah knew, so she kept pressing and watching the flow of blood that pooled below Lizzie on the floor. The drops had become a spot, and then a pool overflowing. Mariah pressed harder.

"You a dead nigger!"

"You a dead white lady if you bleed like this. You stay still."

Calm, just like her mother had taught her. So calm that Lizzie listened to her. She gasped. Mariah knew the pain was terrible, but the little girl just born would have no chance in this world if left alone with the lumberman, Mariah knew. She needed a mama, even this one, this trashy and dirty backwoods bitch.

"Nurse the child, Lizzie." And Lizzie nursed the child. The little girl suckled greedily. Everything flowed from this mother at once, Mariah knew, and she felt a little sorry for her.

Maybe it was a half hour, maybe it was an hour, Mariah couldn't say. Her arms and hands were numb when it was over. But by some miracle the blood, now having washed over her feet to form a puddle six feet across, slowed its flow. Lizzie had gone pale and shallow-breathed, but now began to get her color back. Sometime later there was no blood, and Mariah gently, gently, pulled her hands off the white lady. There were bruises on that pale white stomach where the butt of her hands had dug in.

Mariah folded clean rags together in a wad and placed them between Lizzie's legs, and took Lizzie's free hand and placed it there to hold. She pulled her to sit up at the edge of the table. The little girl sucked hard at her mother's breast. Lizzie swayed, got lightheaded, nearly fell, and Mariah held her up until the stars and darkness cleared and Lizzie could see straight again. The white lady looked down at the blood and vomited. Mariah looked for more blood then, but there was none. It was dark outside. Hours had passed. "Got no rags for the blood, Miss Lizzie."

"I was going to die," Lizzie said wonderingly, ignoring her.

"No you wasn't."

"I was. I should have died."

"God had a different plan."

"You kept me from dying."

"God did," Mariah said. "Now, I can go get something to clean up this blood—"

"Get out," Lizzie said. "Don't come back. I'll clean it."

"I can help."

"You've helped enough. Right now you got to get out. Bill won't like any of this."

"Yes, miss."

"He'll think you tried to kill me."

And that was all Mariah needed to hear. She understood more than needed to be said. She gathered her things. At the door Lizzie called after her. Mariah looked back and in the dark could see the ghostly glow of Lizzie's nightgown perched on the edge of the table.

"Thank you."

The memory was still as fresh as the day she made it.

◦———◦

That was the Crutcher Mariah thought she should go see. Bill hated Governor Brownlow, hated seeing the freedmen taking his land, or anyone's land, or having anything at all. He thought they would also take his money and his rights. Theopolis had been one of those men. Bill would not be helpful.

Down the path to the cabin, tendrils of creeper and wild blackberry had lain down across the way, as if it hadn't been walked in ages. In the clearing around the cabin, Mariah smelled the tang of vegetation crowding in, grass growing man high, more vines, wild onions, foot-high pines already reaching up. The forest was moving in to claim it, but there was smoke from the ramshackle chimney, and Mariah knew that the woman and child had not succumbed, not yet.

Mariah knocked and heard scraping and scurrying.

"Who there?"

"Mariah Reddick."

"What you want, witch?" The voice said the words, but the heart wasn't in it. Mariah could hear a note of excitement.

"Just come to check on the baby."

"Well, I ain't get rid of you until you do, reckon."

The door opened and Mariah walked inside. What she saw she hadn't expected: a cabin swept and washed, every chair and bowl in its place, a fat child sleeping under crookedly sewn quilts, tucked in neat beside the woodstove. The child glowed.

Lizzie was no longer so pale nor so hard-faced. She wore her hair loose and had brushed it so that it lay full in front of her shoulders. Her green eyes were clear, her freckles not nearly so livid. Her apron was clean.

"What you looking at?" she asked, taking her hair in a fist and pulling it behind her.

"The child looks healthy, sure enough."

"And you wondering where the man is."

I am and I ain't, Mariah thought.

"He's been gone a week, maybe more. And I'm about to go, too."

"What you mean?"

"I love that girl right there more than I love anything in this world."

Mariah nodded.

"Kind of funny you showing up when you did," Lizzie went on. "'Cause if you came tomorrow we be gone. We ain't staying here. We gone go to New Orleans. My sister live there. We gone to the big city and we gone dress in proper dresses and have tea and learn to read things. We changing, Lucy and me. She ain't gone be Lizzie, she gone be Lucy."

Ain't nothing wrong with not naming a child after yourself, Mariah thought.

"She ain't gone grow up with a father like Bill, with a man got fists like that."

Now Lizzie got a tight look on her face, her mouth was drawn. She sat down at her little table. There was another seat across from her, but Mariah stood. The child wheezed a little in her sleep. Her mother squinted at the midwife, the Negress looming in her house. Mariah was patient to wait. Her instinct had led her to Lizzie Crutcher, and her instinct told her it was about to become worth the trip.

"Sit down."

Mariah sat.

"She alive because of you, and so am I, and I don't like it one bit, but I owe you a blood favor. I got a debt to you."

Her brushed hair began to curtain her face when she leaned forward. "You lost your own boy."

"He was murdered."

"Your only child."

"Yes ma'am."

"You ain't got anyone else in this world."

"No ma'am."

Lizzie leaned back in her chair, rethinking what she had begun. She shook her head and leaned forward again. She had been eating better, her face was full like a moon, but her eyes were hard as crystal. And yet Mariah didn't have to ask her a single question. Just her presence brought out the words she wanted to hear.

"I don't know nothing about how your boy died. But I know men who couldn't hardly talk about nothing else. And Bill, he were one of them. They was all spun up about your boy and what would happen because of that day they had them speeches in town. They was all spun up about all you niggers, truth is, but they was particular worried about your boy's dying."

Somehow Mariah had known this. She had dreamt of this cabin, and of the light through the chinks between the logs, and of the stove. She had seen the wild-eyed backwoods girl shining in front of her. The great hand—of God, fate, the roots and cures—had drawn her. She sat quiet and listened, not needing to ask any questions.

For the two or three days after the rally, Lizzie said, Bill wouldn't stay still as the Army patrolled the town, taking depositions, writing down names. His comings and goings were constant, unless he was out back near the fire pit with that raggedy crew of strange men he had taken to hosting sometimes. All told there were seven men, though no more than four ever appeared at the cabin at once. She didn't know all their names. They each arrived separately on horseback, at night, all of them heavy with beard and wearing black. These strange men rode horses saddled tight and high like cavalrymen. Some limped, and none of them talked very much near the cabin, only way out by the fire pit. They were polite, they tipped their hats to Lizzie if they saw her, and quietly thanked her for the biscuits and ham Bill insisted she give them when they left for home. They seemed the sort of men who worked very hard not to be noticed. They squinted over their beards and flexed the muscles in their jaws, but remained quiet until they stepped into the firelight. Lizzie recognized some of their voices.

She especially recognized Elijah Dixon, the fancy man from the fancy house with the fancy wife. He talked the most.

"Mr. Dixon was there," Mariah repeated. "You sure?"

"'Course I'm sure. He was the boss man. They all listened to him."

Mariah let Lizzie's words pour over her like a shadow. *The boss man*, she repeated to herself. Elijah Dixon hadn't just been talking to those men, chastising them for killing the *one good cobbler*: he was their leader. She wondered if Evangeline knew this. Lizzie continued.

A week before, Lizzie had taken a basket of bread and cheese out the door and crossed the woods to the fire. There was an old hickory log along the path some distance away from the fire pit, which was where Lizzie usually left the food wrapped in a clean towel. By some trick of the woods, the echo of their voices was clear as anything right there at the log, and she could hear them as plain as day. Every other night she just left the food and walked back, uninterested in the talk. But that night, the last night she saw Bill, something caused her to sit down on the log, beside the basket, and listen.

She heard pacing, shoes scraping and thumping on the hardpack. She heard the bright ring of a jar—of whiskey, she thought—put down, *clink*, upon a rock. It took a moment for the sound of their voices to clarify.

"You goddamn will do what I tell you," came Dixon's voice, rough with power but mannered. "I tell you I have it all handled."

"Said that before, didn't you?" Lizzie thought this was the voice of Aaron Haynes, who lived over near Hillsboro.

"Gonna be a big payday for all of us," Dixon said. It sounded as if he'd said the phrase several times already.

"For you, you mean," came another voice, shriller. "You just want us to do the dirty work."

"Ain't that dirty."

"The Army is coming back," said Haynes. "They catch us—"

"Why would they even think of looking?" Dixon said. "Just keep doing what you're doing. Get the land."

"Those people don't want to sell. Poor niggers never had a place of their own."

"I'm sick of repeating this to you," Dixon went on. "Just do what I tell you. Scare the hell out of 'em. You know how to do that, at least."

"Don't see you out there scaring hell out of 'em."

"I'm the one who's going to make you rich," Dixon said. "Got to stay above all that. Stick with me and you'll be fine."

They began to move, and Lizzie understood at least one of them was coming her way. She whipped around, nearly tripping on a pea vine, and ran—leapt—back to the cabin. Then she stood in the doorway as if nothing had happened.

When Bill at last came through the door and sat down at the kitchen table, he seemed much smaller than he had ever seemed before. The next day he left for a three-day logging trip, and was three days past due. She took this as a sign she should leave.

"I don't want that blood money, if there even is any," Lizzie told Mariah now. "Ain't my business, and I don't want no part in it. I'm going to New Orleans, I'm going up in this world. All this place soon be dead and past to me. But I ain't been able to take my eyes off this little girl here. She everything, Lucy is, and this weren't something I knowed would happen to me, and now I wonder what any woman, even a Negro woman, thinks when she loses a child. And I owe you something at least, which I don't like but that's the damned truth. So I don't know if it help to know this, but I know your boy were killed by them men and my husband. They meant to do it, it weren't no accident or high spirits. They set out to kill themselves a nigger. Mr. Dixon was their puppet master, making them dance and do what he wanted them to do. Bill laughed about killing your boy, said that was one thing Dixon hadn't planned. But Bill is a stupid man. I myself know what happens when you send weasels into a chicken house. What happens ain't no surprise."

She took a breath, stood up, walked over to Lucy, and took her up in her arms.

All the air in the house seemed to vanish. Mariah slipped through the door and out toward the path that would take her far away. Lizzie stood on the threshold looking after her, Lucy nuzzling at her bosom.

Now Mariah knew them. If she didn't know all their names, she knew where they walked and what they said to each other. She knew she could find them and touch them. And, most shocking of all, she had names: Elijah Dixon, Aaron Haynes. She had known Dixon was meeting with the big men from Nashville, but she had not known he was one of the brutes who yanked the life from her son.

"I should have strangled your child, Elijah Dixon," she whispered to herself, and this thought so shocked and nauseated her that she had to stop by the side of the road and wait to be sick. When the waves of nausea passed, she continued on. *Just a baby*, she told herself over and over again as she walked. She vowed she would take no revenge upon babies, but men were another matter.

CHAPTER 22

TOLE

July 23, 1867

From the beginning, Tole and Hooper worked, or Tole went out to Carnton to help the women with their cemetery and around the house. But some days he had to himself, and on those days he went to the woods in the pockets of wildness that still ringed Franklin here and there. He came to know the wildflowers and to know how certain of the animal tracks—deer and raccoon, the smeared trail of the beaver—would lead him to water. He knew to avoid the under-story of cedars and redbuds in the early spring, lest he find himself crawling with the inchworms suspended down on their tiny strings in curtains of the lower air's own green stars. This was hard-won knowledge of ordinary things.

On occasion, while he was working in the yard at Carnton, he liked to take small breaks, wipe the sweat from his brow, and watch the lady of the house, Carrie McGavock, step out the side of the house near the kitchen and take a few puffs of tobacco from an old pipe. The smoke curled around her head and she periodically waved it away from her face like she was shooing horseflies. Tole imagined she thought no one could see her taking respite from her well-known occupation of public mourning over in the cemetery, and for this he liked her better. Down the creek from Carnton he sometimes watched the Negro tenant Caruthers family on their new share stake, and the big Caruthers boys tearing around field and wood, sometimes tossing each other over the end of the porch and rolling down the hill.

Most often, however, Tole joined Hooper on his rounds. They chopped wood, made deliveries, and collected junk that could be fixed and sold in the Bucket. Why the people called Hooper "the ragman" was a mystery to Tole; he saw not one rag in all that time. Hooper collected old dresses, too, and perhaps that's what people meant by rags: the old dresses of white ladies, torn and stained, which he would bring back to sell at April and May's place, or to the market. He hardly ever had success selling those dresses, Tole noticed. Black women walked right on by. "But this fit you!" Hooper would call out after another who had passed them by in the market, nose in the air. Tole would look over then and Hooper would be smiling. It was a joke Hooper kept running, it was something that amused him. Days later they'd burn the dresses. Lace burnt quick and bright, crinoline smoldered.

Another thing Tole noticed: Negroes were always stopping Hooper to take him aside to ask him questions, or to beg for some advice, or to whisper something in his ear. Every day Tole watched Hooper baptize himself in the Harpeth in the name of the Father and of the Son and of the Holy Spirit, which in Tole's book made the ragman crazy, but nevertheless the black people of Franklin treated him as a wise man. It took some time before Tole understood.

Hardly a single white person ever noticed Hooper when he walked in the back through their kitchens to talk with cooks and maids about firewood and junk. They just kept carrying on their conversations—in their sitting rooms and hallways, in their libraries and dining rooms—as if Hooper weren't standing right there, hands in his pockets, trying to figure out how to carry a desk with a broken leg out through the door and kitchen to the cart. But by God, if Tole walked in to help him lift the desk, all conversation stopped and all eyes turned to him. Men put down their forks and stared at him. He and Hooper would carry the desk out, and as they passed through the kitchen he would hear the white talk begin again.

"You a strange nigger, thasall," Hooper said once, as they pulled away with a full load. "They notice you. 'Who the hell is this one?' they say. 'Don't know him. What he want? Which people his?' They keep quiet. Strange niggers scare 'em. There wasn't never no strange niggers before. Back before, if there was a strange nigger walking through the town, he be locked up quick and they try to figure where he come from and who he got to be returned to. This ain't New York City. A black man don't just appear.

"But, if you not a strange black man, if you a black man they known since they were little and got used to ignoring, well"— Hooper smiled—"you hear a lot. They say any damned thing in front of you. When you young that make you mad. When you young and you strong and you stupid, you hate it and you want to fight it, you want to say, 'I'm standing here, missus.' But when you get old and you can see the long stretch of time, you see what you got: a gift they don't even know they made to you. And so you keep even quieter and let them talk."

Tole began hanging back in the kitchens so as not to disturb the delicate balance of known and unknowns, so that Hooper and the black ladies who worked in those big houses could go about their business like ghosts and the white people could keep talking. And they talked. Tole began to notice how, when they were done, Hooper would take a cup of water from the cook or the nurse, and they would stand close talking low for a few minutes, and then Hooper would stomp out of the house whistling.

The realization of what Hooper was came all at once to Tole, so fast he laughed out loud while they were driving away from a big house one day. "You the town gossip." He poked Hooper in the chest.

"I hate towns," Hooper said. But he didn't deny it. "There ain't a thing them black ladies don't know about them they work for, and there ain't a one of them black ladies I don't see every week."

It was true. Through Hooper, over time Tole met the whole network of maids and cooks and nurses of Franklin, the whole network of Hooper's informers. He came to have knowledge of white men who drank too much, who cheated at cards. This wasn't knowledge for mere amusement, Tole realized. Hooper believed white people needed watching. Most of the time the news was exactly like gossip, the whos and whats and whens of white folks. Sometimes the gossip was good to a white man or woman, someone who was kind or generous, and Tole noticed that such news gave Hooper pause to recalibrate the system of relations he had been mapping for many years. But most men, white and black, never did much on principle, never acted crosswise with the crowd. Hooper—and Tole, for that matter, now that he thought about it—didn't care what was in a white man's heart or what he said; he cared about what a white man did.

Hooper sat up straight in his cart, as if he were in command of all he surveyed, and when they drove the mule down this street or that, he tipped his hat to the people and the Negroes tipped their hats back.

Tole admired the operation Hooper had going. It made him laugh at the misplaced confidence of white people. But he had his own ways of keeping track of such men, especially those who snuck around meeting in smokehouses and sheds and plotting their little revolutions.

CHAPTER 23

LETTER

July 24

Dear Mr Bliss,

I been listenin around to see what Dixon is up to and I think I found out sumthing good. Sound like he and his men been scarin foke, maybe to sell sum land he wants. I herd about 1 family they was workin on, think they name Wilson. They live near Brentwood. I gess Dixon wants their land real bad.

I hope this helps you and I will keep listenin for mor.

GT

CHAPTER 24

MARIAH

July 23, 1867

The day after she met Lizzie, Mariah went to Franklin to deliver a beautiful baby girl—seven pounds, six ounces—soon born, named Annabelle Rose, and latched on to the mother's breast. Dusk was falling by the time Mariah washed herself and decided to stop by the Thirsty Bird Saloon for a visit with April and May.

Inside, the saloon was lively with chatter and laugher. In the corner, a young Negro boy, no older than thirteen, sat and banged rhythmically on a bass drum; beside him a heavy black woman with a long braid down her back played the clarinet. Eben Payne and his mother, Eloise. Mariah had birthed Eben. She and Eloise nodded to one another, but Eloise did not stop playing.

April was behind the bar, pouring drinks, chatting to customers. At a corner table, Mariah saw familiar faces: Hooper, May, and, surprisingly, George Tole.

"Mariah, come on over!" May hollered over the noise and chatter.

Tole stood up, stumbled backward toward the wall, and offered Mariah his chair.

"I don't mind standing, Mr. Tole."

"Please sit," he said, and Mariah did. Tole pulled another stool over and sat beside her.

When Tole stood up, Mariah noticed the shoes he was wearing. "Your boots," she said.

Tole looked down.

"Those the shoes my boy made."

"It was my idea," Hooper said.

Mariah smiled. "They look a little handsome on you."

"What brings you out this way?" May asked.

"I need reasons for visiting friends now?"

"'Course not. Except I know you and I know you ain't jus' come all this way to see little old me."

"Old is right," Mariah said.

"Don't you go runnin' that lip now," May said.

Hooper leaned over to Tole. "I seen these two go at it a time or two. You don't want nothing to do with it. They scare even the toughest men."

"I believe it," Tole said, before asking Mariah if she would like a drink.

"I'm fine, Mr. Tole."

Tole nodded and gestured for April behind the bar to bring him another. Hooper and May shared a look.

"So Mariah. What brings you out here?" Hooper asked this time.

"Baby come. Ashby house over off Walnut," she said. Tole glanced over at her, mesmerized. "Pretty little thing," she said. "Her little palm barely fit around my finger."

Tole finished his drink too quickly.

"You all right there?" Hooper asked him. "Maybe you need to go sleep it off?"

Tole nodded without speaking.

"You need some help getting home?" Hooper asked.

"I manage."

Tole looked at Mariah. "It's a pleasure hearing your stories about bringing babies into the world. See you back at the McGavocks'."

"You will, Mr. Tole." Mariah looked at him, worried.

Tole stumbled out of the bar, grabbing hold of barstools scattered about and finally reaching the door, before slipping out and stumbling his way out of sight. Mariah caught herself staring too long after he had gone and broke her gaze to look back at Hooper and May.

"What's goin' on between you two?" May asked.

"What do you mean?" Mariah snapped.

"You spending a lot of time with him."

"He helps out around Carnton."

"And?"

"And what? And not a damned thing."

"Oh come on, Mariah. You hear the way the man talks about you."

"We ain't children, May."

"Trust me, I know it."

"We just friends."

"You fancy that man!" May said, teasing her. "Mariah got her a man."

"You stop that. Actin' like a damn fool."

May's face turned serious. "It's okay if you do."

"It ain't like that, okay? I just buried my son. I ain't about to go start up some romance with a stranger. George Tole and I get on just fine. But it ain't more than that, and I'll cut that nonsense out your mouth if I hear it again."

Where had this rage come from, flooding over her out of nowhere and leaving just as quickly? She asked May if she could have a sip of her water, and May nodded.

"Only having fun," Hooper said.

"Y'all watching me. That's what this is about."

"Yes," May said. "We worried about you. You just lost your boy, and nobody gone say nothing if you enjoy a man's company."

"Would that be so terrible?"

"Not at all. We just not sure about him, is all."

"You not sure about Tole? Somethin' I should know?"

"You already know," Hooper said. "He likes that drink too much."

"Says the man sellin' it to him. I gonna remember that one, Hooper."

"He a drunk," May said. "And who knows what he saw during the war, Mariah. Men like him ain't all put together right."

"I do," Mariah said, coming to Tole's defense. "I know what he's seen and I know where he's been. I know why he drinks, and if I'm the only person who understands, then so be it. He might be all those things you say about him, but that ain't *all* he is."

"We wasn't trying to—"

"Oh hush," Mariah said, interrupting. "I know what you was trying to do."

"He the saddest and angriest man I know," May said. She was not afraid of Mariah, not like the rest.

"Well, I'm sad and angry, too, May. Maybe that's what I like about him."

May placed her hand on top of Mariah's. "You do what you do and I'll shut my mouth."

⸻

Mariah left the Thirsty Bird an hour or so later, after full dark. The air was sweet and cool against her face. She turned the corner onto Main Street and caught sight of Elijah Dixon ahead. She thought about avoiding him, but he seemed unavoidable, like an avalanche.

When they drew abreast, Dixon stopped her. "Mrs. Reddick," he said. "I had hoped the next time I saw you would be as joyous an occasion as the last."

The last time Dixon had spoken to Mariah, she had handed him his new baby boy. Now she said nothing, just looked him up and down in his fine seersucker suit.

"I suppose it's the tragedies in life that bring people together more often than not," Dixon said.

"Or chops them apart," Mariah said.

Dixon looked shocked to hear her speak so directly. "I suppose that's true."

"Please excuse me, sir—"

"Heard about your boy," Dixon went on.

"Yes sir." He would never know how close he was to being strangled to death right there.

"So very sorry. A real tragedy."

Mariah said nothing.

"I knew your son, Theopolis. Did you know that?"

"Oh yes, he spoke very highly of you, Mr. Dixon." She had never spoken to Theopolis about Dixon. Her loathing for him was like acid inside her.

"I am certain we will find the evildoer who did this," he said.

She could feel her fingernails biting into her palms. "Yes sir," she said.

"We must also be careful not to rush to conclusions lest an innocent be strung up."

"Wouldn't want no innocents to be strung up," Mariah repeated, thinking of innocent little Augusten and his other four children, innocently playing in their beautiful house with their innocent servants and their clean carpets and innocent regular meals. She trembled with rage and was glad it was too dark for him to see it.

"Can't have the town getting it all wrong," he said. "Can't put the crime on a man who ain't done it, I'm sure you understand. It's a damn terrible thing, no mistake about that, but these things take time to sort out and make right. Got to make it right and got to start not making it wrong. Patience, child, patience. Go to church and pray."

"Oh yes, Mr. Dixon, thank you, sir."

He frowned, not being a dumb man. Was she mocking him? A former slave, albeit a midwife, mocking the magistrate? Surely not.

Men across the street called to him. He flapped his hand at them like he wanted them to shut up and expected them to shut up when he said so.

The men went into the tobacconist. Dixon paused as if he had just forgotten something that needed to be said. He cocked his head at his feet, inserted his left hand into his waistcoat, cocked his head the other way. Mariah wanted so desperately to get home that she nearly ran. But she stayed, her freedom a relative concept.

"Your son was…" Dixon began, but let it trail away. He opened his mouth and shut it tightly again. His mustache danced, flecks of tobacco in it. "The smallest things have a way of turning into the biggest things of all. Have you noticed that?"

He turned and crossed the street before she could answer.

She refused to stare after him, so she stared at the ground in front of her, a few dandelion leaves poking out from a crevice in the dirt. *The biggest things of all.*

She would not let Elijah Dixon breathe this air that had filled her son's lungs, that had touched his arms and cooled his sweat as he bent, exhausted, in front of a cobbler's bench. She might be a Negro and she might be a woman, she might be a former slave, she might have belonged to someone like a spoon or a vegetable peeler or a shoelace, but sometimes—as he said—the smallest things have a way of turning into the biggest things of all.

Yes. She had noticed.

CHAPTER 25

LETTER

July 25

Refrain from eavesdropping on Dixon and his men any longer. You'll get caught and you're unlikely to turn up much of any import. The only way to get what we need is to access documents I imagine he keeps in his office rather than at home, or perhaps in some other location entirely. That's where the real information is, not out in the open where you can see or hear it.

I have learned from my contacts in Nashville that he has bought a substantial amount of new land around the state in recent months in addition to what he already owned. This includes the Wilson property in Brentwood, thank you for that information. But I have not yet been able to deduce what he means to do with it. Therefore you will have to go into his office and see what he is hiding there. Make no move yet. I will write soon with further directions about what to look for once you enter his office. You will be rewarded for this work.

Dixon is a dangerous man, do not forget.

CHAPTER 26

MARIAH & TOLE

July 28, 1867

The stars made the mud puddles shine, but he walked straight through them, coming back from working with Hooper, who had dropped him on the road past Carnton. They'd gone to some outlying farms collecting junk and making whiskey deliveries, and now Hooper had headed off to the woods while Tole returned to the light and flash of Franklin. All was dark and he was bone-weary.

And then the voice came out of the grove next to the road and nearly made him drop dead right there. He reached for his knife and flashed it.

"You'll get my son's boots dirty and wrecked, you keep doing that."

Mariah.

"You should put that knife away, too, ain't polite."

She took his arm, turned him around, and walked with him. His heart calmed. He kept walking and she kept walking, and soon he knew where they were going—back toward Carnton, back to Mariah's small two-story brick cabin behind the main house. They took their time walking there.

The shadows from the stars and the moon wavered on Mariah's

179

face, which seemed boundless. When she spoke again, it was as if she had already been talking to him for hours. It seemed as if he'd heard these words before, carved somewhere in some nameless place inside him that only she could reach. "It ain't enough to know that my boy been killed, by accident or by purpose, and that it was some kind of white men who done it," she said. "Who don't already know that? No one got to be told that."

"Always the white man at the heart of it," he agreed.

"But," Mariah said, "it's better to know *for sure* than to wonder. Wondering gets to worrying, and that gets to poison, poison like anger. Eat you up. Eat me up."

"True."

"He was a good boy." She paused, corrected herself. "Wasn't a boy. A man. A good man."

Tole saw a sky of stars and noticed how they painted her gray and flat. She looked old, suddenly, and bent. "He was."

"Ain't paid attention to his mama, though," Mariah said. Tole watched her. Did she smile when she said that? Her mouth turned up at the corner.

"What you tell him?"

Mariah looked up, wide-eyed. "What I tell him?" She shook her head and looked back down again. Tole watched her shoulders slump forward. The night was silent and cold around them. "I told him not to go speak in front of men, to keep himself down and happy and safe. I told him the world wasn't ready for him, and that it was dangerous."

"He be alive today, if he listen to his mama."

"Maybe he would."

For a moment the only sound was their feet, scuffing through the dust and weeds. Carnton loomed over them, then behind them, and they circled the porch, the boxwoods smelling rich and sad. The ground sloped down, and Mariah's cabin sprang up before them, a light glimmering in the downstairs windows.

"I was right," Mariah agreed, opening the door and letting him in before her. One candle burned on the table, with a scent Tole couldn't quite place but that smelled sharp, something he could feel in the back of his nose.

"But," Mariah said, now staring holes into the floor, her eyes bright and hard and aflame. "I weren't right. And he knew that, and he smiled at me when he left me the last time and said he hoped I would come to hear him speak. But I didn't even have *that* much courage, to go hear him. I can never know what he sounded like up there, giving his speech and making his arguments and doing his preaching. I never saw him. I only saw him dead."

"He was good, Mariah. Real good. Better than a preacher." Theopolis had never had a chance to speak—the crowd had begun to riot around the time he took the stage. Even if he had spoken—and Tole knew that he had tried, he'd watched the boy's lips move—Tole had been too far away, too high up, to hear a word. But even so, perhaps the young man had been changing the world with his voice. Tole didn't know, but he wanted Mariah to think it anyway.

"I was wrong. He might have lived and I still been wrong. I might have been happy and wrong, I might have had my boy and been wrong, I might have kept to my ways with everything undisturbed and been wrong, and wrong again, and wrong some more."

"You a mama, what you gonna say?"

"I'm a *woman*!" Mariah hissed it. "I'm a grown woman, a real person and not half a one, and so are you. We are real people. No matter what was past and where we was and how we used to think. Real people speak up and do what they can, and the rest in God's hands. Real people speak on two feet and are heard, in heaven and below. Real people made in God's image, breathed into by that God when we was clay, just like the rest of 'em. We got our own powers."

Powers. Did Tole have power, any power beyond that of a rifle and a finger squeezing gentle on a trigger? Was there anything else, intrinsic and deep inside him, that would call out to the world and make it different? "Yes ma'am," he said to her. "We got our powers. Amen."

Mariah shook her head. "I ain't preaching, I just saying. I was wrong and Theopolis was right, even if he died after being right. Not *because* he was right. He wasn't punished for being right. Not one of them men said to theyselves, 'Let's kill the nigger, he so right about all them things.' He was punished because men are small, the world of men is twisted and fallen, and ain't of God, and they don't think and do as God, and so what? That's the truth and ain't no getting around it. But it don't mean my boy shouldn't speak, stand up and speak as a man. The thing I hate the most is I never heard him."

Neither of them spoke.

"And," Mariah said, finally leaning back and stretching her neck, as if she had just let a weight fall from around it, "the thing I hate almost as much is that them white men going to come here and not give one goddamn about my boy's dying. They won't care for who he was no matter what. They won't even *hear* about him, except as 'the Negro boy,' and that make me angry. We free now. We not slaves. We not *property*."

He could sense she'd been circling what she'd sought him out for, circling it like a pack of wolves would head off a deer, or a fox anticipate the frantic, desperate leapings of a hare.

"Somethin' about that man chills my blood," Mariah said. "Always has."

"Who?"

"Elijah Dixon."

"Why?"

"I remember seein' the way he held each of his babies the first time. He just has the blankest eyes. He smiles, says all the right things a new father supposed to. But his eyes—they just dead."

Tole understood, but he lied, told her he never much paid attention to the man's eyes.

"I heard something about him. About him and my boy."

Tole was quiet. Here it would come. She knew. She knew of Dixon, and him. He knew this would come out, and accepted it, but he hadn't anticipated the fierce love of Mariah and her fearless pursuit of the truth. He had long ago accepted that he was a dead man, and his actual time of dying was just a matter of luck and happenstance. But he never thought his consequences would become Mariah's. She was too brave for her own good.

"I heard that Mr. Elijah Dixon set up the whole thing."

"Killing your boy?"

"Yessir. Loud and clear. Seems my boy wasn't the real target—he was mad that his boys killed the only good cobbler in town, I heard. But Mr. Dixon was the one who arranged everything. The magistrate is the big man who's killing niggers and white boys who get in his way."

"You have proof?" Tole asked.

"No." A pause. "I know it was him and half a dozen other men. That Aaron Haynes out in Hillsboro was one, and Bill Crutcher was another. Not sure who the others are."

"Why?" It seemed an awfully small word for such a question.

"Money," Mariah said. "Always is."

Tole thought about the letters from Bliss.

"One of them took a gun and shot him," Mariah said, thinking out loud. "It was one of them. They might have come to shoot some other poor bastard, but it was my son they shot."

"You sure?"

"I'm sure. I feel it in my bones."

Tole watched her face as if each twitch and wrinkle could tell him whether she knew the whole truth. He prayed she didn't.

But hadn't them white men done the killing, really? They were the guilty ones, not him. They had been beating the boy to death.

He remembered the pattern of blood down the side of Theopolis's face, where a broken bottle had hit him.

Mariah was speaking, barely audible, as if it were a struggle: "I'm scared, Mr. Tole."

His eyes softened. "I didn't think you were scared of nothing."

"I wanted this tribunal. I wanted justice. But I know men like Dixon. I know they won't let such a thing happen, and they won't hesitate to kill a worthless old nigger like me to keep themselves high up on that hill." She was right, and Tole didn't say anything.

"I'm scared. I can't lie about that. But I want justice. I want those men who killed my son to be punished. But they won't be, and I don't think I can live with that."

And at that moment the path before George Tole became clear.

They were kin, Tole and Mariah—the killer and the midwife. Death and birth, both began and ended in blood and pain and, most of the time, in hope. They were alike in this way.

If Mariah could hear that thought rattling around in his head, she would laugh at him while cutting it out with a dull blade. And yet this is what he thought: that he belonged to her, like he was a part of her. They had been matched by the same mysterious Creator, that indifferent and inscrutable God that had amused himself by making him, a killer to the bone, into a tender of Confederate graves, and by causing this grave-tender to lose his mind over a woman who breathed life into the world while he snuffed it out. Tole knew what he needed to do.

"You ain't got nothing to be scared of, Mariah. Those men, whoever they are, ain't got no reason to bother you."

"Not worried about them bothering me. Worried about them finding justice."

"They'll have justice," Tole said.

"You're an optimistic man," Mariah said. "Too optimistic I reckon. But maybe, when you're riding with Hooper, you'll hear things. And if you hear any names, if you learn who those men are with Mr. Dixon, you tell me, you hear?"

He knew he would get those names. He would get them and never tell Mariah he knew them.

"What good will having those names do you, Mariah?" he said. "If you can't believe they gone get justice, then what use you got in having their names?"

"Because I ain't going to be grieving *and* ignorant. At least I will know the truth, and that's the thing people like me ain't never get from white people. Never the truth, never the whole truth. And maybe if I have the whole truth and can say it out loud in front of people, then maybe I'll be free."

Neither of them spoke. And then, finally, Tole said, "I have some ideas. I think I have some ideas." He reached over and placed his hand on hers, and she turned her hand so it was palm up, warm in his grasp. They sat like this for a long time, neither of them moving, both bound by grief and sorrow and a desperate desire to, just once, make things right.

Tole would find those men for her. He would bring them justice. He would bring them a reckoning beyond what them white men from Nashville could hand out if they were so inclined. And they would *not* be so inclined, he suspected. This justice, this reckoning, required blood. He would get that justice, and would probably die doing it, but he would get it for her.

———

When he awoke in the very early morning in his own cabin, surrounded by his underworld made of wood and glue and string, he couldn't remember the long trek back to Franklin, couldn't remember coming in the door, but could see the muddy footsteps. Songbirds sang, brittle in the cold predawn light. He had slept the easier, dreamless sleep of the almost-forgiven.

185

CHAPTER 27

TOLE

July 30, 1867

First, Tole decided the swig of sharp whiskey he'd had on the porch with Hooper would be his last. He was three days sober, which was three days longer than he'd gone in years. Since the war, he had been sober only one other time, just after Miles died, those first couple of weeks when he couldn't bring himself to even look at a bottle. He'd thought, then, with the optimism of the damned, that perhaps he'd never have another drink his entire life.

And then the terrible dreams—that one terrible dream—began. The same dream every night: him in a dark shed, building a baby's crib with pieces of lumber he'd found on the side of the road. But when he finished, what he held was a coffin. He could feel the warmth of the coffin's wood as he pushed it toward the shallow hole.

The night of Miles's ninth birthday, just a few weeks after they buried him, Tole started drinking again.

And here he was now, trying again. He doubted any man had failed at getting sober as many times as he had. He knew the first few days were the hardest, and he was well past that point. His hands were shaking less. He stopped choking up blood and vomit into the bucket next to his bed. He started aiming a bit straighter, steadier. He knew if he could make it past that first few days, he might be able to call himself a sober man.

In the park by the Presbyterian church, he'd seen the old minister having lunch now and again, usually sitting alone on a wooden bench, throwing crumbs to pigeons. And while Tole wasn't one for church, he had some questions he needed answered, reckoned maybe he ought to have a talk with God, one last time, before he saw about what he'd planned for next—seeking revenge for Theopolis Reddick.

In the tree-softened streets, with a light breeze painting the leaves, the park felt becalmed, peaceful, out of time. The minister had a mouthful of chicken when Tole reached the bench, and Tole removed his hat and waited.

"Can I help you?"

"Yous a priest?"

"Minister," he corrected. "Something troubling you?"

"Your church here, it let Negroes inside?"

"No. Your church is down the street, in the Bucket."

Tole stood, waiting.

"But perhaps I can help you," the minister said finally, swallowing.

"Thank you."

"How can I help?"

"Name's George Tole."

"Elder Dawkins. You from Franklin, Mr. Tole?"

"New York."

"A Calvinist Negro from New York?"

"My mama raised me and my brother as Baptist. That mean you can't talk to me?"

"No," he said. "It doesn't mean that."

"I ain't been inside a church since I was a kid."

"Your relationship with God is very strained, I take it."

"I ain't got no relationship with God."

"You do, whether you believe that or not. You're talking to him right now."

"No. I talking to you. You a man I can see. I don't believe in no God who hides up there in the sky."

"He understands that. People sometimes go their entire lives not speaking to him, but he'll be there to listen if you change your mind."

"I ain't gonna change my mind. Already told you I don't believe in him."

"Then I guess I'm confused why you're here."

"I guess I just wanted him to know that."

The minister was quiet.

"Can I ask you something?"

"Of course."

"My little boy. He die when he just eight years old. You know if he's up there in heaven?"

"My condolences. I'd have a hard time thinking of too many reasons why God would deny a boy so young. You say you don't believe in God. You believe in heaven?"

"I think maybe I do. For people like Miles, I think there's a heaven."

"May I ask how he passed?"

"He dead because of me. He had dysentery, and then one night he found my bottle of whiskey, just eight years old, and choked to death on it till his face turned a kind of purple I won't never forget."

Tole stared down at his feet, at the fine pair of boots that a dead man had gifted him.

"I ask you one more thing?"

"Certainly."

"Every night before I go to sleep, I tell him I'm sorry. You think he can hear me? Or I just wasting my time?"

"I don't think anyone can answer that for you, Mr. Tole."

"All right then."

Tole thanked the minister for his time.

"Mr. Tole, remember, the door to that church in the Bucket is always open for you, should you change your mind."

CHAPTER 28

MARIAH

July 29–30, 1867

The backwoods woman, Lizzie Crutcher, had mentioned sheds. So had one of the women who cleaned the lumber family Hayneses' house. Something about men, meeting in a backyard shed. Plotting.

It was enough for Mariah.

The Dixons had a shed, and Mariah decided she would discover the truth for herself. To hell with the white man's tribunals and circuses. She had faith she could do that much. She would discover those names.

She wouldn't rely on her spies and informants—Hooper and May and George Tole and all the rest. She wouldn't sit idly by, waiting for a name to roll into her ears and a great ringing bell to start its peal. She'd figure this out for herself. She'd ask, and hunt, and find those men, and she'd take their names like rare jewels to the tribunal, and the tribunal would smite the evildoers into everlasting darkness. Or they'd just hear her say the names, at least. She had given up predicting the actions of white men long before.

When she entered the Dixon house that morning, let in the back way by Margaret the cook, she noticed that Margaret averted her eyes as if she had something to hide.

Evangeline was in the parlor, her brood nowhere in sight or hearing. The mistress lay stretched upon the couch, propped up against pillows. Mariah looked at Margaret, recognizing Evangeline's symptoms, and Margaret nodded. *Yes*, Margaret's eyes said. *The lady been in the laudanum.*

Evangeline shifted and stood up on teetering legs, and without speaking began to putter around the house, straightening the tea service.

"Wanted to ask you something, missus," Mariah began.

"Oh, Mariah, delighted to see you." Evangeline didn't seem delighted at all. "The baby's doing fine. Just fine. Margaret will make you some nice lemonade and a snack. Would you like some nice lemonade and a snack?"

"No ma'am. Just came for more information."

"Information? What are you talking about?"

Margaret disappeared into the depths of the house. Evangeline watched her go.

"You want to know more about my husband," she said when Margaret had gone.

Mariah said nothing.

"They'll be out there tomorrow night, I think." Evangeline waved her finger toward the window facing the shed. "That's where they'll be. Who knows?"

Mariah nodded, knowing who *they* were, just not knowing their names. Her husband and his cronies. The men who had murdered her son. The men who were trying desperately to keep the world the way it was, the way it had always been, the way one now-dead black cobbler would have understood and stood up against and would have said: *No more.*

"How you know?"

"My husband said something about visitors coming by after dark. That's what he always means."

"After dark they be there?" Mariah asked.

Evangeline didn't seem to hear her. "I have become resigned to the disappearance of my husband into something I don't want to understand. I take care of this home, but at times what I see fit to do with it is to burn it to the ground and salt the earth."

What could Mariah say to that?

"And this is the last I'll ever speak to you about it, Mariah Reddick."

———

The next evening, after dusk, they each arrived separately on horseback, all of them heavy with beard and wearing black. There were fewer than she'd expected. Elijah Dixon bustled around greeting everyone. Mariah watched from the kitchen, where she had commandeered from Margaret the food meant for the guests. *I'll do the delivering*, she'd told Margaret, taking her headscarf. *They never look close enough to recognize me.* She crossed the yard to the shed. Below one of the shed's high windows, an old bench faced west, and there she sat down with the basket of food. If she sat still with her back against the wall, it would be impossible to see her through the window. For a moment she was afraid that the smell of the biscuits, steamy and sweet, would give her away, so she draped her skirts across the top of the basket.

Pacing, shoes scraping and thumping on the bare floor. Their voices clarified out of the foggy murmur.

"—family out on Lyon Road. You so sure you need it?" This voice rattled and squeaked, like its owner had ages before lost his voice from shouting.

Voices chimed in.

And then she heard Elijah speaking. "Of course we need it. We have the two parcels adjacent, so it's not even a question. How much did you offer?"

"Eighty," said Squeaky Voice.

"Eighty? Christ, you'll bankrupt me."

"No I won't, because they turned it down."

"They turned it down? Eighty?"

"Let's burn them out." Deeper voice, gruff. One she recognized. Dixon: "You threaten them?"

Squeaky: "Sure I threatened them. Then I offered the eighty."

"What they say?" another voice, younger.

"I tell you they turned it down. They're homesteading and they're not wanting to leave, the husband said. Man by the name of Polk."

Gruff Voice: "They got a barn?"

Squeaky: "Yeah."

Mariah could tell that they all understood what that meant: that they didn't have to even say what that meant. Mariah knew, too. *If they have a barn, the barn can be burned down.* Several barns had gone up in flames recently—farmers bringing in their hay, packing it too closely, some people said.

"Aaron, you go out there later this week," Dixon said. "Ask Mr. Polk one more time, nicely. Go up to eighty-five. Just ask them once."

Aaron's was the higher voice. Aaron Haynes. "Ah hell," he said.

"Just do it," said Dixon. "You're good with a tinderbox. Just hang around that night and take care of the barn. Then stop by there in a couple of days and offer them sixty." He guffawed.

The talk went on. Mariah didn't understand much of it, reference to land and stock and railroads wanting to be built, but she understood the gist of it: Dixon and his men were buying up great forested tracts of land, selling the lumber, and preparing to sell the land to the railroad as it expanded from Nashville south to Franklin.

Finally the shed went quiet, and Mariah could only hear the sound of a whiskey jar being slid across the table. A shuffling of feet, more creaking of the floorboards. They were getting up. She lunged from the bench and ran down the path just as she heard one of the men say, "So, I'll let you know what Mr. Polk has to say."

And then Mariah remembered the basket on the bench. She saw it there in the dark under the yellow glowing window. She saw it steam, and the door begin to open. She could feel the tears beginning to form at the corner of her eyes as she ran—leapt!—back to the bench and snatched the basket into the crook of her arm. The door had opened but no one came out. She could no longer feel the cold air, she felt hot all over, and when finally one of the men had turned to go down the step from the door of the shed, she was there at the bottom waiting with their traveling food, breathing hard, her scarf pulled low to just above her eyes.

A skinny man was first down the steps, a limp in his right leg, face covered in black hair nearly up to the bottom of his eyes. He was saying something in his squeaky voice about feed and drought, something entirely innocuous and false, as if he knew she was listening. When he saw her there, smiling and bearing gifts, still catching her breath, he grabbed a biscuit as if it were all he ever expected, to have Negro women standing by handing out food.

CHAPTER 29

TOLE

July 31, 1867

On muggy days, the forests just outside of Franklin were rife with gnats and mosquitoes. Tole was used to the woodlands, to hiding in heavy brush or behind tall oaks wide as mud wagons. The smell of the dirt was made thick by the humid summer air. He had learned how to stalk quietly, how to keep his boots from crunching on leaves. He knew how to step, how to breathe, all without making a sound. That was the part about killing most sharpshooters didn't get: you have to learn how to be invisible, and nobody knew how to disappear like George Tole.

A few hundred feet ahead of him, Aaron Haynes was sawing a big white oak. A white boy from Hillsboro, a village just outside Franklin, Aaron, like his daddy, was a lumberman. He had a reddish, auburn beard like his daddy, too. Tole had heard that Dale Haynes was the best damn lumberman in the state. His wood had made the cannon wheels and the barracks for the Confederacy, had built towns where the boys in gray were raised, and when it came time for them to die, his wood had made their caskets, too.

Tole had also heard that Aaron wasn't the lumberman his daddy was. No head for business, he'd heard. And no head for the sawmill either—he had only two fingers on his left hand. He'd lopped the other three off in a sawmill accident.

Tole remembered Aaron's disfigured hand from the courthouse square, how the lumberman took his punches with his right hand. When he threw a bottle at Theopolis, he used his right hand, again—holding his left out awkwardly. The awkwardness marked him in Tole's rifle sights.

And Tole remembered this: bearded, friendly Aaron Haynes had kicked Theopolis in the ribs and in the mouth until the boy was spitting blood and tooth and flecks of bitten tongue onto the stage, clearly visible in the rifle's sights. Tole knew he'd never forget that auburn beard. That grin.

Today Haynes was working with a team of other lumbermen, but he'd gotten separated from them—they were behind him, down in the valley, and he'd gone on ahead to mark the next big stand of timber.

Around the two-mile mark Haynes's footsteps veered right, along a rougher track. A handsaw rasped, cutting deep.

Killing in the wild had a natural order to it. Tole crouched down behind a scrub oak, peering through the mess of twigs, his pistol held close. Ol' GT was strapped to his back, but he didn't think he'd need the big rifle.

Haynes was there, his back to him, twenty yards away, sawing on a tree, not looking around, not noticing Tole even when he stood just ten yards behind him, only half hidden by a little paw-paw. The tree swayed above Haynes, swaying more as the saw bit deeper; and then all the leaves trembled and there was a moment when everything stood still, Haynes stopped his saw and the tree stopped its trembling; and then like a gasp it was falling, collapsing forward into a roaring mass of leaves and branches and snapping boughs. At that exact moment, Tole took his shot, the pistol's echo lost in the tree's death roar.

Haynes let out a guttural scream and reached down to grab his leg.

The shot must've blown a hole straight through Haynes's right calf, Tole thought. Precisely where he'd intended. He looked around to make sure they were still alone, listened for yells and rushing footsteps, but heard none. In a moment he loomed over Haynes, who was bent over, scrabbling, looking at the wound. He probably didn't even realize he'd been shot.

Tole put the pistol up against the back of Haynes's head, the cock of the trigger suddenly loud and terrible. "Don't you move another inch, son."

Haynes froze, blood slipping down his leg, pooling in the leaf mold.

"Mr. Haynes, here's how this gonna go. I'm gone to ask you a few questions and you gone help me understand a few things. I don't want to drag this out, hear?"

Haynes nodded vigorously.

"Just so's you and me understand each other, just want you to know that if you start shouting and carrying on, I will shoot you in the head. You understand me?"

Again, nodding.

"Sit down. Against the stump there."

Haynes crawled to the newly made stump, put his back into it. He cupped his hands protectively around his calf.

"Listen now. You and I have a friend in common," Tole said. "We're both in business with a man named Elijah Dixon. You know a man named Elijah Dixon, don't you?"

Haynes's lips trembled through the forest of his beard. His eyes darted back and forth but didn't meet Tole's. "No, no I don't."

Tole lifted the butt of his gun and bashed him in the jaw. Haynes's head flew back. Tole carefully placed the tip of the pistol under his chin, where it disappeared into the beard, and raised his head for him. "I'll give you the one because we aren't acquainted, but you only get the one."

197

"The one?"

"You lie to me again and you'll be dead before you finished talking."

Sweat poured down Haynes's face. "I do know him," he whispered. "Everybody knows him, so what?"

"You call him a friend?"

Haynes nodded yes. "He know my daddy since they was kids."

"That's real nice," Tole said. "Mr. Haynes, do you know the name Theopolis Reddick? Don't answer. I know you do. Theopolis was my neighbor. He was also that poor nigger you damn near beat to death in the courthouse square about a month back. You remember almost beating a poor nigger to death, Mr. Haynes?"

Haynes nodded. "I—I didn't kill him. I swear."

"No, I know you didn't. See, I was there that day, too. I watched you beat on him. I remember you in particular. You hit him over the head with a bottle. Broke that bottle right over him. I saw that, son. You could've killed him fast, but that ain't no fun now, is it? Ain't no fun unless the nigger suffers."

"That ain't how it was."

"Yes that is how it was. That's exactly how it was. You beat a poor shoemaker so there weren't nothing left of him." Tole paused, his voice and eyes full of Mariah. Then: "You need to tell me who your friends are. I want names. You tell me who else was there that day in the square."

"I don't know nothing."

Tole pushed the pistol up farther, bent Haynes's head back so all Tole could see was that beard, pointing up to the sky. Haynes struggled to stay upright, thrashing with his hands. Spots of blood sprayed in the leaves. "I told you not to lie to me."

"Please, God, no!"

"You gonna tell me right now who else was there that day in the courthouse square. There was a whole gang of you boys with blood on your hands, and I wanna know every single one of their names."

"I said I don't know!"

In a movement so quick that Tole didn't even see it himself, the pistol came off the chin and pointed down to Haynes's other foot. Tole pulled the trigger.

A mess of smoking leather and blood and flesh, and a hole appeared where his foot had been. Haynes wailed into the trees. "James!" he screamed. "He threw the first bottle! Not me!"

"What James's last name?"

Aaron's teeth chattered.

"Mayberry."

"James Mayberry. Where can I find him?"

"West Margin Street. I hear he still lives with his mom. Beyond that, I don't know where. I swear on my life."

Tole replaced the gun under Haynes's chin. "All right, all right. You done good. Sorry about your foot there."

Aaron shook, holding each wound with each hand. "My goddamn legs!" He sobbed, spitting and crying and heaving. "How'm I going to get out of here?"

"First you gotta get through this. Then we'll figure out how to get you out. Who else? I want names. All of them."

The names came:

Joshua Knight from out toward Garrison.

Samuel Shaw, who hung around the factory store.

Bill Crutcher out toward the grove.

Daniel Whitmore from Hen Peck Lane.

When the names had all rolled out and Tole had memorized them, he said, "Thank you. Just so you understand, Mr. Haynes, that boy's mama deserves justice. She thinks she's gonna get it from a court. Thinks those white men are gonna listen to the word of some nigger who spent more than half her life as a slave, polishing silver and waiting on the white folks."

Blood was leaking steadily between Haynes's fingers, especially from the leg. *Probably hit an artery*, Tole thought. Haynes's pants leg wicked up more blood, red creeping upward into the home-spun.

"Truth is, Mr. Haynes, justice ain't a thing you ask for, it's a thing you take."

And then another deafening blast of Tole's pistol echoed through the rough Middle Tennessee forest that went on for miles and miles and miles. By the time the rest of the felling gang finally heard that last shot and went looking for Haynes, Tole was long gone.

CHAPTER 30

LETTER

July 31, 1867

I may be wrong. Dixon's buying up far more land than he could ever need for a railroad. I need to know what the land is really for, and where he's getting the money. So here are your instructions for burgling his office, as I promised: look for deeds of trust, stock certificates, ledgers, records of sale, and bank notes. He will have hidden them, I trust you're familiar with the places men hide their valuables. Be prepared.

If you are arrested I will have you killed before you can speak, but if you succeed you will be a very rich man indeed.

JB

CHAPTER 31

MARIAH & TOLE

August 1, 1867

Mariah kept thinking about a day she had once spent with Theopolis. She remembered wearing her favorite tattered linsey-woolsey dress that she wore for washing days. The coarse fabric had grown so soft from the years that it felt on her skin like the silks and velvets that Carrie McGavock hung in her own closet.

Mariah had been hanging out the laundry, feeling oddly like a queen in her stained and worn shift, and Theopolis, six or seven years old, maybe, had been playing down in the ravine with some of the other slave children—and, quite possibly, some of the McGavock children as well—and he'd come running up to her, laughing, out of breath, in the middle of some chase. He'd grabbed her skirts and pulled himself behind her, hiding. Distantly the children's shouts and calls floated out to them.

Her son's small hands gripped tight to the folds of her dress. She looked up, pointing into the sky. "You see that cloud there?" she asked Theopolis. "That's where your daddy went. That's where he lives now." Theopolis followed her gaze up into the clouds, which glowed brighter than clouds should, as if lit by candles hidden inside them. He still held tight to her rough homespun dress, and his voice was clear: "I miss my daddy."

"I miss him, too," Mariah said absently and went to pull Theopolis close, but he'd released her and was running off again, down to the ravine, where his playmates shouted and called his name.

Now Mariah lay abed, thinking. She never saw her son's face in the dream—his head was bent, or his back was to her, or she didn't think to look down. He'd been right there, and she never thought to look down. *We never think to look down*, she thought. *We're always looking ahead or looking behind, but never see what's standing right beside us.*

She wondered if it was true, her missing Bolen Reddick, her dead husband. He'd been dead for nine years; sometimes she had trouble remembering him. Colonel John had bought him in Montgomery, brought him back to help train the horses. He'd been kind, and the right age, and it seemed right to marry him when he'd asked. Had she loved him? She couldn't remember. Love often seemed like a luxury to her, something not quite essential, what with laundry always needing to be done and the washerwoman never reliable, and the cook who'd get into sulks if she wasn't complimented on her roasts, and the gardener boy who'd avoid weeding the patches in the corners of the flowerbeds if you didn't stand right behind him and make him do it properly. How could love blossom or even exist, confronted with weedy flowerbeds and dirty laundry?

She sat up. No tears, just a calm silence and the sounds of the outside wind blowing through an open window. She hadn't allowed herself to think much about Theopolis, but she did see him now, and there he was a ghost following her in her thoughts. It was time she stopped ignoring him.

After supper, she took the horse-drawn cart from Carnton down to Franklin, bumping over rocks and potholes and wishing she'd just walked. She tied up the cart near Theopolis's house. Mariah would put the house up for sale sometime—perhaps sell it to some young Negro couple from the country, perhaps with a baby of their own. She liked the idea of a family living there. Her shaking hand gripping the railing for support, she walked herself up the few steps to the front door. She closed her eyes, took a deep breath, and stepped inside. It was empty and her shoes were heavy on the wooden floorboards.

There was no trace of Theopolis anywhere, but Mariah remembered the day he moved in, how proud he was to have his own house. She remembered he kept forgetting little things from home, shoes and cooking tools, and each time, he would have to come back. Mariah thought maybe he was forgetting on purpose, afraid to leave home. But he had not been afraid.

Carrie was right. The ghosts and the pain didn't lessen by confronting them, but they did grow more bearable—as if you yourself got bigger, able to hold more grief.

On the way back to the dogcart she paused. George Tole, she knew, lived somewhere nearby. *There, that* house. Just up the way. She marched up the three steps to the tiny porch and banged on his door. Immediately she hoped he wasn't home.

Footsteps sounded from inside, and a moment later the door opened. Tole stood there, one hand in his pocket.

"Mariah, you all right? Somethin' the matter?" Plainly he was startled to see her.

"I was visiting Theopolis's house, thought I'd say hello before heading back."

"You want to come in?" He opened the door more fully.

"Thank you," she said, and did.

"Coffee?"

"No thanks. Just being neighborly and saying hello."

Out of the corner of her eye, Mariah saw the model town sprawled out before her, and she moved toward it, gasping, amazed.

Tole walked up behind her, shyly, as if embarrassed. "It's just something I do to pass the time, that's all."

She'd heard talk of this tiny town, fashioned from carved wood and pieces of glass and bits of trash, but had no idea of its scale. All around her and hanging from the ceiling were tiny figurines carved from wood and twigs or molded from melted wax and glue; old pieces of tin and copper, some of them welded together and painted, sloppily, but there was a beauty to it. In the center of the room, square in the middle of the floor so it was impossible to walk directly from one side to the other, lay the entire town of Franklin, miniaturized and bastardized, splayed out as if seen from above, from a great distance, from God's own view.

She wondered how a man who barely knew the town at all could know it so well. She stepped closer, gazing down Church Street, studying the roof of the Thirsty Bird Saloon on a tiny, winding block of Almond Street, the colored grocery on Fourth Avenue, the small park where she had sat with Theopolis so many afternoons, handing him stale bread from Carrie's pantry to feed the birds. She could hear her younger self call out to him: *Careful, baby, don't get too close now!*

In the courthouse square, a tiny stage no bigger than a playing card had been erected, and on that stage sat a tiny wax figure, painted black, maybe with tar; he was sitting beside another figure, this one painted much lighter.

Mariah wiped the sweat from her face. "How long this take you to build, Mr. Tole?"

"Oh, I don't know. Guess I been workin' on it some months

now. Off and on. Started when I moved to town. Could be over six months now or so. Not too long."

"It's a powerful thing." Her eyes followed a miniature horse pulling a miniature cart down a miniature Main Street, where they'd just installed the miniature streetlights. The businessmen's bowler hats were constructed from what looked like tiny metal thimbles, melted down and polished. Almost unconsciously she looked for Army men, to see which uniform they would wear, blue or gray. She couldn't find one. She looked closer.

"I don't see any Army boys. You forget to put 'em in?"

"No ma'am. I didn't forget."

"I wondered if you'd put them in blue or in gray."

"I wouldn't put them in either. Wouldn't have an army here."

She skirted the wall, surveying the—what was it, sculpture? art? a crazy unbelievable anomaly?—town from another angle. Miniature schools, barber's parlor, taverns. Miniature churches bristled with toothpick steeples.

Yet something was off. It took her a moment to realize what the issue was: miniature trees grew in places that should have held buildings. The police station. The jail. Both missing. Miniature trees grew there. Where the old jail should have been, Tole had carefully designed a garden park.

Perhaps Tole had simply forgotten to add them. Maybe, she thought, he was working from an old map, before the jail was built. In the corner, by the trees he'd built with wax and sticks, she saw a man painted black and a smaller man, most likely a boy, sitting beside him. A man and his son, perhaps.

And then, only then, it struck her. She realized what she was looking at. It wasn't a miniature. And then she realized this wasn't a replica of Franklin as it was; it was Franklin as it *could* be. In a better world, a more just world, maybe in a different time.

"It's beautiful, Mr. Tole." Tears pricked at her eyes, old fool that she was. "Seems like such a happy place. Doesn't seem to matter how much killin' and sorrow goes on. I want to remember it just this way."

"Good."

"You think a place like this could ever exist, Mr. Tole?"

Tole nodded yes, as if he did believe it.

She noticed a man, made of twisted baling wire and with a tiny, bright red cork head, perched on Dr. Cliffe's house. He seemed to be holding a long stick—a wand or a staff, or a tiny rifle. Some initials seemed carved, infinitely small, into the staff, but they were too minute for her to see.

"Who's he supposed to be?" Mariah asked.

"Just somebody I added. I like to think of him as a guardian of the city."

"A guardian? What's paradise need a guardian for?"

"Don't know. Maybe he don' trust it."

"He a magician? That a wand he holding?"

"Maybe."

"Or a rifle?"

"Maybe."

"If it were my town," Mariah said, "I'd take that rifle from his hands."

CHAPTER 32

TOLE

August 2, 1867

A warm, windless Friday evening, and George Tole squatted at the edge of the roof of the Billard Saloon on Main Street. It had been a warm day, but the night was brisk, with a sky black with hostile gray swaths and an occasional grumble that seemed to threaten rain. Well after dark, Tole felt a cold drop land on the back of his hand, and another on the barrel of ol' GT. A flash of lightning cast a blue shadow along Main Street. Not a single person on the block.

The saloon was just a few blocks from West Margin Street, where James Mayberry lived with his mama. Some of the black folks around town said Mayberry usually drank himself half to death in this bar here. They said you'd be more likely to find him falling down in the saloon outhouse than you would in any church on Sunday mornings. And now, perched just a couple of stories above, kneeling on the thin shingled roof, Tole could hear the men laughing and getting on, a little rowdy and beer drunk.

Another rumble from the sky, a bellowing *barroom* of thunder. Tole threw an oilskin over himself and the rifle before it started to drizzle—a warm summer rain that quickly soaked the roof. Tole didn't mind the rain so long as his powder stayed dry. Miles, oddly, had learned to walk in the rain. He had taken his first steps in such weather, naked and unsteady, a chubby baby boy waddling, barely able to stand, and Tole on his knees with his arms stretched out wide, ready to catch him if he fell. The years passed and Tole could remember chasing Miles through thunderstorms, the same way his mama had chased after him and his younger brother—*You boys get back here now, before you go and catch yourselves a cold!* Tole had sounded just like his mama, calling after his son the same way. And when they'd return home, he would wrap Miles in the blanket his mama had knitted.

Tole never thought of those days now. Almost never.

A glass shattered below him and wooden doors swung open. He took a knee at the edge of the roof and saw two men stumble out. The man on the left was Mayberry, stumbling drunk, barely standing. *If a stiff wind comes rollin' down this street,* Tole thought, *this boy gone fall and break his neck, save me the trouble.* He didn't recognize the other man. He figured he wouldn't kill any man he didn't know for certain to be involved with Theopolis's death. He lifted the rifle butt to his shoulder and squinted through the sights. The rain came down a bit harder now, cold on his legs and feet, which were still exposed.

"You go on home, ya bastard!" Mayberry shouted and slurred. As he turned into the moonlight, Tole could see his cleft lip. "Tell the missus we're expecting her for Sunday dinner."

The two men parted with Mayberry heading east, a few wobbly steps before he stumbled down, first to his knees, and then onto his back, laughing, his belly heaving, and talking nonsense to the clouds. The second man, tall and gangly, made his way around to the back of the saloon.

Mayberry mumbled and cursed, trying to reach his feet. Tole had him, sighted in on his forehead. He waited for Mayberry to make it up, watched him fumble with his belt buckle and piss right there on Main Street. Mayberry fell backward, stumbled straight, whistling something that sounded like a lullaby.

Tole thought of the man's mama. He thought of what he was taking from her. She would be changed forever, but her son was a killer and a cruel man. Maybe someday someone would tell her this.

He took his shot. Mayberry crumpled like burning paper. The boom from the rifle should've been enough to wake the whole damn town except for the thunder.

Tole climbed down and walked over to the body. The man lay still, facedown in a puddle. Tole reached into his pockets and found some coins and paper money, and a small yellowed bank check signed by Elijah Dixon for thirty-three dollars. He stuffed it all back in the pocket. He had no use for blood money.

Time to haul the body away. Tole was glad the river wasn't far.

CHAPTER 33

MARIAH

August 2, 1867

"Do we have the 9th Regiment from Alabama here, Mariah?" Carrie asked. The two of them stood in the cemetery, Mariah still a little shaky from the evening before at Tole's house. She still wasn't sure what she had seen. Now she checked the book. "No."

She trailed behind Carrie, Book of the Dead in hand, a bundle of letters in the front pocket of her apron. These letters came from all over the country, Texas to Maryland, and in them parents and widows plaintively asked if, by some chance, their man had come to rest there at Carnton.

We never knew where he could be, but we want to come visit if he's there.

Got a flower to put on him.

His daddy ain't the same, it would do him good.

Maybe he run away, but I prefer to think he died. I may go to hell for thinking that.

Every few weeks Carrie put on her veil and the two of them went out into the cemetery to check on these missing men, to see if their records in the Book of the Dead matched the names and fighting units given in the letters. They would sometimes find a few, and when Carrie wrote back to those families she wrote in joyful bursts and left great blots of ink everywhere. But most of the time there was nothing to report. In the cemetery lay a large grassy emptiness marked by an obelisk, containing the remnants of hundreds who had never been named. When Carrie wrote back to the others, she would tell them of this monument to the unnamed dead, how pretty it was. She always invited these people to come visit it, and sometimes they did. Carrie would turn their visits into an event: invite them into the house, serve them tea and pastries (if Becky Ann, the semi-incompetent cook, had prepared something edible). The families always left awed and pleased that their son or husband had someone like Carrie McGavock to watch over him.

In between the rows, Carrie, and now Mariah, had worn thin matted paths in the grass. From the top of the cemetery, Mariah looked down and thought they looked like the trails of ants, or the sort of meandering line a child draws in his puzzle book.

How well she knew these paths, that sky, the fences and slopes of Carnton. Every other place of her life had faded, but not Carnton.

Carnton, in that moment of revelation, seemed to Mariah removed from the rest of the world, protected as if walled off and ringed with moats. Here she stood not far from her boy, and however hard she squinted through the trees she could not see the town, or its smoke and brimstone, its mud and shit, its hurrying and shouting, its men with knives. Franklin might have been the moon.

Carrie approached up the wide main path between headstones, no longer floating. She had her skirts gathered in her right fist. She came over and stood in the shade of the old oak with Mariah. "Do you have the letters?" she asked.

Mariah nodded and pulled the bundle out of her apron pocket. Two squirrels squabbled in the limbs above them. Carrie sat down under the tree, arranged her skirts around her, and held her hand out. Mariah sat down, too, a little heavier and more tired, not worrying about her dress. She handed the first letter to Carrie, who began the ritual.

Though she had already read them once, Carrie liked to read the letters again in the cemetery.

Dear Missus McGavick,

I herd from my nayber Louisa Mae Bollingbrook that you have her son berred in your gravyard and I want to know if my son be ther two. His name is Donald James Burns and he was 20 in 1863. Hes a tall boy with a shock of yellow hair that he got from his daddy and hes rite handy with a harmmonaka or a kazoon in case you a boy playing music. He enlist with Tommy John Bollingbrook and was in the Alabama Volunteer Infantry under Colonel Julian Bibb. I nit him a gray skarf speshul and Lila Rose his girlfrend nit him gray sox too. We aint herd from him since a letr in Octobr 1863. Plese mam if hes ther can you plese let us know. His daddy and I miss him somthin feers. I keep riting letrs but nobody know wat happin to him.

God bless you,
Rita Burns

"Donald James Burns isn't here, is he?" Carrie asked.
"No."
"What about the friend? Bollingbrook?"
"Ain't no Tommy or Thomas John Bollingbrook either."
"No matches today," Carrie said. "Poor things."
"You tired, Miss Carrie?"
"Today I am."
"I mean"—Mariah looked away—"I mean tired of all this?"

"What this?" Carrie always liked the terms spelled out nice and neat. "Which part?"

"Most of it. All of it?"

"The letters are a bit much. But perhaps I think this because I've got seven of the hard letters to write when I go back to the house. Those people will have ghosts upon them always. What else becomes of the son who just disappears, as if he'd never walked on the earth? Sometimes I think I am condemning them to a haunting. That's tiring and dispiriting, yes."

Carrie bent down and picked three twigs from Theopolis's grave and tossed them away. Mariah nearly grabbed her by the arm to stop her and had to check herself. The familiarity of the gesture boiled her blood. *How dare she? That is my son.* She thought Carrie might be trying to say something to her about the nature of motherhood and sons, and one's obligation to the dead. She knew Carrie meant to chastise her, even if Carrie herself didn't.

"You act like they was all your sons," she said, when Carrie stood straight again.

"And why not? I have my own dead children in this cemetery, just like you and all those seven mothers from today, plus the thousands of others. I say 'my own,' but what is really different about my own now? They live in my mind, but here…" Carrie leaned against the oak. "There's nothing to distinguish them from the others except for their grave markers, and those they never saw in life. They were carved by strangers. These planks have nothing to do with those people, they are not them, and so what is one marker apart from another? Nothing. Our children's are stone and the soldiers' are wood, but they both serve the same purpose. I could be, you could be, mother to all or none in this cemetery. I've chosen all of them."

Mariah imagined all of them as children, tagging along after Carrie, climbing into her arms until her back bent. And then still more, tugging and pulling until her mistress could not move, until she had been pinned to the earth like a lacy black butterfly, ecstatic to be finally motionless. She looked down at her son. *This is not for me, Theopolis.*

She was not mother to them all. She was mother to one. He was no ghost, but he was alive in a way, and different from every other in that cemetery. It surprised Mariah that Carrie could suggest otherwise. Mariah had memories, felt obligations.

Mariah said slowly, "I been trying to find out the truth, Miss Carrie."

Carrie kept her head bent over the letter she was reading and twiddled a loose bit of lace in her other hand. "Truth of what, dear?" she said. "Have you begun going to church?"

Carrie would call her "dear." The mistress had always imagined herself old, older than Mariah, though Mariah could remember the day Carrie was born.

"Not church. The truth about what happened to my boy."

Now Carrie looked up. "For what reason?"

For what reason, indeed? Because, after all, he was just another black man. To most, he didn't even have a name—he was "the cobbler" if he was anything at all.

Tears burned like bile in the back of her throat. "To know for sure."

"What good would that do?"

"Other men coming to investigate next week, from Nashville, but I don't trust none of that."

"Those men are worried about the man who was killed, John Sykes, they're not coming for some black shoemaker," Carrie said absentmindedly, and she was right, but Mariah felt stabbed by the words anyway. Carrie could see what she'd done, and let the letter flutter from her hand to her lap.

"I'm sorry, Mariah," she said. "I care nothing for the grocer, he was a rude little man. I cared for Theopolis."

"I know."

215

"But it's the truth, even so. It's how that world works."

"I hope they want to know about my Theopolis. But whether they do or not, I do." Mariah said this with lips drawn tight, looking straight at Carrie, watching for a reaction. She thought, *You didn't expect this of Mariah, did you?* But Carrie didn't flinch, merely folded her hands in her lap.

"You're alone."

Of all the things Mariah expected to hear from Carrie, she hadn't expected this. Lectures about danger, the futility of confronting men—that was what she had expected. But she *was* alone, she had been alone listening to Evangeline Dixon and Lizzie Crutcher, and she'd been alone hurrying away from them. She was more alone than she and Carrie were at that exact moment, not another living soul in sight and thousands of bones beneath their feet.

"You won't make them interested in anything they aren't already interested in," Carrie said.

"Theopolis didn't kill no one. He was murdered. They ain't interested in that? They ain't interested in all the other black folk hurt that day? Twenty-six they was, Hooper told me." She knew the answer to her question even as she said it.

"No. They won't care."

It infuriated Mariah to know not only that Carrie was right, but also that she was so certain of being right. How could she be so certain when she never left this place and never invited the world in?

Because she knew her people. No matter what else she did, no matter how perfectly Carrie McGavock closed the circle around her and her thousands of dead boys, she would always have that knowledge of her people bred in the bone. What they thought, late at night when they were snuffing the candles in the windows of their houses—that was no mystery to Carrie. And she knew that her people, out there in the world beyond the fences and the tree line, would not care that Theopolis had only wanted to speak and had never owned a pistol and had been murdered by cold men from this very town. Never done anything out of the ordinary except have his own house and a little business, and on occasion visit with his mother. They would not care.

A dark, breathtaking thought crossed Mariah's mind: *Maybe Carrie doesn't really care either. Maybe she cares more about keeping me close.* Mariah sat still and listened to the squirrels, watched the long grass in the field roll and shudder in waves of breeze, watched the tree line for the hog or whatever it was. Carrie left her hands in her lap, now intent on Mariah. What would her own life be like, Mariah thought, if she stayed there at Carnton forever? It would be exactly like this every day, she knew. She would grow old trailing behind the widow of the South, carrying the bundle of letters. The world would recede like a tide, and no news would disturb the rhythm of their days. They would remain as they were, evermore, because that's how Carrie had always wanted it. They would grow wrinkles and that would be it.

I am alone right now, Mariah thought. *And I'll be alone forever if I stay.*

"Still got to know," she said.

Carrie kept reading the next letter.

"And when I find out, maybe I go to testify for the Nashville men."

Carrie still kept reading.

"I will find out. I ain't gone stop." Mariah had not known this until she said it. But now she knew she would go on just as she formed the words.

Carrie finished tracing her gloved finger across the lines on the paper, carefully folded the letter she had picked up again, replaced it atop the bundle, and ran her thumb across the edge. "Of course you will find out," she said.

"Just so you know."

"You didn't have to tell me."

Now Mariah was silent. This was true. Why had she told Carrie anything? A second time, Carrie's words stabbed her, but this time she felt the knife going in tenderly, like it was removing something.

"Just being friendly," she said, for want of anything else to say.

Silence.

"Are we friends, Mariah?" Carrie said this with force, with fire in her voice. Mariah could not answer that question aloud. It had never been asked, only assumed, from the time they were children. More than assumed—assigned. She had been assigned to Carrie as friend and helpmate. There had never been the question. She was unprepared to face it spoken aloud, baldly. She knew somewhere in the core of her mind that it had never been a question for her, only for Carrie. She said nothing.

Carrie watched her for a moment. Then she leaned over, letting a couple of letters spill from her lap, and placed her hand on Mariah's arm.

"No, we are not," she said. "We are not friends."

Mariah said nothing but looked Carrie straight in the eye. She saw a woman gathering herself, lining things up in her mind, releasing the bonds of thoughts long tied down.

"We are not friends, and I dare say you know you have no obligation to confide in me. *Confidence* is not the word for what passes between people like you and me. *Friends* is not the word for what we are. What we are I can hardly contemplate, and there is no word for it. The Greeks would have had a word, but I do not. Whether or not we are friends, you know me better than anyone, and you know what goes on here in this cemetery."

What could Mariah say? She had listened to Carrie and her soliloquies à thousand times over the years. "I am the mother of a murdered man," she said. "The mother of nobody."

"As a midwife, you're the mother of everyone in Franklin," Carrie pointed out.

"Sure don't feel like a mother anymore."

"But I suppose you must nose around after the truth, whatever anyone else thinks or cares?"

"Yes."

Carrie sighed and picked up her letters. "I will help you when the time comes."

"If I think you're needed."

"If I'm needed. And even if I'm not needed, Mariah, I will help you. Know that. Whatever you need. I am here."

CHAPTER 34

TOLE

August 4, 1867

There had been seven conspirators. Five had met unfortunate accidents, their bodies hidden in the Harpeth River or buried in shallow graves or slid into ditches; one—Bill Crutcher, husband of Lizzie—seemed to have lit out days ago, and no one knew where he was, but talk was that his wife had left him, and he'd gone south to hunt her down. Crutcher was out of Tole's hands.

Only one man—apart from Elijah Dixon—remained. Tole was saving Dixon, the man most critical, for last: he would cut off the head so the beast would be dead for good. This would be the one killing that would probably get Tole killed in turn. The world didn't miss backwoodsmen and drunks, but it would miss Elijah Dixon. There would be a price to pay for taking that one's head, and Tole thought he was almost ready to pay it now. Almost.

But first he had to visit the last of Dixon's men. Daniel Whitmore, out on Hen Peck Lane.

Whitmore was a fisherman from Louisiana. Far as Tole could tell, he lived alone, was missing his right leg from the war, and spat tobacco so constantly that his beard had been permanently stained red on his chin. These days, he made his living hobbling around on errands and scouting land for Elijah Dixon, but he still got himself on a fishing boat any chance he could.

Tole spent the early morning scouting the Harpeth where Whitmore kept his boat. Time was slipping away from Tole; the tribunal was just two days away now. Late that morning a heavy, bearded man with a limp stepped unsteadily down the hill and climbed into the rowboat Tole had been watching. The man held on to the edge as the boat wobbled. The lettering on the side of the boat said *AB Fishing Co.*

Hello, Daniel Whitmore.

Tole crouched down, took cover, stalked and crawled as he had in the war days when every rock concealed an ambush, every steep hill a cover for movement, every tall tree a potential lookout. The war had created a different world, and in that new world all things arrayed themselves as friend or foe, even the inanimate ground and the unconscious beast. He himself had been his only friend, isolated from all things. He was at war again.

Whitmore spat, happy as anything. Life was indeed good. He didn't hear Tole circling far up the hill behind him, always downwind and covered. He didn't feel him getting closer, so close Tole could watch his chest rise and fall with every breath and could smell the dull reek of sweat and tobacco stain. What did a fisherman have to fear? It was broad daylight hardly a half mile from town. Tole assumed this was why the man seemed so oblivious to the threat. But though they were close to town, they were also hemmed in on two sides by steep river-cut banks, and on the third by a severe bend in the river. This was a great fishing hole, but hardly anyone fished it. They might have been a hundred miles away from Franklin.

Tole sank into himself, integrated and indistinguishable from leaf and bud, no boundaries between him and rock. It was a kind of pulling apart of body and mind.

He could hear Whitmore's whistle, louder than before. He watched the man tend his hook and listened to the unintelligible hum of someone in constant conversation with himself.

Tole raised his rifle. This was what he did best. The August sun seemed to burn the top of his head, the tips of his ears. Sweat poured down his brow. He tried to concentrate on his target while gnats chewed away at the back of his neck, his ankles. He watched as a gust of cool summer wind, strong from the west, blew the leaves of the sycamore across from the river. He was invisible in the bushes. Whitmore leaned over, doing something with his line, and when he lifted his head, Tole took his shot. A thunderous explosion.

Whitmore slumped down and the boat drifted into the current.

Tole stood from the bushes and checked his surroundings. No one around. Should he let the boat just drift downstream? Having the body so visible, floating along with a bullet wound to the head, made him very uncomfortable: he wanted it out of sight, melting away into dust and maggots.

But Tole couldn't swim.

The boat floated out farther, picking up speed in the current, and he shambled after it, stumbling over rocks and logs at the river's edge. To the west the Harpeth ran for miles, winding through farms and fields and forests, and then becoming the Cumberland, and then the Ohio, then into the Mississippi. Tole imagined Whitmore's body, fleshless and baked in the sun, making its way back home to Louisiana and then out to the gulf and beyond, riding the waves forever. It seemed like a glorious way to pass into whatever comes next.

Tole was about to give up following the boat when, about a quarter mile downstream, his luck turned. The boat hit a submerged log and bumped along, sliding almost to shore—close enough so Tole could wade in and pull it to shallower waters.

Blood had pooled like falling shadows at the bottom of the hull.

Whitmore was lifeless on his side, and Tole rolled him onto his back.

The man's face transformed Tole. He'd seen death before, of course—so many times. He was used to how the eyes seemed to look straight into him and know something even Tole refused to understand. Was there a smile then, a smirk? No, just the mouth relaxing. The whole face had relaxed and had gone from hard to soft. The eyes kept on him, though, they sought out Tole's face. They looked into his own eyes. The eyes insisted on watching him and seeing him; they rebuked him. *I know you, I know you.* The eyes remained open, even if they stared straight into nothingness, the light gone.

It came to him that the men and boys he had killed knew him better than anyone in the world, better than his wife and son, better than his family, better than Mariah could ever know him. Better than he knew himself.

When he pulled the body out of the boat and dragged it down to the beaver dam and hid it underneath the dark wet branches, he cried as if this were the body of someone dear and loved.

He was a killer. He could never love nor be loved.

⸻

Throughout that afternoon, he wandered. He didn't dare see another human being until he knew he had control of himself. When he was hungry, he stole rock-hard turnips from an old garden. He pulled out that old boy's Bible and tried to read, but every passage was a rebuke. He had made the mistake of seeing his quarry and being seen by him, both of them humans living and breathing until one was not. Morning slid into afternoon and then night. He had seen death, watched it take over a man's body. He had watched it free him! He envied the man in the water below the beaver dam. He tried to shake this thought out of his head. He would leave him there to float, facedown and lifeless, his blood coloring the water a murky red, until he'd either sink for good or wash up on the dock.

He climbed trees and sat in them looking over the town. Higher and higher he climbed until all there was to see were toy houses and ants on two legs moving about their business. In the trees he began to breathe deeper, calmer. After the shame and horror came a degree of pride. At least he felt something, he thought. This thought gave way to other thoughts, and he became more certain of himself. He was a human, just a terribly tangled one—a human whose sins were great and whose soul was in mortal danger. But tangles could be traced backward and made straight again, he pleaded to God.

CHAPTER 35

TOLE & MARIAH

August 5, 1867

The next day Tole spent the day at the Carnton cemetery. He barely saw Mariah—she was in the house, and then he caught a glimpse of her walking down the driveway toward Franklin.

Late that afternoon, however, just as he was putting away his tools in the shed near Mariah's cabin, Mariah appeared out of nowhere with a bunch of goldenrod it looked like she'd just gathered.

"You go and hurt yourself, Mr. Tole?"

He had: dragging Daniel Whitmore's heavy corpse out of the boat, he'd sliced his arm on a sharp piece of wire fencing that had gotten hung up on the waterline.

"Just cut myself doing some yard work, is all," he said, but Mariah squinted suspiciously.

"And the bruise there on your face? I reckon a tree reach out and sock you?"

Tole set the bread down. He still had so many secrets from her. None of it seemed real as long as he harbored the burden of knowing what happened to Theopolis. "Maybe so."

"Interesting news from town," Mariah said, almost conversationally. "You hear about the body wash up ashore?"

Tole did not move. "No."

"Everybody's talking of it. They say it's that Haynes boy, out from Hillsboro."

"Don't reckon I know him," Tole said.

"You don't?"

"No'm."

"He's one of the men I told you about, the ones who are working with Mr. Dixon."

"Oh."

"He was shot, they say. Bunch of times."

"Oh."

"Terrible thing," Mariah said, staring at him.

A long pause between them to consider the death of a man who helped kill her son.

"I know something…" Tole said, and his voice trailed away.

Her hand reached across the space between them and touched his shoulder. Almost instinctively he put his hand on hers. Warm.

"I got something to tell you," he said.

———

The sun set and it turned to night. Mariah listened and looked hard through the big, worm-shaped crack in the bench outside her cabin, through which she could sometimes see things moving on the ground. Tole kept his hands folded in front of him, only occasionally looking up to catch her eye.

He had been a criminal, he said. He'd seen evil. He had been a fraud. He said this with great drama in his eyes, looking straight at her.

But who hadn't been a fraud themselves? she thought, listening to him run down the particular stations of his descent. He told her about the lying and stealing, a lifetime's worth.

Mariah stood up and laid the goldenrod on the bench behind her. She stood up straight, and in doing so she realized that she *always* stood straight, and she wondered why she did that. The world had got heavy on her, and she deserved a bend at the shoulders. But no. She walked head up without tripping. She fixed her eyes on Tole. Then she went over to the water bucket, drew Tole a tin of it, and walked over and gave him the cup. He thanked her. He made her tired, with his reservations and little secrets—his obvious secrets.

"That ain't all the evil you seen, Mr. Tole," Mariah said, as plainly and menacingly as she could.

He watched her face. She felt naked, and offended that he thought he could look at her so directly. She stared back until he turned away.

"No, that's true. I seen your boy get killed. I seen it." He ran his finger around the rim of the tin cup, three times.

"How did you see it?"

"No particular way, just…well, everybody seen it, ain't they?"

"I only saw the very last moment," Mariah said. "I only saw him dead on the ground. I put my arms around him, and then he died. But I didn't see what happened before that, or who done it."

Mariah got up again. She seemed unsure of where to stand. She went over to the porch rail and stood with one hand resting lightly on its surface. "Tell me everything you saw." She had almost convinced herself she never wanted to know, but that had been a lie, too. Now she wanted the truth that would hurt.

Tole watched her eyes, nodded, and closed his eyes for more than a couple of beats, before opening them again.

"I saw him come up on the stage." He had seen the crowd collapsing and expanding in little knots that grew into bigger knots until the whole space in front of the stage had been filled in. He had seen people he recognized, and some he didn't. He had seen the tops of their heads. He had seen arms thrust in the air, and he had seen fists. He had seen a group of black-hatted men standing right at the foot of the stage, just underneath Theopolis. He had seen the podium splinter apart. Tole had seen grown men running scared in every direction. He had seen the men drag Theopolis down.

"How you seen this?" Mariah asked, squinting hard at Tole as if she could concentrate the truth right there in the air in front of them. As if she might scare it out of Tole and into the open. But Tole just shook his head and ignored her. He was not intimidated.

"Why you never told me you were there that day?" she asked.

"I didn't want to upset you."

"Upset me?" She had wildfire in her eyes, flared nostrils, a look of outrage he had never before seen. "You sit here with me for weeks now, and you don't think to tell me you seen my boy up there right before he murdered?"

"Me seeing him die don't change the fact that he dead."

"I have searched this town high and low trying to figure out what happened that day, and all this time, you seen it all. That what you tellin' me?"

"I seen him take the stage. I seen the crowd get bigger, fulla white folks, angry folks, filled in. I seen the tops of their heads."

"The tops?"

"Yes ma'am. I saw your boy try to speak. I saw some white man with missing fingers throw a bottle at him. I saw them pull him off that stage."

Mariah's eyes filled with tears. Tole stopped talking. "This why I didn't want to tell you. Those tears in your eyes the reason I been so quiet."

"Nevermind no tears. You finish your story. I want to know. I don't care if blood comin' out my ear by the end of it. You don't stop."

This is what he wanted to say to her: *I seen terrible things in my time, all them things that take place in the dark and sometimes in secret, and you don't hardly realize how twisted up it all is until, right then, it happens, and all them souls go floating off in their terrible states, like the earth done gone to crack open and drag 'em down if they don't get going quick, so they gone.*

"I saw the mob riot, I saw five men, maybe six, pull your boy off that stage and beat him until he bleeding from his mouth and his head. Seen them drag him down and he gave the good fight. Do that make things better for you, that he kicked some teeth? He did do that, they threw three of them men on him like they was wrestling a hog, and the hog got the better of it. He were a whirlwind, every leg and arm swinging out, *pop*, catching someone in the ear or the gut. He was going good, but then I seen a bottle catch him in the head and he went a little more limp after that, still swinging but like he were in water or something.

"I only seen Theopolis once or twice after that, just flashes, and each time I seen him, he a worse bloody mess. Then something hard and quick happened, and them men went to pulling away like they got burned, and then you come through into the clear of that circle and take up the boy, though he already gone. I seen him go. The doctor came through, too, but there weren't nothing to do. What was going to be done had already got done."

Tole looked down. He could see Mariah's tears thudding against the wooden porch floor. Heavy tears. "There so much noise but I thought I heard him scream for help. I thought I heard him scream for you."

"For me?"

Tole nodded, lying. Lying for a good purpose, for once.

"And what did you do? You just sit there and watch like a god-damn coward?" Mariah leaned against the porch, stood up, and took a deep breath as the reality of what she'd just heard sank in. And then went to sit down beside him.

The light, Tole thought. *The light goes out* snap *in a man's eyes. It's on and then it's off. You don't even got to be looking in their eyes, you can be watching their leg or an arm or their backside, and maybe nothing moves at all, but all the same you* know *they gone, and all that's left won't never move again. Maybe the color changes, or whatever was vibrating in 'em just gone and stopped.*

"I don't believe much in a life after life," he said. "The life you got is what you got, and in war that life ain't much to talk about. Spend the war looking out for the last moment, wondering where and when it coming. Maybe it's the most merciful thing to bring that end quick. This is what I said to myself sometimes, up in those trees and in those haylofts, picking them men out. I said to myself, *You are a mercy.* But I don't know now, and I never did know. There weren't ever anyone to *ask.* The dead were gone and who was left? I never knew. But maybe Ise wrong. Sure like to think so."

"So you seen the men who did this, is what you're saying, isn't it? When I asked you to be on the lookout for those men, you already knew, didn't you?"

"Didn't know they names."

She ignored him. "You had seen them when I told you I wanted them to face the justice they deserve."

"You ain't gone find them anywhere, Mariah."

Now she heard him. "What are you saying precisely, Mr. Tole?"

He looked at her out of the corner of his eye, the bruised eye, cut and swollen. "I said, you ain't gone find those boys walking this earth."

"That's what I've been thinking, this whole day, ever since April said the name Aaron Haynes to me." She looked down at his bandaged hand and up again at his bruised face. "I been thinking, 'I wonder where Mr. Tole was when that man disappeared?'"

"That's not the only one."

"You been killing them," she said. It wasn't a question. She knew. "How many?"

Tole sucked his breath and looked at her.

"You been killing them who killed my boy. Don't say nothing."

Silence. Tole shut his mouth and watched her. She seemed like she might split apart, not certain if she should be angry or grateful. It made her look older than she was.

"Why?"

"Because they deserve to die."

"So now you the Lord? You decide who lives and dies?"

"I did it for you."

She stood up, pulled away from him. "Don't you dare say that to me," she hissed. "I never once asked you to hurt no one. I just asked you for *names*."

"You're so sad. Any man who put that on you, who cut that hole in you, he don't deserve to live."

"Don't you dare say you did it for me."

"I did it because it need to happen. You deserved justice, and you ain't gone get it from no court fulla white men who don't even know you exist."

"You gone stop killing them men."

"I already stopped."

"Liar. Can't trust a killer. Say you *will*! You ain't going to lose no more of your broken little soul, hear? Not on my account. That's over. You stop."

More silence.

"Say you will."

"I will."

"They ain't the reason my boy dead, anyway. They just the

weapon, the dumb and ignorant weapons. Are you too stupid to know that? Or maybe you just like them."

It was quiet. What Mariah had said was true. It wasn't any one man who killed Theopolis—it was the hatred of the world they lived in that killed him. He could've been any Negro standing there and they would've killed him just the same. All this time she held tight to her anger because it gave her purpose. She didn't have any time for tears, not until she had her justice. But now, sitting here in silence beside Tole, she had to face a hostile truth that the kind of justice she had imagined would no longer be possible. Tole felt the shame burn him.

"I thought it would be easier if there was somebody to blame," she said. "As long as I was hunting those men, I wouldn't have to face myself. I'm embarrassed to admit this, but I was happy when I heard it was Elijah Dixon. I finally had somebody to hate. But the truth is, he didn't kill my boy. He just a greedy man like all the rest of 'em. My whole life, I was a slave. My reason for getting out of bed in the morning was to serve somebody else. I didn't have no purpose of my own. There was no me. Not ever. And when I had Theopolis, that changed. I was a mother. I was still a slave, sure, but not to him. To him, I was Mama. When he was young, he didn't understand all this bullshit. The politics. He didn't know white men could trade me like I was cash. I wasn't a *she*, I was just an *it*. Theopolis didn't see me as a thing. He saw me as his mother. And all of a sudden, I had a different purpose for getting up in the morning."

Tole nodded. "I understand."

"I figured you might. And I figure you'll understand this, too. When that purpose gets ripped away, the only purpose you have left is justice. That's the reason I get up now. It's to find the men who killed my boy and bring them to justice. But what happens when there ain't nobody left to go after? What happens when there's nobody to blame, Mr. Tole?"

Mariah remembered Carrie's words: *Some of us turn and face them, look them in the eye. And when you finally turn around, you'll realize they're not here to haunt you, my dear.*

"Someone was in charge," Mariah said.

"Maybe."

"You know who?" she asked.

"I know who."

"Well then." She glared at him. "What's the name? I want you to tell me."

Tole wiped his shining forehead with his sleeve.

Mariah stood over him with her arms crossed. *It all gets so complicated and twisted up so easily*, she thought. She wanted to stab him and kiss him; she wanted to run away from him; she wanted him to disappear, and she wanted him to stay.

"You know the name. Why you afraid of giving it to me?"

"Because if I say it out loud it'll just make everything harder for you."

"Harder for me? Harder than it is right now?" She laughed. "Can't imagine that." She stared at him. "Why don't you just come out and say it's Elijah Dixon?"

He stared back at her. "How you know that?"

"'Course I knew. I've known for days. The justice of the peace, the city magistrate, done ordered the death of my son, even if he didn't mean my son to die."

"Why you pretend you didn't know?"

"Wanted to see what you knew, didn't I?"

"Are you going to tell the Army boys at the tribunal?"

"Sure am."

"He'll be sitting there. He'll be sitting there with them."

"So he'll be sitting there. He can hear it right from my mouth."

"You think they'll believe you?"

"I don't rightly know. But I have to try, don't I? I have to try. That's what my son was doing. He was speaking out, he was trying to get a better world for us Negroes. I have to do it, too. I have to believe that the Army men will listen."

He watched her, saying nothing. "White men always protect they own," he said finally. "They ain't gonna help niggers like us."

"The whole world's changed!" she hissed. "We ain't slaves no more. We free. We can know and say the truth and not care what white people do."

"You always got to care. There ain't no not wondering and worrying about what a white man will do, not for the Negro."

She stared at him blankly.

"And you know this, because you didn't go hear him speak. You was scared for him, and you didn't think he could make it, a poor black cobbler boy playing at being a white politician. And that was the terrible truth."

He could see the pain in her face. She had wanted the painful truth.

"Them Army men won't listen to you. They won't protect you."

"No more killing, you hear me? You promise me no more killing. I'm not going to have Dixon's death on my conscience. Not with him having five babies at home."

At last he nodded. "I promise. I will not kill Mr. Elijah Dixon. But I ain't putting my trust in any white men either."

"What you mean?"

"Means I have some other plans for Elijah Dixon. Means that you can tell all you want at the tribunal, but I'm not going to put my trust in them. No ma'am."

"What plans?"

"Can't tell you," he said. "You and I gone to take our roads, see who gets to justice first."

He stood up, stared at her in the darkness for a moment, and then turned and headed down the long road back to Franklin.

She watched his back as he hiked out of the yard toward the woods. He marched with a purpose, like he had something to do.

She cursed his back, pleaded with him to stop. She fiddled with the bunch of goldenrod in her hand. Finally she leaned out and tossed that bouquet over the rail of the porch as hard as she could, as if she might with a mighty heave bring down the man disappearing behind the ash trees.

CHAPTER 36

MARIAH

August 6, 1867

The morning of the tribunal, Mariah Reddick stood out on the porch of her small house that used to be the slave quarters and now was the house she was living in, and she noticed things she had never noticed. She could see pollen where she had never seen pollen before, and the shades of green in the woods were infinite. The vegetative green of leaves and vines was a texture as much as it was a color. Turkey tracks across the mud at the foot of her stoop were larger than she had imagined, and surprisingly symmetrical. Off in the woods—her sight had no end, apparently—ferns appeared wedged among the unlikeliest of wet rocks, in places that seemed to contain no soil. The ferns slowly unspooled their delicate fronds, and Mariah believed there might still be mysteries, which meant there was hope.

She could sense the various qualities of air—scent, temperature, weight, humidity, movement—and could catalog those slight adjustments. This day smelled different than others, the air lay on her arms and cheeks differently. She thought she noticed the distinct, dense quality of endings. Things would come to an end today, and she shivered.

She thought there were some things, like testifying before the tribunal, that a person did because they had to be done, without regard for whether they were important or not, and that most things aren't as important as they seem. Some things you did because it would humiliate Elijah Dixon. Her testimony would do that, she hoped, if nothing else.

She walked out her cabin door and down the steps, following the path until she got to the town road. She tried to rehearse what she would say to these white men. What was a tribunal, anyway? All she knew of tribunals was from the Bible, and a line from Matthew kept circling her head: *While he was sitting on the judgment seat, his wife sent him a message, saying, "Have nothing to do with that righteous Man; for last night I suffered greatly in a dream because of Him."*

Those tribunalists would do the same—why would they want to listen to a freedwoman? They would of course have nothing to do with her. They were all white.

When she passed the big house she hardly looked over to see it, though it had been her home for twenty-seven years. She thought for a moment of visiting Theopolis's grave, but pushed it from her mind. Was she headed to town for Theopolis, or for something else? Maybe something else, or maybe for no good reason at all. But she wouldn't make Theopolis responsible for it, whatever the reason was, and so she kept on down the road and only looked up the hill toward the obelisks that marked the family cemetery. No sign of Miss Carrie. She knew she'd be already up and picking out a black shawl for the day and wondering what fool's errand delayed Colonel McGavock another day, another month, and whether he was still actually alive. Perhaps today Carrie would look in the mirror, or up at the portrait of her dead children that hung beyond her bed, and choose a black veil, too.

Mariah went to town and toward the tribunal because she could. It was complicated, but it was also that simple. If she were free, this was something she could do. A free person needs no other reason than that. She was putting the world, and that freedom, to the test.

The sun came out and ducked behind clouds again, over and over. Sometimes it warmed her face. The path became the road, and the road was rutted with roots that she descended like steps. Juncos tittered in the underbrush, and tiny insects floated up in the columns of light that broke through the oak and hickory. Every step became easier, and the road widened. Past the last set of white oaks, the territory opened up ahead of her. The roots plunged deep into the ground and the macadamized road went smooth. Little fields—barely more than clearings—gave way to larger fields. The hills were no longer deep and dark, having been mowed and harvested by farmers. The trees, where there were any at all, were now planted in orderly windbreaks. Mariah took to the center of the road and swung her arms. She smelled smoke and saw it drifting up in every direction from cooking fires, and as she walked along she imagined the men in their dungarees combing out their long beards and the women worrying their chickens. Morning in the fields.

Mariah walked closer to town and could feel the sun on the back of her neck. When she put her hand to her neck, it felt moist. Carts began to pass her on their way into town, carrying every manner of goods for trade. She imagined the town was itself alive and awake and calling forth for tribute to be brought to its altar. The closer she got, the more people and horses and carts she could see pouring into the town. It required their presence. The town now loomed above her, up the hill and past the old Cunningham place and its smokehouse.

She would spend the rest of her life in that town. That knowledge came to her in a rush. She knew it as if it had been augured in the flights of sparrows over her head. She paused in the middle of the road at the foot of Academy Hill, right at the edge of town, and then moved off to the side of the road where there was a post she could lean on. She looked around half expecting an angel to be on hand to explain the meaning of the prophecy that had just taken her.

She closed her eyes. Some places are just meant to be the last stop, the final place of arrival. What she had left to do in this life would be done in this town. She realized she had lost the ability to imagine, in any vivid way, the world outside. It appeared to her that there could *be* no going on into that wider world. The drama of this town would occupy her forever.

She did not feel anchored to the town by Theopolis and his grave behind her, but she *could* feel how she had become entwined in the story of Franklin, and it in hers. She hadn't the energy to extricate herself. She would be married again and she would grow old there. It was just a feeling, but it was strong. She saw herself living back in her house in town, but every day walking the cemetery with Carrie. She would talk about the death of her son with that woman who had also lost children. In this there was no distinction between them. Carrie described herself as a widow, but Mariah thought of herself as orphaned: orphaned from both her elders and her own child, alone, the last possible orphan in her line. The orphan mother.

She started up the hill again and felt light. There was relief in revealed knowledge, she thought, and though this knowledge had come to her in a vision, it already seemed inevitable and substantial. It had weight. Just then she heard the squeak of the trap's seat and the rattle of the rig and knew what she would see when she turned around. There was no trap that sounded like that one. Or, rather, there was no trap she had heard so often that every creak and scrape of it was familiar to her.

"Tried to sneak off, did you?" Carrie called. Mariah turned. She wore no veil, and no black either. She wore a plain green day dress with white piping and pockets. With her brown napped boots and round yellow straw hat, Carrie looked like a flower. She looked like she was headed to a carnival, or parading for Mardi Gras. Mariah hardly recognized her.

"I know where you're going, and I'm taking you there, Mariah," Carrie McGavock said. "I mean it." She brought the horse to a stop and looked down from the gleaming leather bench. Everything shone, every buckle and bit and knob. Mariah wondered why she hadn't noticed the trap being polished.

"Walking suits me."

"Now get up in this cart next to me. I will not have it otherwise." Carrie McGavock, even when she was young and certain of everything and bossy, had never spoken to Mariah that way. She had never demanded she do a thing. She had only ever suggested things, though even those suggestions were not *suggestions* as white people understood them. But Carrie had never taken this tone, which sounded for all the world like the sound of her father, master of plantations. Mariah studied Carrie's face and decided she was being tested.

"Don't take no orders no more."

"That was not an order, just the invitation of someone trying to look out for you."

"Going to that courthouse on my own legs, to do *my* business. Ain't your business."

"All by yourself."

"Got to."

Carrie shrugged her shoulders. Then, after thinking for a second, she leaned over until her face was on Mariah's level. "No one does anything by themselves. Or, what I mean is, no one ever *finishes* anything by themselves. No one *succeeds*."

"Don't believe that."

"It's been my experience."

"Your experiences ain't mine."

"No, they aren't." While they talked, Carrie pulled the trap to the side of the road. Two other carts passed them by, one full of green rye and the other loaded with barrels. The white men driving them looked over, but Carrie fixed their attention back on the road with a glare. The sun kept coming up over the trees, and Mariah could feel the beads of sweat on her spine.

Carrie continued. "But you've had experience of the world. You have some idea how it works, for good and bad."

"Yes." Mariah began to suspect she knew where this conversation was headed.

"And you think they're just going to let you march yourself into that courthouse and say your piece? Like you were anyone else?"

"If they stop me, they stop me, but I'm going to try."

Fierce eyes from Carrie. "So you just want to *try*? You just want to get seen *trying*? Oh, that's going to accomplish everything. *Mariah tried*. And who will give a damn about the fact that you *tried*? Not one soul. You might as well have stayed in bed."

"I done more in this life than you ever did. More than just *tried*." The words were out of Mariah's mouth before she could choke them back, and when they hung in the air between them she was glad they were out. "I cleaned up your children and your house, I carried your things halfway across the country, I washed your dead babies and dressed them and laid them in their coffins, I wiped the blood up from all them hundreds of dying boys you laid out on the floors, I *listened* to you for most of the minutes of my life."

Carrie leaned back, no longer fierce. "You did."

"I done plenty."

"You did that, too."

"And I'll *do* this just the same."

"No you won't. You know the world. You know they won't hear you. Talk all you want—that won't change."

Carrie was right, as Tole had been: they would not hear her. A poor black woman, recently someone else's property: she didn't have a voice yet. And if she did, they wouldn't have the ears to hear it.

Mariah did not know how to reply. Carrie irritated her, angered her even. She wanted to pull her down by her well-fixed braided bun and let her see what it was like down on the ground. The feeling passed. What would happen when she arrived at the court-house? They would let her in, that was true. They would acknowledge that she could sit there. They would know her name, or they'd at least pretend to know it. But what else?

"You sure you couldn't use me?" Carrie asked.

"How could I use you?"

"Let me arrive with you. Let me walk in with you. Like I'm someone who would not stand for having you be insulted and ig-nored. Like a friend."

"You already said we ain't friends."

"Not *yet*, and anyway they don't know that. If you were with me, if we went in together, they would have to hear you. They would have to pay attention. You know this. This is the truth of the world. You should take advantage of this fact."

"Like I'm a child."

"*No*," Carrie hissed, and then calmed. "No. Not like a child. Like a woman who knows how to outwit those who would hold her back."

"And what will they say about you, Miss Carrie?"

"Don't know."

"They say, 'She not right in the head. She a nigger lover.' And the white ladies say, 'She ain't getting invited to no teas no more.'"

"And I'll say, 'Oh, thank God.'"

An impasse had arisen, a decision had to be made. Did she want to testify, or did she merely want to be seen trying?

Mariah climbed up into the trap.

Carrie drove her into town like she was the servant and Mariah the mistress.

They didn't speak.

At the railroad track they continued down Lewisburg Pike past the boys' institute to Main Street. People watched the trap go by. Mariah wondered if they knew what she was going to do.

At Main Street they turned right. There was the Billard Saloon, and the men standing around in front. The men stepped back from the edge of the sidewalk when the trap came abreast, but they didn't acknowledge what they saw. Not even a tipped hat. Across the street Mariah saw Mr. Smithson the newspaperman standing by. He seemed smaller than she remembered. He watched them the whole way past. Down ahead Mariah began to hear voices, real voices, murmurings and singing.

Now Mariah could see the courthouse and the front door through which she would enter. From her vantage, across the square she could see several things at once. Off to her left, down the straight road from Nashville, she saw white men on horses trotting closer. On her right, up from the Bucket, she saw fifty or so men and women—black men and black women—approaching on foot from a few blocks away. Carrie urged the horse on, but the crowds met at the courthouse before they could get there. Black men and women surrounded the courthouse, facing out, daring anyone to try to interfere with the proceedings. They parted and Carrie drove forward. She parked the cart at the foot of the courthouse steps. They hadn't rehearsed this, but somehow Mariah knew to wait in the cart for Carrie to descend and come around.

Carrie helped her down, Mariah's naked palm covering Carrie's gloved hand.

Together the women marched up the courthouse steps, eyes on the courthouse doors, the crowd quiet. Soon they were through the doors and into the dim and looming vestibule. To the right was the main courtroom, where the tribunal was already in progress.

Carrie walked Mariah to a seat in the courtroom. "This is as far as I can go with you," she said. "You don't need me anymore."

The time has come, Mariah thought. *Going to be heard, so I hope I got something to say.*

CHAPTER 37

TOLE

August 6, 1867

The entire town would be preoccupied most of the day, Tole knew. The U.S. Army had shown up yesterday, soldiers bivouacking in tents out by the Nashville Road, and a few of the higher-ups bunking in the Parrish Hotel. Tole made it a point to know where they were staying, and to know the schedule of the tribunal, which would formally begin at ten o'clock sharp at the courthouse—presided over by the city magistrate, Elijah Dixon, as well as a lieutenant and lieutenant colonel of the U.S. Army, and two others.

At seven o'clock that morning, Tole was on the roof of the opera house across the street from Elijah Dixon's office, with a clear view of the front door and the side streets on either side of the building. He could also see down the block a hundred feet in each direction. Conceivably someone could creep through the back alleys, enter a back door, and take the rear stairs to reach Dixon's office, but would anyone go to such trouble, especially on today, of all days? Tole doubted it.

The next few hours passed slowly, but Tole was in a mental state that he recognized and welcomed: the moment when he dwindled to something less than "I," when he was part of the brick parapet

244

in front of him and the gritty graveled roof beneath him, as if each pebble recognized him and cried out to him and embraced him, so he became part of them. He knew neither boredom nor anxiety—he just waited.

All of Franklin flowed in one direction: toward the courthouse. Groups of freedmen and bands of white men poured past, some with signs and horses, some on foot, laughing and chatting as if they were going to the Williamson County Fair. A girl in a yellow dress tied with a green sash adjusted her hat brim and Tole thought for an instant that she'd seen him, hiding here, but she turned and smiled up at her companion and the moment passed.

At 10:05, Tole descended the opera house stairs and out into the street, meeting no one. Most shops were closed. He crossed the street as if crossing a river, wading against a tide that threatened to bear him off downstream, fought his way across, put one hand on the front door, and pulled it open.

Upstairs, the doors to Dixon's office were locked, but the locks were simple and basic, he'd brought a screwdriver and Bowie knife. It took almost nothing for him to open one.

Once inside, he rifled through drawers—dozens of them. All he found in the promising drawers—those that were locked, in the desk—was liquor, Hooper's better stuff. Two of the eight file cabinets in one of the antechambers, however, surrendered gold, quite literally: the big wooden four-door cabinet (locked, until it met Tole's screwdriver) on the far right side yielded the real estate transactions, hundreds of them, thousands of acres, it seemed to Tole. Too many files to carry, so he searched through the documents and pulled out those that reflected the largest transactions.

Combing the four drawers in the right-hand file cabinet took him the better part of an hour. He had a stack of documents about eighteen inches thick, and wished he'd brought a sack to carry them in.

He waded into the other cabinets. More documents—much of

them from the city of Franklin. As magistrate, Tole knew, Dixon was a sort of judge who could hear certain matters, review arrests. Tole also knew that Dixon had much to do with the financial rebuilding of Franklin after the war. He didn't know the details, but had heard that Dixon was instrumental in obtaining loans from the U.S. government, and otherwise facilitating the rebirth of a town decimated during the war. Now he found details, far more than he wanted—lists of contractors and supplies, correspondence with government officials both in Nashville and in Washington, D.C., orders for building and orders for rebuilding—the files seemed endless. But nothing struck him as odd or problematic. He remembered Bliss's suggestion to look for ledger books, and he found them lined neatly on a shelf near one of the cabinets—long lists of entries and figures that he didn't quite understand.

Was this everything? It was probably enough. All those real estate transactions would be of interest to someone, surely.

Just to be on the safe side he pulled the rugs away and walked the room board by board, listening. The board he was looking for wouldn't sound hollow, he thought, just different. The sound of his foot would have an odd timbre; it would ring out different from the other boards. He methodically walked the boards lengthwise, heel first, striking each in the exact same way until, finally, the sound he heard was slightly muffled. He checked to make sure there weren't extra nails. He bent over and took note of the lack of dust in the joints. With one of Dixon's letter openers, he pried the board up and found, hard up against the joist, a metal box about the size of a very thick book.

Before he opened the box, the lock easily broken, he replaced everything just as it had been—rugs, drawers, pictures. The whole operation had taken him another half hour.

When everything was settled again, he opened one of Dixon's drawers, pulled out a bottle, and poured a few fingers of whiskey into a tin cup. He settled himself into the soft, high-backed chair near the fireplace, rested the cup on the mantel, and pulled the papers out of the box.

Stock certificates in the Louisville and Nashville Railroad Company, on fancy paper: olive-green border, black lettering, an engraving of men in a switchyard, trains flying past trailing steam. Tole found a whole pile of these, and gave up trying to calculate the value. This was worth more money than he had ever thought a man might hold in one hand. He guessed this was most of what Dixon owned, and it made him laugh. Just paper, but so much trouble!

He put the papers back in the box, shut the lid, placed the box on the rug in front of him, stared at it and the sheaf of real estate documents. This was exactly what Bliss was talking about. He'd done well. It was time to get over to the tribunal before Mariah's testimony.

Bliss had asked him about where Dixon's money came from, and Tole realized nothing he'd found had the answer. All that stock and land would have required a vast sum. The Dixon family did not live in an extraordinary mansion, and he wasn't known to have inherited extraordinary wealth.

Again he returned to the file cabinets, flipped quickly through each drawer, looking for something, anything, that seemed wrong, strange. Nothing. Then he reached up.

A three-inch space lay between the top of the upper file drawer and the cabinet top. Tole's fingertips grazed leather binding. A book had been slotted into the space. It took him a few moments to figure out how to extricate it, but he found some straps and a tie. The book tumbled into his hands.

Another ledger book.

Each of the eight file cabinets held another ledger. Each ledger was neatly organized—more rows of names and figures. Each of the ledgers was labeled: *City Tax Revenue. Building Reparations. Water & Sewer.* Quickly he found the ledgers out in the main office—dozens of them, but a few labeled similarly. He compared them, side by side. They did not match.

Tole wasn't quite sure what he was looking at, but he could guess. Mr. Dixon, magistrate of Franklin, had his hand in the till. The magistrate of Franklin was pilfering funds of Franklin, and funds meant for Franklin. This was where all the extra money was coming from.

He allowed himself a breath of exultation. They wanted proof? He'd gotten the proof.

In fifteen minutes he'd left Dixon's office, hidden the documents in Theopolis's old house, and headed to the courthouse. If he were lucky, he'd hear Mariah speak. *That would be a perfect day.*

CHAPTER 38

MARIAH

August 6, 1867

Mariah emerged from out of the darkness at the back of the courtroom and could feel the sun through the high windows. She had not been called by the men at the bench far ahead of her, and she nearly turned back, but then she thought she might have been called by powers greater than those of mortal man, and who knows the mind of such forces? They create worlds unimaginable, even worlds in which a woman such as she walks down the aisle of a white man's tribunal and takes her place in it. Such is the mind of God. The minds of men twist and knot around the impossible task of understanding.

A thousand faces, it seemed, watched her way. Probably a hundred, but it felt like more. The faces she passed flickered from dark to light, in the shadows that passed over the windows, shadows of men on horses and other men and women. The courthouse was a ship at sea, buffeted by agitated and irreconcilable waves.

Ahead of her rose five chairs on the dais, older men looking down at the room in judgment upon a town that had murdered two of its own, a white and a black. On the left sat Elijah Dixon, magistrate. Mariah did not recognize the other four, but noted that the bald one in the middle was clean-shaven, with a high-bridged nose and delicate glasses perched on the end of it; the one between the man with glasses and Elijah Dixon seemed gruffer, with thickset arms that bulged with muscle beneath the blue U.S. Army uniform.

Dixon met Mariah's gaze as she stepped forward. "Who is this?" he said. He knew full well who stood before the tribunal.

The room turned as one, to follow his gaze and look upon her, dressed in a linsey-woolsey dress, as if she'd just then walked right off the plantation, out of the past. She wore the boots of a man, but polished mirror black. All the room looked at her, and knew her. She was every Negress they had ever seen, and none of them.

Silence. Two spots of color flushed red as rose on Dixon's face. He craned his head around to watch Mariah.

Mariah Reddick stood with her spine straight, hair like hard silk pulled back from her face. Her mouth was set in a straight line, but even so she could feel the anger in her own eyes and she tried to squint it away. She held her hands before her, then at her sides. She stood in the aisle at the back of the room, and those in the audience who had been wandering about took their seats but quick.

"You are?" the bald man asked her, speaking for the tribunal.

She walked slowly up the aisle, enunciating every word as if wanting to be heard clear to heaven. She spoke to the bald man as if born to it, as if there were never any question that a Negress could stand before a tribunal of white men on her own authority. The audience murmured.

She began with a booming "*I.*" The sound of it, like the note of a choir, echoed into the rafters, as if causing little birds there to twitter and leap and seek shelter. "I—" she said again, and paused. "I am the mother of the dead man. Mother of Theopolis Reddick. I am Mariah Reddick."

The bald man called her forward, but she only stood there looking at him. She cocked her head, inspecting him, her eyes took his entire measure. The bald man—all of the tribunal, in actual fact—had seemed bored and hard before, barking out instructions, taking pleasure in their power. But now the lines of the man's face softened, as if chastened. He slackened, he leaned back against his chair. He never quit watching her, nor did she quit watching him.

Then he asked her if she would please come forward and take her place in the witness's chair. The audience tittered and whispered. *He afraid of this Negress.* Mariah knew it wasn't fear. But what did he see in her? Did he see the future, and was that something to fear? There was no time to think about it.

She walked forward.

Six windows stood on either side of the courthouse. A row of high windows stretched far above the judge's bench where the five sat. Off to the right of the bench a chair had been placed. Mariah took the chair and turned it to face the audience directly, instead of the men on their bench above her. The windows glowed. She was silent. Shouts came from beyond the walls. From the back of the room came a hiss and a curse. Several people giggled. But Mariah stared down the culprit until he ceased, until it became apparent that there would be no one, that day, who would lay a hand on her. She was shocked, though she didn't show it. It wasn't just the fact that no one *would* lay a hand on her, but that it soon became apparent, the longer she sat there, that no one *dared*.

On that day and in that moment, the world ended as she had known it, and who could know the future? The firelight in the windows flashed and doused, chaotic and uncertain. There was a fearful tremolo in the sound of the shouting outside the courthouse. The future was as unknowable as God himself.

Before she spoke she removed the scarf from around her neck and tied it up over her hair as if she were going to work. When she was done arranging herself, she was every Negress who had ever stooped over the long, lonely field rows, or nursed the lady's child, or cooked the master his food. She wore it as a costume, as if play-acting. Mariah meant it as a revelation and a scandal, the gesture of a prophetess.

She had imagined that the only thing in her mind would be a rebuke and a great reordering of time, history, and that town. The colors of justice would flow from her mouth to dazzle the gathered. The audience would be captured and made to see the world differently. Theopolis would become a hero and then a martyr. There would be great wailing for the injustice done. Her words would be inscribed in marble.

But this was not what was in her mind at the moment she took her place, and these were not the words that came out of her mouth.

"Mariah Reddick? That is your name?" The bald man spoke as if from the bottom of a well. She heard the words but paid them no attention. She looked into the audience. How long had they all been sitting there? Eons. They faded, darkened. The faces lost focus, became shapes and then only brushes of color.

"Do you have something to say, Mrs. Reddick?" She heard the impatience in the man's voice, but she couldn't begin yet. She had to see.

"Well, she can't just sit there." Dixon dragged himself to his feet, but she held up her hand and watched him freeze. He looked up at the bench and sat down slowly.

This was a real place. There was a seat here, in the middle of a courtroom, and she sat in it as a witness. She, a Negro, sat in the middle of the courtroom. She had the right to sit there. She had words, whatever words, which would be taken down in the record like any other man's or woman's.

"Yes," she said, finally. "I have something to say." She looked up at the bald man, who smiled in relief, pointed his finger at her, and sat back in his chair. He listened for her words, but she had already said them. She had already spoken: she had taken her seat. Anything else she had to say wasn't all that important.

There were consequences of freedom; the world had not been miraculously transformed by paper declarations of independence. Nevertheless, she was not afraid. Others would have to carry it forward from there. Things would get worse before they got better, she thought. As they always do.

But if she had not taken her seat, the seat would have disappeared.

"Please begin your testimony."

"My name is Mariah Reddick. My son was Theopolis Reddick. My boy was killed by men who ain't had the courage to hear him speak. He were no murderer. He was a free man."

Only then did she realize how long she had sat there with her eyes closed. When she opened them the light flooded in, all was foggy. The faces in the audience came into focus slowly. She saw eyes first, then faces.

"Did you see who killed your son?"

"He was just dead and that's all I seen."

"What about the men in the black hats?"

"I knew they were there, didn't look too hard at them."

"Would you guess they killed your son?"

"One of them, surely. And surely all of them were helping."

"Why would anyone kill your son?"

"You'd know better than me."

"I'm asking you."

"Truth is, sir, I don't know who killed him. I been trying all this time to figure out who, and it turns out, it don't matter who."

A pause. Then from Dixon: "Mrs. Reddick, if you don't have any relevant information, please remove yourself."

"I ain't going nowhere," she told him. Then to the bald man with the glasses, in the middle of the dais, she explained, "See, I'm afraid you asking the wrong question. It don't matter who killed my son, because I know *what* killed him."

"Ma'am?"

"It's odd," Mariah said, almost dreamily, and drifted off to silence again.

"If the witness has nothing to say, she is dismissed," Elijah Dixon put in again.

She ignored him. "I know the truth about who killed my boy. I know names. I know faces. But knowing them wasn't as simple as I hoped. It took a lot of men to kill my son. It took a lot of years for their hatred to be passed down, from daddy to son and again."

"The witness needs to step down," Dixon insisted.

And yet the other men kept listening. Something about her earnestness, the way she looked at them directly, through grief and rage and numb incomprehension, froze them and made them hear her.

"I've heard some stories about that morning. They say there was a riot. Gunshot rang out. And my son just happened to be the Negro standing in front. They say it could've been any nigger standing there. Maybe they right. Those white men, wherever they are now, they beat my boy within an inch of his life and shot him, and for what?"

She slammed her hands onto the oak railing.

"Because they still fighting, and they mad some nigger wants to get up and talk the same way they do. You tell me, what do you think is going to happen if you let us speak? What are you so afraid of, you tell me?"

"Who are you talking to, Mrs. Reddick?"

"I'm talking to all of you. You killed a nigger ain't got no name and no face. And now that he dead, how you feel? Is it over now? What if I told you the boy you killed was my heart and now he's gone? Would it matter? Maybe I just as much a ghost sitting here now as my son. What killed my son is being strong when all around you is cowards, and they own everything even they don't own you no more."

To Mariah's appalled astonishment, she found she was weeping. Tears were sliding down her cheeks. She had to wipe them away to see the men sitting there, staring at her, unblinking.

"Do you know who killed your son?" the bald man asked again.

"I just said."

"Do you have names?"

She drew a deep breath. "Yes, I have names. But they're not the real culprits, don't you hear that?"

"What names do you have?"

She repeated the names she'd heard, whispered from the maids and cooks and farmhands, from the smiths and bricklayers and carpenters, from all the black folk all over Franklin, some who'd spoken and some who hadn't, but the names had made their way back to her, one way or another, and now she said them:

Aaron Haynes. James Mayberry. Joshua Knight. Samuel Shaw. Daniel Whitmore. Bill Crutcher.

Those six names she spoke, and when she was done she sat back and breathed.

"How do you know it was these six men? Do you have any proof?"

"There's one more name," she told them. And pointed. "Elijah Dixon."

There. It was done. The poor Negro woman accused the magistrate himself, in front of God and the tribunal and all of Franklin.

She expected an uproar. She expected Dixon to leap to his feet, protesting. She expected weeping, and a rending of the heavens.

Instead she found silence.

"Mrs. Reddick, you realize that Magistrate Dixon was not even on the stage when your son was killed?"

"I know it. But I know he ordered it."

"You are saying that the magistrate conspired with a group of men"—they consulted their notes—"these Misters Haynes, Mayberry, and so forth?"

"Yessir. That's what I'm saying."

"Conspired with these men to kill your son?"

"Yessir." She paused, and thought. "Well, no sir."

"The witness will explain herself," broke in the bearded man on the far right.

"What did you hear, Mrs. Reddick?" the bald man with the glasses asked her again. "Are you accusing Magistrate Dixon of conspiring with these men you listed to kill your son?"

"He conspired with the men to kill someone. Maybe not my boy, but that's what they done."

"Who did Magistrate Dixon allegedly conspire to kill?"

"I don't rightly know. He got his own business, he crooked."

"Where did you hear all this? How do you know this?"

"People talk. People tell me. I know it. Why don't you just ask him?"

The bald man looked sternly at Dixon. "Mr. Dixon, do you have anything to say?"

Dixon had remained quiet till then, his face gone white, staring openmouthed at Mariah. Now he came to life, sprang up, pointed. "I haven't the least idea in the world what this Negress is talking about. I think she's made it up out of whole cloth. She wants to besmirch my reputation and destroy my life, and I haven't a clue why—oh." He paused, staring. "I do know why. She's angry at me."

"What for?"

"She's the town midwife. A month ago my wife, Evangeline, gave birth to my son Augusten, fifth child. Evangeline had brought her in to assist, but I didn't like how things were going and I called for the doctor." Then, to Mariah: "That's it, isn't it? You're jealous and spiteful, angry at me for bringing the doctor in to point out your incompetence."

"I saved your baby's life!" Mariah told him. "He would've died if it wasn't for me."

"If it wasn't for Dr. Cliffe, you mean," Dixon said.

The bald man looked from one to the other of them. "This woman's allegations will need some investigation," he said.

"Don't be absurd," Dixon sputtered. "This woman has lost her son and she's looking for someone important to blame, so she says I'm responsible for her son's death. She gets up here with a crazy story about me trying to kill someone, and she points at me because she thinks she can with impunity."

"That may be true," the bald man said, "but we have to determine—"

"You have to determine nothing," Dixon said coldly. "You all were sitting here when she said I didn't kill her son. She says I ordered it, but maybe not. She names six men, so call them. *Call them!* Where are they? They haven't been seen for days, but I'm sitting here doing my duty. And *I'm* responsible? Do I act guilty? Go find those six, let's talk to them."

Mariah could see the bald man wavering. "What about these other names? Mayberry and so forth?" He looked out in the crowd. "Where are they?"

"Fled! That's what they are." Dixon began to relax. "And this one"—he pointed right back at Mariah—"this one bedeviling your investigation with libels and her Negro midwife houdou theatrics. I say enough is enough."

"I'm here for all the people I've birthed, white and Negro, so they don't have to live in a world where men like Mr. Dixon here can cause chaos and kill people," Mariah said quietly, knowing she had been beaten. She was not surprised.

"You're here because you're a lonely Negro who has a grudge against your betters," Dixon said.

"That's not true!" Carrie McGavock stood up with her hands on her hips. She glared at Dixon. "And you know better, Elijah. Mariah is one of the smartest, truest people in all the world, and she bears no one a grudge!"

The bald man banged on the table with the flat of his hand. "Madam, please sit down. We'll call you if we need you."

Reluctantly Carrie sat.

The bald man turned next to Dixon. "Elijah, how do you know those six have not been seen for days?"

Dixon spluttered and had no ready answer.

The bald man waved his hand. "Never mind, I'm sure this all can be explained. But we cannot have you on this tribunal. You are formally put on leave until we can determine if there is any merit to Mrs. Reddick's claims."

Wordless, Dixon gathered his papers, turned, and left by a side door.

"As for you, Mrs. Reddick," the bald man said, "am I to understand that you believe these six men actually caused your son's death?"

"Yes."

"Is there anything further you wish to say?"

"No sir."

"You may leave, then."

She looked out onto the courtroom and couldn't get anyone to meet her eye. She recognized them, white and black, and felt them turned to stone. She stepped down off the platform and looked up one more time. Now she saw April and May in the Negro section and they were smiling and pointing and beckoning her. George Tole was there, too, but he slipped away as she drew closer.

It was done. Mariah had spoken. But had she been heard?

CHAPTER 39

LETTERS

Letter, unsigned and undated, slipped under the door of the offices of Elijah P. Dixon, magistrate, city of Franklin:

You has lots more to loose then I do. You gots a nice family and lots of moneys. I seen all five of yor chilren. You lay one fingr on her and I will take erithing from you. You stay away far away from her.

⸻

Bliss,

I found them papers. You got to come here to get them. Bring my money too.

GT

CHAPTER 40

MARIAH

August 6, 1867

Outside the courthouse, people shuffled down the steps, looked around, and went off in every direction, down the several streets that radiated outward from that center. The town seemed to recede before Mariah's eyes. Windows were shuttered here and there, doors closed quietly, awnings rolled up. In the quiet the town seemed solid, immovable and ancient.

The verdict had come down, and it had come down as they'd expected: regrettable chaos. Two men accidentally killed, thirty-two wounded, no one responsible, everyone feeling very guilty and very sorry.

The magistrate Elijah Dixon on leave, pending further investigation.

Mariah, for a moment, was a hero—swarmed by friends and colleagues congratulating her. This was a victory, they knew. Today history had been made: a Negro ex-slave had pointed her finger at one of the wealthiest men in town, and she was not (yet) dead. Whether or not there would be long-term consequences, no one could know. But for the moment, a victory. Whites might listen to

Negroes with some respect, there might be peace, there might be hope. Or something bloody was coming. It could go either way. In that moment euphoria reigned.

After the throng had thinned, Carrie made her way through. "Do you want to come back to Carnton with me tonight? I think you should."

Mariah looked questioningly at her.

"You embarrassed Elijah Dixon today. I'm worried that he'll act out. Better that you're out in Carnton, with our people around you."

Mariah nodded. But she could not spend her life hiding at Carnton, could she? And in the meantime, all of the U.S. Army, it seemed, was flooding the Franklin streets. Was she really in any danger?

Still and all, she was exhausted, and Carnton seemed very welcome right then. "We going?" she asked Carrie.

"Yes." Carrie moved toward the horse hitched at the post.

"You, too," Mariah said, pointing at April and May. Carrie didn't say a word when all three of them climbed up into the trap and the horse began to pull them down the street, through the Bucket, on the way out to Carnton.

When they passed the sisters' tavern, Mariah signaled for Carrie to stop, and she couldn't help marveling when the trap really did stop. Carrie and the sisters exchanged pleasantries as they climbed down. Then Mariah climbed down, too.

"Where are you going?" Carrie asked, frowning.

"Have some business."

"Will it take long?"

"Not this kind of business."

"I'll wait," Carrie said.

It would not normally have been good for the tavern's business to have the widow of the South perched on her trap outside the house, but there was already a little crowd inside. Hooper had let them in and was running the pouring and the taking of money for

261

the till. *Ain't a thing that man can't do*, Mariah thought. *April know it, too.* She watched April slide behind the serving table and poke at the man and bump her shoulder into his.

They were all there, standing around or sitting on the benches that lined the big room. Country people and people who shined their shoes and polished their watches. At one time they had all been the same in one crucial way, bound and trapped, but since that moment Mariah had watched them all split off and transform, each becoming stranger and more intriguing, an infinite number of butterflies from similar plain cocoons. One of them, or maybe several of them, would be the next to stand up and try another run for office. Maybe April and May would start a hotel. Maybe they would all do something. Not everybody. Some would flutter and sink.

It was not proper, she knew people would talk about it, and April would think about slapping her face for it, but Mariah leaned over and wrapped Hooper in her arms and kissed him softly on his right cheek. Even after kissing him she wouldn't let go. She had known him forever, and she wished Theopolis had followed him and done what he did, and become a man like Hooper, quiet and easy, able to make do, able to fit in. But people would be what God made them to be, she thought to herself. Hooper could only be himself, and Theopolis could only be himself. Finally she let him go.

"Thank you," she said.

"You can hug me like that anytime."

"No she can't," April hissed, having slid over to listen. But she blew Mariah a kiss, too.

"I'm leaving," Mariah said. The words had no weight in that air, filled with singing and shouting and laughing. They nearly stuck in her throat, too heavy to raise up, but once they were out, they just floated off and disappeared. There was nothing more to say. "But I'll see you all right soon."

Outside, Carrie sat straight, reins in her hands, studying the poplar in front of her. If they had still been children, Carrie would have told her all about how the leaves shivered and spun, and about the orange ring on the poplar blossoms, and how there were fairies standing in the crook of the tree way up there, *can't she see them?* But now they were old, or older, and such things a woman like Carrie McGavock, mistress of Carnton, did not say aloud to a Negro, even Mariah Reddick. Not in public, anyway. Mariah wondered if that would ever change. *Not before we dead*, she thought, climbing up and sitting on the bench of the trap, to Carrie's right.

Soon the Bucket was far behind them, and they followed the road through the woods, up and down two hills, off to the side of the old trenches, and onward toward the house. It had become a gray day, and in that light, Carnton seemed smaller. They came up the front drive, where Mariah spied the brief flash of blue from the underside of the front portico ceiling. She was a little surprised when Carrie didn't stop at the house but continued on down the hill past the smokehouse to Mariah's cabin.

She was even more surprised when Carrie got down from the trap there, at the base of the steps up to her quarters.

"What you doing?" she asked, joining her.

"I have something to show you," Carrie said. She began to float, to walk without bobbing or swaying in that strange way she had whenever she felt possessed of ancient knowledge. Mariah clunked up the stairs behind her.

At the top of the stairs, leaning against the wall to the right of the door, Mariah saw a large rounded piece of finished stone on which some words had been carved:

Theopolis Reddick
Beloved Son, Free Man
1842–1867

263

Mariah had not been able to afford a proper headstone for Theopolis. She thought she might be able to afford one for herself if she saved her midwifing money for a year or so, but found herself quite willing to accept the gift.

She turned to Carrie. "Thank you."

"You don't need to thank me. He had a name. He wasn't just your 'Dead Son.' He was your Theopolis. And now the whole world can know."

Had he known he was a beloved son? she wondered. She hoped he did.

"Anyway, it's not a gift, it's just something I thought you should see. But there's a gift inside," Carrie said, pointing toward the door.

"Why you giving me gifts?"

"Gift. One."

"And?"

"Because I know you're leaving, and that's what you do when you're sorry to see someone leave. You give them a gift."

"I didn't say nothing about that."

"What else would you do, now? You're a changed woman, Mariah Reddick. People who sit up in courtrooms don't live in slave cabins. And this won't ever be anything more than that. You weren't going to stay here, I knew that. You did, too. And anyway, we didn't buy that house for you so no one would live in it."

They stood on the threshold for a moment more, considering the way the words they had just exchanged had reordered the universe. And then Carrie walked down the steps, got into the trap, and rode it back up the hill until she had disappeared around the corner of the house.

Mariah wanted to call out one more thing, but didn't know what to say. There are no good goodbyes.

She pushed the door open, went in, and lit her lamp. On the bed was a padded leather box. She sat down on the bed beside it.

The black leather nearly shone, and it dimpled where it had been tacked down to the box. A simple brass latch kept it closed. She flipped it open.

Inside she found a square thing wrapped in light muslin like a shroud, like something from the afterworld. She was afraid to touch it until she reminded herself she didn't believe in the things that made her afraid. Then she unwrapped it in her lap.

It was a framed picture, a tintype. Mariah could remember when it was made. They had all been much younger. Carrie had not yet experienced the death of a child, for there they were in the photograph, the littlest cradled in Carrie's arms and wiggling so much that she became a foggy blur, as if the camera had predicted the child's death soon to come. The whole McGavock family stood on the walkway between the cedars that led to the front of the house and up upon the portico. There were John and Carrie in the middle and the children gathered around. Off to the right side, at a noticeable distance from the family, Mariah stood stone-faced in her best house uniform, and for some reason, she held an empty silver tray before her.

And off to the left, as if he had just materialized out of the fog at the edge of the photograph, a creature soon to return to the trees, stood little Theopolis. He was seven, maybe. He held a hayfork in his left hand, tines standing far above his head. The tintype made his eyes sharp and dark. His hand on the hayfork stayed steady, but his mouth had moved, and now it was just a smudge. She saw his strong nose, his puffed chest, and allowed herself to cry.

She lay down on the bed and held the photo and cried for a few minutes. Perhaps she drifted off. When she looked down again at the photograph, she laughed. Here she was crying over a picture of *the McGavocks*. A tintype of the McGavocks had been placed in a leather-padded box and wrapped in muslin as if it were a gift fit for the Christ child himself. And here they were, mother and son, the Reddick Negroes, standing on either side of that family bearing the tools of their work and staring dutifully into the camera, only little Theopolis couldn't keep from running his mouth into a blur. This was the most precious and ridiculous gift, and she loved it.

CHAPTER 41

LETTER

August 8, 1867

Thanks for sindin yer addres. Glad yer bak. Meet me undr the Harpeth brige by 12 st. I bring the papirs and we will see how we can get him.

GT

CHAPTER 42

DIXON

August 9–10, 1867

The last of the late summer sun, defiant and fire orange, quietly blued behind the distant mountains of Pulaski, Tennessee, a small Methodist town some sixty miles from Franklin. It was suppertime. Way down on Cleveland Street, a mud wagon slowed to a stop across the way from the old post office, and Elijah Dixon, the only passenger, stepped gingerly down onto dirt and pebbles. Dixon walked south to meet a Confederate veteran named John Lester. Lester was a cousin of James Mayberry; their mothers were sisters.

Dixon hadn't planned on coming until the next day, until the Army was safely out of Franklin; but word came down that the unit was heading out early, would be gone by early afternoon. Franklin was undefended.

Dixon couldn't wait another minute. He'd stewed in his study, pipe lodged in his mouth, puffing tobacco smoke and running the tribunal through his mind. The illiterate letter threatening his family gave him pause, but Elijah Dixon was confident that he could resolve the situation favorably.

He set out. He wanted their nigger houses burned. He'd been embarrassed enough. And he could use the land.

The letter from John Lester, the one Dixon had received that morning, said he and his boys gathered in some veterans' club close to the church. He said the building had no sign, but Dixon would know it by the white, chipping paint and the wooden stepladder out front. Dixon walked through the gray-blue of fallen dusk and well into night before he finally found the old church and, across the way, just as the letter said, a small house and a ladder, shrouded in blackness but for a small oil lamp lighting the porch steps.

The door opened as Dixon approached, and a young man stepped out onto the porch and lit a pipe. "You lost, sir?"

"Name's Dixon. Came to see John Lester."

The young man's name was Calvin, and he blew smoke out the side of his mouth as he took a step down toward Dixon.

"John's inside. You the man from Franklin he been talkin' to?"

"That's right."

"You some kinda big shot he tells us." Calvin stamped out his pipe, blew the excess out the side of his mouth, and gestured with his head for Dixon to follow him inside. The small house was mostly bare: just a few rooms, a small space with a coal oven, a wooden table, and a few chairs. In the main room, a few boys sat around playing cards, maybe nine or ten of them.

John Lester stood first when Dixon entered the room. He was a tall, thin man—Dixon pegged him at six foot four—with a gaunt face covered in a dark brown goatee.

"Mr. Dixon," he said in a gentle southern drawl. "See now, you weren't s'posed to be here till mornin'."

"Well I'm here now. Decided to head out early. We got business can't wait till morning."

"Understood."

One of the veterans stood and offered his seat to Dixon, who nodded and sat, waving off a pint of beer.

"You walked in just as we were finishing a hand of rummy. We can deal you in next hand if you want."

"All due respect, Mr. Lester, I'd prefer you put the cards away so we can talk. My patience isn't what it used to be."

John Lester stared steadily, calmly at Dixon from across the table, threw his cards down, face up. "Okay then. From what I understand, you got some renegade nigger that needs killing, that right?"

"The way I feel right now, that whole goddamn town needs to be burned to the ground."

"Why you come to us? I'm curious."

"Most of my boys are dead. Gone. Not sure which, and it doesn't matter. I think they were all murdered."

"What happened?"

"Don't exactly know," Dixon said.

"You wrote us that it's just one nigger. It's just the one, right?"

"He's the worst. Mean fucking nigger."

"What he do?"

What did any of them do? Dixon thought. They were parasites, beasts. "You boys have been making a lot of noise these last couple months around here," he said, not answering the question.

"Somethin' happenin' in this country," Lester said. "You know that feelin' I'm talkin' 'bout, Mr. Dixon? When you walk outside and you feel like the country you knew, the one your daddy raised you in, the one your granddaddy died for, it ain't quite the same. It don't feel like it belong to us anymore."

"Yes, I know the feeling."

"We ain't ghosts, Mr. Dixon. We just want our country back. Since the war we seein' these uppity niggers walkin' 'round thinkin' they can just take what we and our kin worked our whole lives for."

"Uppity niggers. That's right. That's exactly it."

"But what you got against this one nigger? What so special 'bout him you can't do this yourself?"

"I think he killed your cousin, for one thing. I told you that. He's a mean son of a bitch. Good with a rifle and quiet as a snake."

Lester took this news with remarkable calm, and Dixon wondered whether the man had any feelings for his cousin one way or the other.

"What make you think he killed James?"

"Can't find him anywhere. He just plumb disappeared. And a bunch of others I was working with. All vanished. Body of one of 'em turned up a couple weeks back, all shot to hell. And that nigger I'm talking about, he's good—really good—with a gun. Couldn't be coincidence."

"Lots of folk are good with guns."

"Yeah, but all my men have disappeared. Most folks don't have the skill for that. Or the patience. This one does."

"You think this one nigger killed all of them? How many we talking about?"

"Not sure how many he killed. Maybe five. Haven't heard from a couple of them, but that don't mean he got them. Maybe they took off."

"Hellfire."

"Time to teach this boy a lesson," Dixon said. "Frankly, you ought to want him dead worse than I do."

"Funny thing about my cousin James. I wasn't all that close with him, if I'm bein' honest. I always found him a bit queer, you ask me. But you tell me some nigger blew a hole in the back of his head, and I guess I figure my Aunt Jo deserve some restitution. That's why I invited you down. I could tell by the way you answered my letter. You sounded like a man I'd wanna know."

"Then if it's all the same to you, I'd like to get this done."

"How do you find this special nigger?"

"He live in a part of town they call Blood Bucket. You can start there. It won't take long to find him."

Lester nodded.

271

"But I don't want you to just stop with this one nigger. I want all those niggers to learn a lesson. Torch the fucking cesspool where they live. The Bucket, it's called. The Blood Bucket. What kind of name is that?" Dixon didn't expect an answer. "And Mr. Lester? I'll pay you well for this."

"Well then, that sounds like some good fun."

The Bucket, well past midnight, sweltered in August heat.

Hooper, slumbering beneath his cart down off Indigo Street, woke to the smell of smoke, the distant sound of galloping horses.

Six blocks east, behind the Thirsty Bird Saloon, April and May, closing down for the night, walked outside and saw the eerie glow of fire. Smoke billowed into the sky.

Fire.

Hooper slid from beneath the cart, grabbed his pistol, and listened. He saw the same orange glow. He ran barefoot down the dirt road, glass and pebbles digging into the soles of his feet, leaving a trail of blood as he raced toward the light. He turned the corner to see a small wooden church awash in bright fire. The flames' reflection bounced off his skin, which was shining with sweat. He turned to look behind him. In the distance, the same glow. A house on fire, and the hard gallop of horses getting closer.

"Get out! Run!"

Several houses—shacks, most of them—were aflame. The houses emptied ten at a time, two and three families tumbling onto the streets, some barefoot, naked children in their arms, running, screaming.

Gunshots.

A few riders kicked open doors, dragged women into the streets. Hooper could hear them screaming and then silenced in a thunderous roar of a shotgun. Even a street away, Hooper could feel the gunshot blasts in his stomach.

Negroes swarmed for safety. They ran down the street carrying whatever they could—dishes, hoes, sabers, children.

The roof of the Thirsty Bird Saloon caved in, consumed by smoke and flame.

"No, no, no!" April yelped and ran for the saloon.

"April, no!" May ran after her, tried to stop her. "It's too late! It's too late!"

April threw herself to the ground and pounded her fists into the earth, face wet with tears and snot and spit. She screamed at the fire before her while May wrapped her arms tightly around her. "You can't, baby! You can't save it."

———

The Bucket burned on. There were blocks of flames, and in the absence of any moonlight, its whiteness lit the sky like bright lightning. Hooper lay on his belly, mouth full of dirt, the burn of sweat and tears in his eyes. He counted the bullets in the chamber of his pistol. He only had six shots, and his hunting knife in his other hand. He knew he wasn't much of a killer, but he wasn't a coward either. He had principles. He crawled on his forearms and peeked around the edge of a house, a house that had not yet burned, a house in which he had discovered three children and their terrified mothers, doomed by the sound of those men approaching.

He saw the horses' hooves, and black boots marching alongside them. He was alone, gripping his gun until the handle made a deep imprint in the palm of his hand. The boots were getting closer. Shadows flickered in their torchlight. Hooper blessed himself. He believed in God the way his mama taught him to, and said a quiet prayer before picking himself up to his knees, then to his feet, standing tall behind the corner of the house. He took a deep breath.

When he ran out from behind the house, everything slowed down, he noticed everything. He yelled and they yelled back. He fired his six shots at the men, and they fired back.

He heard the gunshots and saw the blasts from their shotguns, exploding like fireworks. He felt the shards of shot rip through his abdomen and through his leg, just above his knee. *It don't feel like nothing*, he thought and nearly cheered. Another shot entered his chest, but he was moving so fast it caused him to fall forward, onto one of the blackbeards, who looked surprised when he felt Hooper's knife slip between his ribs and into his heart. Hooper rolled over, heaving, choking on the blood that was rising into his lungs. *Stay away from the house, stay away from the house*, he prayed.

The gang surrounded him, hooked a rope around his neck, and attached the rope to the horse's saddle. Blood poured from Hooper's mouth, out of his ear. He choked, he tried to speak. He couldn't form words.

And then one man hoisted himself onto the horse and yelled "Heeawwh!" and the horse surged forward, dragging Hooper for miles across town. The second-to-last conscious thought Hooper had was to thank God that they'd stayed away from that little house. The last one was that he had been right to hate that town.

He was still breathing when they cut him loose and left him at the edge of town to die.

CHAPTER 43

TOLE

August 10, 1867

Tole heard them coming long before they arrived—the drum of horses' hooves, men moving fast. It was almost second nature for him to be off his pallet, pistol in hand, crouched protectively behind the door, listening.

By the time the first of the men stepped into his yard, Tole was already out back, behind a tree with his rifle, a pistol, and one long Bowie knife.

Strapped across his back, a blue-and-red satchel—what had held all his worldly goods when he came from New York—now held all the documents and the box he'd stolen from Elijah Dixon's office. He wouldn't let that satchel leave his side.

He had two ways of retreat, one through the hedge into the neighbor's yard and down the hill into the deepest Bucket, and the second a dark alley that served the blocks of the upper Bucket and led through the south end of town and down toward the Harpeth. *Always have two options if it all goes bad.* The first assassin quietly circled the house toward him. Tole faded into dark, hard up against the tree, not breathing, thinking for a moment to reach out and collar the man who shuffled by too loudly and held his rifle too low.

He could smell the tang of old sweat. He let him pass. The man disappeared into the dark.

After a time he heard voices from around the front. Several, maybe six or seven men. Tole moved down the hedge, keeping the corner of the house between him and the clot of men who had gathered at the foot of his steps.

"Check it again."

"Ain't that big."

"Check it again, just do it."

"Oh, you the boss man now I suppose. Well goddamn it."

At some distance from the others stood Dixon, and he had his hand on something. Or someone. Tole couldn't see, but he recognized how Dixon always kept himself just out of the fray like a good boss man.

Footsteps into the house. Sound of tables crashing over, something metal rattling against stone. Maybe his pot in the hearth. More crashing and stomping. Tole saw the flash of torchlight through the little windows down the hallway from his main room. The door slammed open and then closed again.

"He ain't here."

"What else you find?"

"Nothing. The fire was going, though, and coffee on it. He was here just a second ago. Don't see him now. He a strange one, got dolls and toys and all such nonsense all over."

"How about the floor?"

"You want me to tear up the floor? He in the *floor*? Come on, what the hell are we doing here?"

There was a pause. Tole heard the low sounds of men conferring quietly. Some more argument, and then nothing. He pushed through the hedge and into the yard of the little house next door. He still had a clear way down the alley toward the other end of town and the river, but he also had a better view of the front of his house. They had more torches. Five men stood on the ground, a sixth stood looking down from the porch. He couldn't make out their faces, they all had their hats pulled down low and their coats buttoned tight. Beards on most of them.

"No need to tear up the floor. Just burn it."

"The floor?" This was the man up on the porch. Tole could see him cocking his head.

"The whole goddamn thing. My God, man, get some sense. Burn it all and we don't got to worry about where he hiding. Understand? Either he in there, or he'll come back and we'll get him then."

"Should have done that from the start, if you want my opinion."

"I don't."

The man on the porch went back into the house. Two other men climbed the steps carrying torches. They also disappeared into the house.

Tole knew there wasn't any stopping it, though it made him nearly shout in frustration. Everything he had in the world would soon be gone. He kept his mouth shut, though. He knew how to keep his discipline. He moved quickly down the alley, away from the house, always keeping quiet and his eye on the front door. Finally he found cover behind a line of old grain barrels, and there he set up. By now he could hear the fire beginning inside the house. He knew all of that dry wood would catch fast. The town he'd spent hours crafting together, which he didn't mind saying he'd made *better* than the real one, was just tinder and kindling, and would burn like dry leaves.

His anger clouded his better judgment. He should have run then, but he couldn't. He sighted in.

The first man who came back through the door and onto the porch took a bullet in his shoulder. He fell awkwardly, like he'd tripped in his hurry to get out of the way of the fire, and so the other two behind him didn't think much of it. They came barreling out into the night.

The second man took a round in his leg, which opened up like a flower. He went down, too. By this time the last one out the door noticed something awry and tried to leap over the other two. This carried him through the porch and over the steps. He rolled around on the ground for a moment before standing up.

Meanwhile Tole had been able to load again. The one who had been confused about what to do with the floorboards began shouting that something was awfully wrong, but before he could complete his sentence a bullet shattered his right arm and he went down for good. Tole was impressed with himself. He thought surely he'd kill one of them accidentally and violate his promise to Mariah, but when it counted he was as good as he remembered.

The four remaining men reached up and pulled the two men from the porch and the third from the ground. At about the same time they realized they were being fired on, the house wooshed up and was engulfed by fire. They fell back even farther, dropping the wounded men, who crawled and pulled themselves behind the cedar tree in the front of Tole's yard. The others took cover across the street. Tole knew they were looking for him, and would soon enough have figured out his position, so he moved around the side of the house, feeling the heat curl and burn the hair on his forearms and his cheeks, until he guessed he was behind them again.

He considered whether he ought to finish off the wounded, put them out of their misery. *Out of their misery.* No. Spare their lives. Leave them in their misery. Plus he'd promised Mariah: *no more killing.*

The house groaned. The sound of a fully engulfed wood structure is the sound of a river at flood, currents of flame leaping the banks. There would be nothing left, it would all be carried up into the sky as ash and smoke, and in coming days it would color the shirts and dungarees of his neighbors for a quarter mile around. That edge of Blood Bucket would smell of Tole's disintegrating world, but eventually even that would dissipate, and there would be nothing left.

He knew this much: now that they knew he was alive some-where, firing his bullets at them, they would never leave him alone. Not now. There would always be more to come after him.

And these men, especially, would be after him with a ven-geance.

It had been an enormous mistake to let them live. But if he didn't, where would the killing end?

With me, George Tole realized. *The killing will end when they kill me.*

———

The night dissolved into the quiet pale of dawn as Tole hurried his way out of Franklin and southeast to Carnton, using the Nashville-Decatur railroad track until he reached the McGavock property. He smelled of smoke and fear and sweat. He wasn't sure who had made it out alive. He wondered if Mariah could smell the smoke and see the flames from where she was. He hated the thought of having to tell her the news of the Bucket burning. He reached the driveway to Carnton a long hour after he left Blood Bucket.

Past the cemetery, and to Mariah's door. He tapped lightly. It didn't take her long to answer, wrapping her shoulders in a light linen shawl to cover herself.

"Mr. Tole, what is it?"

"The Bucket, ma'am. They done burned it down."

"What? Who did?"

Mariah pushed past Tole and ran barefoot into the yard. She couldn't see the flames, but the gray-and-black smoke had bil-lowed into the sky, looking like thunder clouds. "No! Who dead?"

"Don't know. Left to come here. I was worried they was after you, too."

"No one came here."

"That's good."

"Let me get my kit, I have some medicines to help. Give me a moment."

He waited on the porch for her. Birds, inexorable as darkness, twittered in the bushes.

In a few minutes she was back, wrapping a heavier shawl around her. "We'll take the cart. I should wake Miss Carrie and tell her."

Twenty minutes later they were on their way in the dogcart, Mariah's medicines and herbals heaped behind them. "I'm sure April and May made it out," Tole said.

"What makes you so sure?" Mariah sounded desperate.

Tole couldn't answer her.

"What about Hooper?" she asked.

"He's probably home sleeping off his moonshine."

"Who done it, George? Who done it?" She was crying.

"I know who."

"Dixon?" she asked.

He didn't say anything.

"Because of me," she said. "Because of my testimony."

They drove into the smoke and ash and heat, and as they got closer, Tole said, "I need you to let me off right up here."

Mariah stopped. She looked at him. And before he could say anything she kissed him and said, "I be waiting."

Chapter 44

Tole

August 10, 1867

Elijah Dixon's office glowed in the early morning sunlight.

It was around six in the morning when Dixon carefully let himself in, closed the door, and locked it behind him. He smelled powerfully of smoke. Then he kicked his chair. And his desk. And his file cabinets. He was very obviously angry just then. When he lit the lamp on his desk he burned a finger.

He spat on the floor. The light seemed to expand into the room slowly, and everything glowed. His desk, the floors, the picture frames, his chairs.

The Negro in the corner.

"Hello again, Mr. Dixon."

Dixon jumped at the sound of Tole's voice. This was what Tole had missed since leaving New York: the fear he could paint across the faces of men. Why had he ever given up this power? A Negro gave a white man plenty to fear and worry about, but Tole was one who could also make them fear for their lives. He was ashamed he had given this up when he slunk off to Tennessee. Look at what he had become, bending and scraping and living in his paper-thin house. He had nearly gone mad with his figurines and his carvings.

George Tole was a man to be feared, and he would not forget that again.

"How'd you get in here?" Dixon asked.

"The door. It just needed a little help to open."

"So you wrote the note?"

"In a manner of speaking," Tole said.

Just then Dixon noticed the safe box at Tole's feet. He leapt at it as if unable to resist its pull, letting out a little shout that was more like a lady's scream. Tole brought the pistol up and aimed at his face.

"Give it." Dixon was so enraged he could barely squeeze the words out, and forgot his fear. He pointed at the box.

"I don't reckon I will. This here is a gift for a friend who done me a favor—saved my life, you might say. The only reason I ain't already gone with it is I wanted you to know who took it."

Dixon stepped back and slumped into his desk chair. He ran his hand over his head, and then he dug the heels of both hands into his temples and squeezed, as if he were trying to push everything out and to start over again. "Is that my whiskey, too?" he asked, pointing at the cup on the mantel.

"Mine now."

Dixon stared at the pistol in Tole's hand. Tole took a sip of the whiskey and kept the pistol trained on him. "You want to meet my friend?" Tole said at last. "He sure want to meet you."

The back door to Dixon's office, the one that went down the back stair and that Dixon used when he didn't want to be seen, opened.

"Hello, Elijah," Jesse Bliss said, primping the orange feather in his hat. "George here has a hankering to kill you. And I can understand him. After all, you wanted *me* dead."

Dixon sat totally still, not even breathing. Then his eyes flickered to life, dancing from the box to Bliss to the door with the file cabinets, to Tole and to the desk, and then back, inexorably, to the safe box, which Tole casually used as a footrest.

"We can chat first, if you like, or just get down to business," Bliss said. He took a chair facing Dixon and Tole. Tole thought he had one of those faces that looked built to face the wind—narrow, pointed, his eyes in a permanent squint, chin sharp but receding, his black-and-gray mustache and beard neatly trimmed. He cracked his five knuckles periodically, one at a time, with his thumb. His field coat draped off his wide body.

"You want me dead, Mr. Bliss?" Dixon said. "I'm surprised."

"I do not. Unlike my adversaries, I don't indulge such crude calculus. I appreciate a more elegant solution to my problems."

"I am glad to hear it."

"Though it is a *useful* calculus when all other options fail."

Bliss stared into Dixon's eyes as if looking for something. Tole thought, *He wants to know which it is going to be: the elegant solution or the crude one?* It was a question Tole had silently put to many men in his time.

"I don't think you will be glad to hear it when I explain my proposal. I'm still irritated that you would have even tried to have me killed. You made a damned mess of it, yes, and I take personal offense."

"You would've been better off taking that bullet, Bliss," Dixon said. "I was a much more pragmatic man back then. More merciful. You don't know what kind of hell you've gone and stirred up now."

"I'd go easy on the threats, Mr. Dixon. We both know what you're capable of. But you and I both know, without your power and your titles, you're nothing but a man."

Bliss reached into Tole's red-and-blue carpetbag, which he'd been carrying, and removed a few of the ledger books that Tole had found affixed to the tops of the file cabinets. Dixon's face drained. He made as if to rise, and Tole leaned forward to follow him, keeping his pistol raised at Dixon's head. Dixon stopped, stiff and unmoving.

"I went through these books, but I only have a rough guess as to how much money you've been stealing. If you'd like, we can all three of us head down to the county clerk's office, get the city's official books, and compare them. Would you like that, Mr. Dixon? Because what we hold in our hands is proof of federal crimes. You understand me? See, I always wondered where a man like you was getting all that money. I should have known you'd be the type to take it from the rest of us."

"You going to trust some lying nigger?" Dixon muttered. His forehead flushed. "He's conning you, Jesse. That's what he does!"

Tole leaned toward Dixon and brought his face within inches. His eyes widened, his mouth bared teeth. "You yourself may be beginning to understand how many ways you've crossed *me*. You should shut your mouth from here on in."

Dixon leaned away. Tole again enjoyed the look of fear on the man's face.

"Thing I still haven't figured out," Bliss said, pleasant again. "Where have you been hiding the rest of the money? You own some businesses I'm not aware of, Elijah? Maybe down south? Somewhere you can scatter the money around so nobody notices?"

Dixon didn't say a word.

"Well, wherever it went, we'll find it. It might take some time, but we're going to find it all."

Bliss turned his attention to Tole. "Open the box."

Tole leaned over, picked it up, and sprang the latch. Inside lay the stock certificates for the Louisville and Nashville Railroad Company. "Take them with my compliments, Mr. Tole. You're a rich Negro now."

Dixon leapt to his feet. "Now that ain't happening."

Tole laughed and riffled through the papers.

"Indeed, this *is* happening," Bliss said. "Sit down."

Dixon sat down.

"To save us time," Bliss said, "the answer to every one of your objections henceforward is the following. If you refuse any of our

284

conditions, I will leave, you'll be shot in the head by this here Negro, and the death of Elijah Dixon, whose friends didn't like him much, will be officially credited to assailants unknown."

"You wouldn't dare."

"Wouldn't I? Wouldn't we? You really want to test us, Elijah? Think of your children!"

"Are you threatening my family?"

"Mr. Tole is squeamish about killing infants," Bliss said, "but not their daddies."

Dixon sagged in his chair, rubbing his forehead. Tole leaned his chair against the wall, reading the stock papers that had just made him rich, and Bliss, who'd risen, sat back down on the other side of the desk. He composed himself, and Tole had the impression of a man who had grown to twice his normal size settling back into his usual shape.

"You're too dangerous to be allowed to roam free in the wilds of Franklin," Bliss said. "As head of the Republican Party in the capital, I need to have control of Franklin. To that end, Mr. Dixon, you'll be appointed to the legislature as the acting Republican representative from Franklin."

Dixon stared at him, amazed.

"Your first act will be to introduce a bill granting the Freedmen's Bureau more enforcement and investigative power throughout the state. They really have been helpful to us. It's nice to have them to send off hunting down old Confederates who seem to believe the war never ended. Those sorts of people, your friends from Pulaski with the masks and the hoods, they won't like this new politics of yours, Dixon. They won't like you as a *progressive*. So you'll require protection, and therefore you'll depend on me. That seems about right, I think."

"No one will ever believe..." Dixon began.

"I am putting my mark on you, and don't ever make the mistake of forgetting that I own you, every greasy bit of you. You backed the wrong horse, and now you've got to pay up. You are mine. I keep my enemies *that* close."

Dixon sank even farther into his chair. Bliss turned and spoke to Tole. "Anything else in that box?"

"Just these certificates," Tole said.

"Put them in your pocket."

Tole set the box on the floor, folded the certificates, jammed them into a pocket. He noticed that Dixon's eyes remained fixed on the box.

Tole picked the box up again. Flipped it over. Tapped the bottom with his knuckle, then the inside. He pulled out a pocketknife and inserted it into the empty box. Up came a false bottom.

"Hell," Dixon said.

Tole pulled some more papers from the box and Dixon gave out a squeak. Tole looked over at him and thought the man might cry; the humiliation must be terrible. He showed the papers to Bliss and Dixon.

"Ah, the deeds!" Bliss said. "All the land another railroad in these parts might ever need, all here in one place." He held them up to Dixon. "These you'll sign over to us, now. As a board member of the Louisville and Nashville Railroad Company, which is one of the perks of being on the correct side of history, I shall receive them on behalf of the railroad and keep them safe. My fellow directors will be very pleased."

He walked the deeds over and spread them out on Dixon's desk. "Sign," he said, holding out Dixon's own pen. "This pile's for me. And this pile's for my good friend George Tole. He may even want to use them to help rebuild half this town, which I did notice you burned down. That's another crime. And the murders..."

As Dixon bent to the task, Bliss brightened and patted Dixon on the back. "Looks like Franklin might get another railroad after all, now that land is so cheap! I have to tell you, it was looking pretty unlikely before, when it became apparent that someone had locked up all the good land. Franklin was important, but not *that* important. Thank God we straightened that out."

When Dixon was done signing, Bliss gave one sheaf to Tole and folded the others away in his own pocket.

"I reckon Mr. Tole might want a final word with you. Don't worry, he won't kill you *now*. So I bid you good morning. I will be in touch to let you know when we'll have the swearing-in ceremony. You're going to make a fine Republican. Mr. Tole, I'm sure we'll be in touch shortly." And then Bliss went out the door, closing it tightly behind him.

When he had gone, Tole and Dixon stared at each other. Tole wasn't sure how they'd got to this place, which he would never have predicted a month before when he'd been *afraid* of Dixon and what the man knew about him. Dixon had been the big man. Now Tole didn't care who knew about him. Things had changed in seconds, in a moment. He felt what it was like to be free *and* in charge.

"I don't expect to hear you doing anything to Miss Mariah or Missus McGavock or anyone else I care about in this town. Not ever."

"I make no promises." Dixon still had some fight in him, some ancient bone memory of how he ought to talk to a presumptuous Negro.

He needed correcting.

"You count on me watching you, from now to eternity. Watching is what I do. I'll be watching and you'll never see me."

Dixon did not speak. But Tole could read acceptance on his face.

"And when you cross that line, you'll never see me then, either. Everything will just go black, forever. *Snap.* Won't hurt a bit, you just be gone."

Dixon nodded, put his hands on his knees, and stared at the floor.

"But Mr. Dixon, there's something else, too. Don't make me threaten those five beautiful babies of yours. Mr. Bliss did that. I don't want to. And I know that you want to see them grow up. And you want them to grow up."

Tole cleared his throat, the next words coming hard. "Don't make me threaten them. Don't make me do anything—*anything*—ever to hurt another innocent person. But I will, you know that? If you do anything to Mariah Reddick or anyone she loves, I will."

He put his pistol in his pocket, lifted his rifle from the corner, snuffed the lamp, and went out the door and down the steps to the street.

Bliss was a cigarette smoker, and Tole smelled him before he even got down the stairs. Out on the street, in the dark of the building's shadow, he spied the burning ember glowing orange. He walked over and joined Bliss walking down the street.

"You know," Bliss said, "you can't stay here."

"I already worked that out for myself, Mr. Bliss. I'll stay for a bit, but not forever."

"Where will you go?"

"Ain't worked out that part." Tole checked the breech of his rifle, double-checking his load.

"I wasn't lying about knowing people in New York," Bliss said.

"Good for you."

Bliss tossed the last of his cigarette into the street, where it flared up and hissed before going out in a puff of pure white smoke.

"You're a ghost now, though," Bliss said to Tole.

"Mmm."

"I was thinking that being a ghost would be an advantage in your line of work," Bliss said. There was a sly note in his voice. "I could use a ghost. In Nashville. Steady work for ghosts up there, if you understand my meaning." He handed Tole a slip of paper. "That's a real address in Nashville. When I'm not in Franklin, I have a little place up there. You come see me if you want the work."

People were coming down the sidewalk toward them. More ambled across the street. Tole needed to go, quick, before he was seen. He picked up his rifle, held it low in his right hand, and with his left patted the papers in his pocket. He took a few steps away before turning around.

"I'll let you know."

"I look forward to it," Bliss said. He lit another cigarette, making his face flash up in shadows and orange, turned, and disappeared down the block trailing smoke. Tole went the opposite direction, down an alley, keeping to the shadows, and headed south out of town.

CHAPTER 45

TOLE & MARIAH

August 10, 1867

Tole had nowhere to sleep, so he wandered. He learned that four people had died in the fire, three of them strangers. The fourth, Ronald Hooper—ragman, whiskey maker—had died in the defense of six others and one of the few houses that had not burned.

Tole had not waited to hear any more about how Hooper died: it would have just infuriated him, and that, he thought, would do no good at all.

Instead he wandered the smoking ruins of the Bucket, saying goodbye to the world he had known, until finally the wind freshened and he knew that morning was come for good. He kept repeating that word to himself, like a prayer: *morning, morning.*

He turned down the street, where Nattie Coyne had her small food shop, just a few tables, Negroes only. Nattie's wasn't open quite this early, but with all the chaos of the past few days, several people were already there.

Tole knocked on the door, held himself up against the doorframe, and knocked again, this time hard enough to shake the windows. Nattie's face peeked through the glass and the door unlatched.

"What you want?"

"You Nattie Coyne?"

"Yes sir, this here my shop."

"I work—worked—with Hooper."

"I know'd Hooper. So what?"

"He told me he used to come in sometimes for your breakfast?"

"He did love my pie," Nattie said haltingly. He noticed her eyes were red. So she knew, as well. Of course she knew. Everyone knew.

"Listen, can I come in and sit for a spell? They burned my house. I ain't got much time this morning. Hooper told me you make a damn fine pecan pie. Was wonderin' if maybe you had an extra slice, maybe somethin' left over from a few days back?"

"You hurt?"

"Nah," he said. "I just a little hungry, is all."

Nattie opened the door to Tole and invited him inside. Tole limped in. Nattie pulled out a chair.

"You said pecan?"

"Yes ma'am, if it ain't too much trouble."

In just a minute or two, Nattie came out of the kitchen with a slice of warm pecan pie on a plate. She set it down in front of Tole.

"Smells delicious, ma'am."

"It's a couple days old."

"Only gets better that way." Tole's fork cut easily, and he took a bite. He closed his eyes and chewed, exhaling. "Hooper ain't wrong about *that*. This some damn fine pie."

"Coffee?"

"Please."

It was full sunrise when Tole stepped back outside and began his long trek out to Carnton one last time. Under his plate he had left a stock certificate signed over to *Miss Nattie Coyne*, and he hoped she'd know what to do with it.

The sky had just turned a pale blue when he arrived at the old plantation. The morning birds were chirping. He knocked softly on Mariah's door, and then again, whispering her name.

Mariah. It sounded like the wind.

Mariah opened the door.

For a moment, she saw nothing but the gleam of early morning. Up near the big house, three or four butterflies traced patterns, runes, in the summer air. If only she could decipher what they were saying to her.

And then she saw Tole.

Mariah had the sensation that he'd been standing there forever, and that he'd be standing there forever more.

"Mr. Tole. It's barely morning. Somethin' happen?"

"I needed to come see you." He looked weary beyond belief. As if he hadn't slept in days.

"Come inside."

"There's something else," he told her. "Something I need to tell you now."

She waited, the almost-knowing a taste on her tongue like ash.

"There's something else I need to tell you about your son."

She had to work to focus her eyes on him, there was so much else to see and everything was so bright. Tole took a seat in one of the chairs. He rocked in place and was silent. The tightness went out of him, the permanent furrow between his eyes eased, and afterward, Mariah would think she had never seen a man so happy and so frightened all at once. *That the Devil fleeing the body,* she said to herself. She knew that feeling. She realized he would soon speak words that would permanently mark a line between the gray world of not exactly knowing, to the sharp world of knowing perfectly. She had tried to live in the gray world and couldn't; now she would see what it meant to live in the clear world.

"If you gone to tell me it was you done shot Theopolis, you can save your breath, because I already knew that." She had not *known* that until she said it aloud, and then it was so solid and obvious she could hardly believe everyone in the world didn't realize it. Everything fit: everything about the toy town and the strange figure on top of Dr. Cliffe's house, Tole's lurking around, his service in the war and the men he'd killed, the implacable sadness on his face, the sharp way he looked around him.

He seemed so lost, sitting there, goggle-eyed at what she had just said. She saw him slump some more, as if the whole structure of the world had begun to collapse and his bones no longer had the strength to hold him up. He shook his head.

"Who told you that?"

"You did, Mr. Tole. You ain't a mystery. Now I'm just waiting to hear you tell me why. I thought it made a lick of difference who done it and why, but now I ain't so sure." The anger surprised Mariah. It worked its way into her voice. "Maybe I don't care the *why*."

"You such a master of death," he said, "it's so simple for you, that you wouldn't want to know why?"

He was right about that, Mariah thought. She sat down. "Yes, I want to know. Though the *why* of killing black folk ain't ever very satisfying in the answer, you ask my opinion." She vowed to remain bold, uncowed, and to go out into her new world with some dignity about her.

For a few minutes, the two of them stayed silent. Mariah could hear the crickets, sawing away in the brush. The future was an utter mystery in that moment, the last moment of her enslavement. She had to get past this last thing.

Tole leaned forward, hands on his knees, elbows locked. Then he stood, picked up his chair, carried it over to her, and sat back down so his knees nearly touched her. Now he could look directly at her face. Her cheeks went hot and she stared back at him. The way he held his hands gripping his knees, he looked as if he were keeping himself from flying into the air. He began to speak.

"I seen terrible things in my time," he said. "I seen the things in war that no man ever sees, you know, all them things that take place in the dark and sometimes in secret, and you don't hardly realize how twisted up it all is until, *right then*, boom, it happens. I killed important men, whoever they said. I looked for the insignia and piping on the rebel officers, which was like the flash of a deer's ass in my sights. Sometimes they tell me who to get, and I got 'em. I killed more than I want to count, and I saw they faces each time. They had good deaths; they never knew what was coming and weren't afraid of me. They were often laughing just before they dropped. Nobody looks out for the assassin when they laughing."

"I've seen war, Mr. Tole. I've seen the light when it goes out in a man's eyes. You not the only one who's seen war."

"I didn't see that with your son, and I'm sorry to say it. I reckon he died just like every man dies, here and then gone, but it weren't quick right up to that moment. It weren't a *surprise*."

"I want to know what you did. What did *you* do?"

"What could I do? When I looked down on that crowd that done sucked up your boy and made him like he never existed, I saw a man in great pain and I stopped his suffering."

"So you the one? Is that what you think? That you the killer?"

"I already given myself over to that particular devil. Your boy was near to death and in great pain. His shirt had been torn off and blood ran all down his chest. He was on his back still holding his hands over his head, and someone kicked him in his back and he rolled over on his right side, toward me, and in just that instant it was like he had offered up his chest to me, and his heart slid before my sights, and that's the sort of moment you don't think about— you just *do*. I put that bullet right through his heart and I stole their kill. I *stole* it. They didn't get the satisfaction of it. They slunk off like kicked dogs after that. And I spared that boy one more instant of horror."

Mariah didn't speak. They sat in silence for minutes as she stared at the ground, trying to understand.

The first thing Mariah felt on hearing this was exhaustion. She had been like any other in the world, a world full of collectors of *fact*, who mistake *fact* for the true substance of life, who mistakenly believe that life is an infinity of fact, and that wisdom is the artful arrangement of such facts. She had known better, and yet she had pursued the facts anyway.

For instance, she possessed no wisdom for having been another's slave, which was a fact of hers. There was no wisdom that had been imparted to her in the McGavocks' house or at the end of the switch. If there *was* wisdom to be earned by being owned by another, if there was some special insight into the doings of man and earth that could only come of being enslaved, well then God was an awfully cruel creature best rejected and condemned.

And yet we all collecting facts like they everything, she thought. She had collected facts to make Theopolis come alive again. And here came a man, Tole, bearing his gift of knowledge and fact, believing that she would relieve him of his burden and bear it up her own self. She felt a shiver of anger.

"When I seen you with his head in your lap," Tole went on, "I knew that what I done had also been done to you. I should have remembered that. I knew it from long ago. There ain't no killing that don't echo out and mark others. And so I reckoned you had a right to know. It's in you, too. So there it is."

Mariah stood and walked over behind George Tole. She took his head and gently held it in her hands, as if a priest laying a blessing on him.

"You know the other reason I come, don't you?"

She nodded, but he said the words anyway.

"I came to say goodbye, Mariah."

"Where you goin'?"

"Hooper's dead. Did you hear?"

"I heard."

"They strung him up and dragged him by a horse."

"I heard."

"It's because of me. And we know about the other men I killed. That'll start coming up soon. Long as I'm here, Negroes in Franklin ain't safe. That's the truth. Those boys'll set fire to everything they see until they find me. Won't be long till they settin' fire to this house."

"Your going away won't change that."

"I think it will. I think they need to not see my face, I think they need to forget I existed and don't need reminding that I beat them."

"Where will you go?"

"Somewhere where they can't find me. Not far, though. I'm going to stay nearby for a while. Make sure that nobody hurts you."

"Why somebody hurt me?"

"You told the U.S. Army about Mr. Dixon, remember?"

She smiled. "I did, didn't I?"

"I think Mr. Dixon ain't going to cause any more trouble. But I want to be sure. You hear me?"

"I don't know what to say."

"I've always been something of a shy man. If I'm bein' honest, I want to ask you to come with me. Leave all this mess behind."

Mariah smiled sadly. "Go where? You don't even know where you goin' and you want me to come with you."

"It don't matter where. Anywhere but here would do just fine."

"This is my home, here."

Tole nodded and began to turn away. Mariah grabbed his hand. "I think I need to put some things together first. Before I go with you."

"Does that mean you'll go?"

"Means I'll think about it."

"So before I leave for good, I'll come find you."

"Do that, Mr. Tole."

Tole nodded, accepting. "I didn't think you'd come with me, but I brought you something anyway." He set a cloth satchel on the floorboards and opened it up. She wondered where he'd come by it—it seemed very luxurious, finely embroidered in red and blue.

Tole rummaged in the bag, pulled out an envelope fat with the deeds and the stock certificates from Elijah Dixon. He handed them to her.

"What is it?"

"It's stock certificates to railroad companies. And deeds to land. You a rich woman now."

"Where you get it?"

"Don't ask."

"You steal it from Dixon?"

He laughed. "In a way, yes. But he knows and he ain't coming after me for it. It's yours now."

"You get outta here with all that," Mariah said.

"No ma'am. This is yours now. You can do a lot of good with it, and I know you will. There a lot of young men, men like Theopolis, like my son Miles—hell, men even like me—who need your help."

"I don't need no money to help those boys."

"Maybe not. But I seen the evil killin' over money bring. We both seen the blood that's spilled over money. Now you take this and do good with it."

Mariah nodded. "I can do that."

"There's one more thing before I go," he said. He reached into the satchel and pulled out a white lily glowing in the early morning like something otherworldly. "This for you," he said.

Mariah reached out and took the stem. She stared at the sky as her eyes reddened and pooled with tears.

"Thank you, George Tole. It's beautiful."

———

Later, after he'd closed the door softly and she heard the sound of his bare feet on the steps, she went out onto the porch.

There, sitting neatly next to the door, sat a pair of men's boots, scuffed and worn, a deep gouge in one of them. She recognized them immediately as her son's, and Tole's.

She picked them up and hugged them to her chest. "You be careful, George Tole," she whispered to the new day. "And you come back, hear?"

CHAPTER 46

TOLE

August 10, 1867

Down the steps he went, then up the hill past the big house, which shone in the morning light like something freshly created, like a gift. The underside of the porch ceilings had been painted blue and glowed as if the sky were right overhead. *Such a world we live in*, he thought, terrible and extraordinary in equal turns.

No one was about, and he picked his way barefoot across the driveway, past the rows of the dead Confederate boys lying calm and easy, wrapped in the care of Mrs. Carrie McGavock, who would do all she could to write to their loved ones, to make the connection, to give peace if peace were at all a possibility. He wondered for the hundredth or thousandth time if he'd ever seen any of those Confederate boys through his bead moving behind their picket lines, laughing at a joke or reading a letter or trying to scrub off the funk of blood and battle. He wondered at the coincidences of the world, that perhaps that soldier and he, a broken Union sharpshooter, a rarity out of the ranks of the Colored Troops, should for an instant share another patch of ground. The sunlight fell in orderly shafts through the trees; the whitewashed plank markers glowed and stretched for an eternity.

He would go, for a while, to Hooper's camp. There he'd find clothing enough, and new boots, and as much moonshine as he needed or could ever want. From there he could watch—watch Elijah Dixon, and watch over Mariah Reddick.

He was now past the brick pile that was Carnton, beyond the fields and into the woods, stumbling down a steep hill to where water splashed in a stream. He thought about the quiet that would come with living so deep in the forest. A woodpecker rattled a tree a few paces away, and insects buzzed. Would life always be this quiet? Would Mariah really come or would life somehow get in the way? Could he be the man she needed him to be? Right now had been too soon for her to come with him, he knew—she'd just buried her son. He would be there when she was ready.

Cicadas whirred in the trees. High summer in Middle Tennessee, warm and sultry and so very much alive. Winter was a lifetime away, and in the meantime there were boots he needed finding at Hooper's camp.

Off to his left a kestrel called, sharp and choppy, repeating its cry over and over as if desperate for understanding. Another kestrel, over the next hill, answered.

The sound wasn't coming from quite the same direction as where he was headed, but it was close enough. Tole followed.

CHAPTER 47

TOLE

August 11, 1867

The moonshine was the undoing of George Tole: gallons of moonshine, neatly stacked in one of the cordoned-off areas in Hooper's camp. Tole had just wanted a sample, just a taste; it had been just a bit shy of a month since his last sip of alcohol, or at least it seemed that long—the longest he had been without a drink for years now. But the sip had turned into a swallow, and the swallow into additional swallows. He didn't remember falling asleep.

But now, suddenly, suddenly he was terribly awake. It wasn't quite morning. The moon was full and poured waves over the woods and the camp. Boughs heavy with leaves blocked the stars. Down the hill the creek poured and poured itself away, onward to the Harpeth and the Mississippi and the ocean; and nearby a drip, drip from the moonshine kettle rang out clear and soft and unattainable.

All of this he was aware of, as if all the universe had without warning invaded his senses.

For what centered his attention, in that last moment, as Hooper's moonshine dripped its song upon the world, was the soft, almost comforting feel of the hand cupping his right shoulder, pulling him up into the air and the light.

A breath on his face: foul, smelling of corn liquor and garlic and fear.

A voice: "Hello, nigger."

And then the sound of the cock of a pistol.

EPILOGUE

MARIAH

December 12, 1912

The tea had been drunk, the washing-up complete ("We will wash and dry, Mrs. Reddick, it's no trouble at all"), and the daylight had begun to fade. It was the time of day Mariah liked best: when the sun cast no shadow, when the world glowed with a last tremulous light before dusk poured in.

Her visitors rose by some unseen signal. Reverend Cravath thanked her yet again for her hospitality. "Time to be going," he repeated for the second or third time. "And please, Mrs. Reddick, come to see us. See how your generosity will be put to good use. We would love to have you."

"Maybe I will. Would be a treat, seeing young Negro men learning and making something of themselves. Reckon I'd like to see that."

"And they would love to meet you," Parmalee Edwards put in.

"Even if they don't know my name?" She couldn't help teasing him a little, him being so kind and humorless.

"Even so. We could host a special dinner for you, introduce you to some of the best scholars—young Whittaker Doolittle, for instance, studying medicine—a fine young man he is, whip smart, with a memory that just eats facts and figures."

"I don't imagine young Whittaker Doolittle would have a lot to say to this old woman."

"Probably more than you'd think." By now they were donning coats, finding gloves in errant pockets. She wondered if they were staying in Franklin for the night or taking the train back to Nashville. Perhaps they even had a motorcar, but she doubted it.

As they moved toward the door she said, "I reckon you forgot the second reason you came."

They stared at her a moment, and then Reverend Cravath recovered. "The condition of the bequest was that someone from the university had to come out here, meet you—"

"I wanted you to come out here because I have something else to give you."

"Something else? But you've already been so generous—really, Mrs. Reddick—"

"This is important."

She left them for a moment but was soon back, carrying a worn carpetbag, its reds and blues long faded to gray and shreds. She needed both hands to lift it and place it in Cravath's own.

For a moment he had to tug it, as if her fingers refused to loosen. But then they did and the handle fell away and the man in the jeweled stickpin, whose hands had probably never held a rifle or a pistol or a plow or a cobbler's hammer, took the bag into his smooth hands. Something in Mariah's chest loosened as if she'd been holding a breath she hadn't realized she'd been holding, and now that breath poured out of her.

He opened the bag and peered inside.

"What is it?" Edwards asked, craning to look.

Cravath didn't answer, pulling out a pair of polished black leather boots. The toes were scuffed, one heel deeply scarred, but the leather shone, soft and supple, as if waxed and cleaned a few hours ago. "These are yours?" he asked her, holding one out.

"In a manner of speaking. They were my son's. They were other folks', too, for a while. But they're mine now. And I want you to have them."

"What do you want us to do with them?"

"You find a place to put them," she told them. "Find a tall place in some belltower somewhere, someplace where they can look out and see all those fine earnest young scholars you've been telling me about. Find someplace where the wind will dry them and the birds can nest in them and in a few years they won't be shoes no more. Just put them somewhere high, you hear me? Put them somewhere where they can see, and if you're looking in the right place, where you can see them."

An odd request, certainly, but an easy one. The men eyed her warily. She wondered for a moment if these founders of this fine university would just toss the boots from the carriage window on their way back to Nashville—but no, they wouldn't. That was why she had summoned them. To look them in the eye and to see them for herself, to size up what kind of men they were.

They were that promise come to life, she thought. All those babies, freshly washed in the air of the world, twisting their fingers and crying out as the force of life shuddered into their lungs for the first time. Those children had grown and they would keep the promises they made to her. Or if they didn't—if the world blew in, raw and ugly—that was all right, too. Because they would try. They were good men and they would try.

That would be enough for Mariah.

OBITUARY OF MARIAH REDDICK

December 21, 1912

The Review-Appeal reported the following:

Much Beloved Negress Dies

The passing of Mariah Bell Reddick at her home on Columbia Avenue on last Wednesday night removes from Franklin one of her oldest citizens, and also a historical character that has been closely connected with prominent and leading events in the South.

"Aunt" Mariah died at the ripe old age of 90 years, retaining her mental faculties and her devotion to her friends until the last. Many politicians and community organizers made an appearance at Mrs. Reddick's funeral, including U.S. Senator Augusten Dixon, 55, of Franklin.

When Col. John McGavock was married to Miss Carrie Winder in Louisiana seventy-four years ago, Col. Winder gave this bright woman to his daughter for a maid. She made her home with the McGavocks after that, nursing four generations of the family and later acting as midwife in the town of Franklin.

Little Negro blood flowed in her veins; she was half Indian with possibly a strain of French blood, hence the strong clear mentality and a combination of characteristics marked and unusual.

Her only husband was Bolen Reddick, a Montgomery Negro (d. 1858) who met her in Tennessee soon after she arrived at Carnton, the McGavock homestead. They had one child, Theopolis Reddick, who predeceased her (d. 1867). She leaves no other family behind. Although many who attended her funeral claimed that they were all her children, Negro and White, since hers were the first hands who touched and delivered them at birth. A fine and remarkable sentiment, indeed.

This exceptional old character has hardly an equal left among her race in this town.

AUTHOR'S NOTE

My agent, Jeff Kleinman, asked me the question that I had been dreading anyone asking. He asked in light of the slaughter of the innocents in Charleston, in light of the events in Ferguson, in light of all the rest that swirls around us these days, how could I, a very white man living in the first quarter of the twenty-first century, justify writing a novel about the plight of a mixed-race woman living in the second half of the nineteenth century?

It's a tough question. I will not try to rattle off some dubious credentials about growing up around black people, as if somehow their "blackness" rubbed off on me. The truth is, while the world I grew up in was painfully unequal for those around me, it was hardly separate. Yet, I make no claim to somehow understanding anyone by proximity.

In truth, I realized, Jeff asked me two questions. The first question is "Why now?"—how, at this point in history, can I even attempt to address the life of this woman in the world we live in? My answer to this is simple. I can think of no better time than today to speak about race and history. Despite all the politically correct attempts by those around us to mask what we see every day, the issue of "race" is always with us. It has been so since the first slaves arrived at Jamestown, and perhaps it will be with us for years to come.

Events in the past few years, however—what happened in Charleston and Ferguson and all the other places of late—has focused me as never before. I believe that we are, all of us, called to examine the human condition—*our* condition—and race remains there, front and center. So that, Jeff, is why this story needs to be told now.

As far as the second part of the question—as to how I, a white man, can attempt to speak for a black woman—well, that's a bit harder. When my first novel, *The Widow of the South*, came out, again and again women would confront me, asking me how I could possibly understand what a mother could go through, losing a child. After all, I was not only not a woman, but had never had a child, let alone lost one.

In the end, all I could say to them was that I had not tried to understand what it was to be a woman so much as I had tried to understand what it was to be human. I was writing about human loss.

There are several qualities required to be a good storyteller. I have never claimed to possess an abundance of many of them, but whatever else I may lack, no one can claim I wasn't given the empathy gene. I say "gene" for, like my dad, it seems to be more than just sentimentality. Even as a child, I was struck by the sadness of those around me and wondered why they were sad.

So, how can I dare write and speak for a black woman? The answer is that I didn't. I have tried, once again, to understand a human being, with the same hopes and dreams, the same responses to sorrow and loss, that all humans have, whatever their circumstances.

I remain fascinated with the themes of transformation and redemption—the kind of transformation, and redemption, that I imagine a former slave named Mariah Reddick might have possessed.

Acknowledgments

The first time I was given the privilege to create a list of acknowledgments, I began by saying that while it would be long, it would never be complete. Nothing has changed. There are so many folks who have pushed—and often dragged—me along over the years to reach this point in time. I could never possibly name them all any more than I will ever be able to appropriately thank, let alone repay, their kindness and support.

At the top of any list of thanks is my agent, Jeff Kleinman, at Folio Literary Management, who's advised, guided, directed, encouraged, and supported me through it all. His greatness is his passion for his clients and his credibility in expressing that passion to the world. I've come to realize that none of this could have happened without Jeff. I can't imagine a better agent nor a better friend.

An enormous, heartfelt thanks to my tireless editor, teacher, and advisor, Duncan Murrell, who consistently went well beyond the call of duty to make this book a reality. And to Kenny Porpora, whose insights really changed this book for the better.

A team of readers lent their time and sage wisdom to this endeavor: most especially, Amy Rosenbaum, Annika Neklason, Natalie Edwards, Hannah Smith, and Corinne Kleinman.

I am forever grateful to Jamie Raab, who is not only my publisher, but has evolved into my editor. While there is no doubt that I am indebted for life to both Amy Einhorn and Deb Futter, ace editors on my first two novels, yet even then I knew Jamie was there for me. She seemed just offstage, encouraging and making subtle suggestions along the way. Now she has stepped onstage as my editor. I am grateful for her taking on this role, grateful for her wisdom, support, and encouragement. Likewise, I am indebted for all the folks at Grand Central who have played a real role in making this happen: Maddie Caldwell, Anne Twomey, Bob Castillo, Abby Reilly, Andy Dodds, Roland Ottewell, and Deborah Wiseman.

Then there is my family, so far away—Marcus and Candy, Nova, Danny and Ivan.

With gratitude to all those who have walked alongside me during this often arduous journey; the best friends anyone could have ever had—Beth and Peter Thevenot, SK and Russell Hooper, Olivia and Justin Stelter, Jayne and Julian Bibb, Susan and Damon Byrd, Trish and Jim Munro, Deborah and Mike Lovett, Susan and JT Thompson, Ann Johnson, Violet Cieri, Estee Pouleris and Monte Isom, Ashlyn and Brian Meneguzzi, Lynn and Ghislain Vander Elst, Elaine and Rick Warwick, Tim Putnam, Jamie Kabler, Carol and Joel Tomlin, Kelly and Bo Bills, Jenilee and Philippe Vander Elst, Nathalie and Tyler Stewart, Evan Lowenstein, Mike Cotter, Andrew Glasgow, Greg Lancaster, Mary Springs Couteaud, Ellen Pryor, Mindy Tate, Elizabeth and Johan Sorensen, Joseph Spence, Emily Volman, Christina Boys, Willie Steele, Scott Sager, Teresa and Danny Anderson, Mary Pearce, Michael Curcio, Cahl Moser, Danelle Mitchell, Dave Wright, Carroll Van West, Kay and Rod Heller, Mary and Winder Heller, Pat and Hanes Heller, and so many, many others.

Thank you, all.